Lowell T

1-5

Going Home

The BATH POND Series

BATH POND

"God promised to feed the birds, but he didn't promise to put it into their nests."

Bath Pond is a story of early Florida pioneers that serves as an important record for future generations. The adversity, warmth, and determination of the Gregson family and their friends working their way through the Depression combine for a great, feel-good read. The Florida of this book no longer exists except within the minds of those who lived through the troubled period it describes—a group that is dwindling at an alarming rate.

FORTUNES CROSSING

"The tragedy in dying is not ever having lived at all."

Fortunes Crossing, the transition volume in the series, carries a moving message. Two young men are facing difficult, life-changing situations. One achieves his goal of learning how to die with dignity and, in the process, discovers the formula for determining one's life mission. The other successfully fights his drug and alcohol addiction and subsequently devotes himself to helping others do the same.

INHERITED JOURNEY

"A candle loses nothing by lighting another."

Inherited Journey tells of the culmination of a surrogate son's promise and the long-ago generosity of an unselfish benefactor. A fateful present-day encounter between two men leads to an alliance between their powerful foundations and forever links their families in bonds of friendship and charitable endeavor. This book focuses on the job of giving: a giving not just of financial resources, but of acts of actual hands-on altruism. It is also filled with the hilarity that can only come through the energy and antics of youth.

PROMISE TO POPPY

"With privilege and resources comes responsibility."

Promise to Poppy is a story of a young professional musician who finds himself in difficult situations. He and his companions succeed in developing a method to help ordinary working people increase their income by educating them in order that they may serve in more responsible positions. This fun-filled volume will warm the depths of one's soul.

GOING HOME

"For it is in giving that we receive our greatest gift."

Going Home, the fifth book in The BATH POND Series, continues the saga of one Depression era farmer's wish to be of immeasurable benefit to his fellow man. The benefit presents itself in the form of education of various kinds to assist others in helping themselves. It also continues the development of the internationally famous entertainer, Derek Davidson, and his son Rob. They enter into venues world-wide, all of which provide increasing funds to continue helping others at home through contributions from those who assist their work.

Going Home

A Life Fulfilled Helping Others

Lowell Teal

Bath Pond Publishing
Windermere, FL

10 9 8 7 6 5 4 3 2 1

Typesetting by Bellerophon Productions
Cover illustrations: John Groth/Michael Komarck
Printed in the United States of America
ISBN: Paperback 978-0-9841035-2-2
ISBN: Hardcover 978-0-9841035-3-9

Library of Congress Cataloging-in-Publication Data
CIP Data on file with the publisher.

Bath Pond Publishing
800 Dillard Street
Winter Garden, FL 34787
407-257-5106

Dedication

The BATH POND Series has been a pleasure to write, allowing me to join a family and to come to know the people as friends. People who write fiction become a part of the characters in the stories, and vice versa. It's a fairy-tale existence for the author.

My sincere appreciation goes to the many readers who have purchased and continue to purchase the books and who pass along kind words and reports of your enjoyment. Your words have encouraged me to want to continue to write—my undying gratitude for your thoughtfulness. I am humbled and most appreciative.

Contents

Author's Note on the Bath Pond Series

Bath Pond was always intended to be a book about another time and place. The story told about tough conditions and tough people during the Great Depression. Success, however, was always on the horizon.

After *Fortune's Crossing* I was primed to write another. Gus Squires is a character who would bring so much to just about any story. He was perfect for *Inherited Journey* since his life was an example of everything it shouldn't be in today's world. He and Jay Gregson were a wonderful fit, since they were doing virtually the same work.

The passage of time and *Promise to Poppy* brought Derek Davidson to the fore. He made his entrance into the world of service by becoming an internationally recognized entertainer. Everyone who heard Derek loved him. His troupe accomplished so much in so many ways; only *Going Home* could do justice to the story of these special generations of people for whom altruism is not second nature, but first.

The delightful and honorable people in the BATH POND series have an almost divine mission in life, yet as with all people's lives, sorrow and trouble present themselves when least expected.

Bath Pond, the lake, is a real place—although it was never known officially by that name. Like many small bodies of water in Florida, it was once clean, white-sand-bottomed, and filled with flowing springs that kept the water ideal for swimming. Unfortunately, Bath Pond today is in an area that's been developed for housing, and it's located on the back lawn of a very large residence. Its shape has been changed from round to lagoonlike. Bath Pond is now polluted.

PART ONE

Kids Become Involved

1

The very special June night was murderously hot. A summer shower slipped over an hour before, and a hot vapor was rising from the streets and sidewalk. The humidity was fierce, and each person was wiping perspiration. Everybody was mumbling about the excessive heat and having to walk so far, since the nearby parking lots were filled to capacity. One of the good things about the night was the fragrance of the multitude of blooming flowers wafting about for everyone's enjoyment.

Inside the Central Florida Performing Arts Center, the graduation exercises were taking place for the most prestigious private school in the area—some say even in the state of Florida—the Langford Academy. The center was professionally constructed for these purposes, with outside lights ablaze, the glow set against the lush landscaping, and trees situated around a magnificent structure.

Its inside parking garage had long been closed to more cars. The streets were filled with parents walking from blocks away on this warm evening in June.

Graduates were lined up along a side hallway in monitored silence, awaiting the signal to begin their march to the assigned seating area. The graduates sat in chairs outfitted with rubber socks placed in front of the permanent seating. This area was installed as a dance floor when the opportunity for patrons to dance presented itself, though this particular night was not for dancing.

Despite the fact that most of the graduates were not acquainted with the music, they could hear the dual pianists, who were busy beyond description. Those listening were introduced to the full introduction to "Pomp and Circumstance" by Edward Elgar. Seated at twin Steinway concert grand pianos onstage, centered and facing each other, were the twins Rob and

Ali Davidson, also graduating seniors. They had the entire rendition well rehearsed and memorized, and they were doing a fantastic accounting of Elgar's work. When they reached the appropriate location in the music, they professionally moved into the cadence and tune of the graduation song so familiar to everyone in the audience. They played this part over and over until all the graduates were standing in their places and the faculty had situated themselves on the stage in front of the twin pianos. At this point, the Davidson twins moved into the finale of Elgar's magnificent work. Most people did not know such a finale existed either.

Though everyone knew of their father, Derek Davidson, an internationally recognized musician, they were not now aware he was in the audience and as close to a nervous collapse as was humanly possible without experiencing one. He knew his kids enjoyed playing together, but this was a very difficult piece that all professionals have problems with, yet they were pursuing its finale with gusto and perfection. They were too young to realize a problem might exist. In fact, it never occurred to them that they couldn't play the piece. Had they known the worried shape their father was in, they would have overwhelming troubles that might have contributed to some sort of cave-in of their own.

When Rob and Ali finished, they stood together and moved to their places with the class. The headmaster approached the lectern on the dais, motioning the graduates to be seated.

Kit looked at Derek, who had an almost fatal case of flop sweat running down his face. The front of his shirt was soaking wet; he was perspiring like a plow horse in July. Kit had known he was almost to the point of becoming a candidate for the paramedics from worry, even though he had played at venues around the world without the same catastrophic results.

He whispered, "Kit, they didn't miss a note. Not a note! Their timing was perfect, and their crescendos were totally out of sight. I'm so proud of them," he gushed.

Rob and Ali were the children of Derek and Kit Davidson.

Derek was not only an internationally famous entertainer but president of two major foundations and had taught their kids all he could. When they reached their very early teenage years, Derek felt that a different piano and voice teacher should be secured. Not only did he know professionally that this was in their best interest, but his schedule did not allow being the teacher they should have. Their talents went far deeper than he could develop given his limited time.

Both kids loved piano and voice, and they were happiest playing and singing with their dad because he was so much fun. When others complimented their abilities, as was constantly the case, this was the greatest comment of admiration Derek could receive regarding their children.

Their graduation would end one phase of the Davidson kids' life and begin another. Both thought they wanted to pursue musical careers. Rob was certain, yet Ali had spent all her available time with Dr. Wendy Squires in Boston and at home just because of their friendship. Their friendship deepened when Wendy came home to rest and look after her parents, Gus and Anne Squires, during their declining years. While Ali loved music, she had a strong desire to study pediatric medicine because of her visits with Wendy. Her decision was yet to be finalized.

There was no question with Rob. His pull was music, and puzzling questions still lingered from time to time about Poppy's ranch out west. And what if Derek needed him? Where would the knowledge to be of assistance come from with no business training?

When the diplomas were awarded, the headmaster approached the lectern and said, "We are going to close tonight's ceremony just a bit differently. I've asked Rob and Ali Davidson to join our other graduating twins, Cindy and Mark Matson, to sing 'The Lord's Prayer,' accompanied by Mr. Derek Davidson."

Rob's voice was almost an exact replica of his father's deep baritone, and Ali was a rich contralto. Because of this, the combination of their four voices blended extremely well. They had been schooled over and over for this occasion. They performed the piece flawlessly.

When the selection was concluded, Derek moved directly into "Pomp and Circumstance," without the full introduction and finale. These were the instructions of the headmaster, who allowed the Davidson and Matson kids to march out with their fellow graduates. Kit had instructed Derek to play Elgar's rendition just as it was written. She did not want him to take the opportunity to flower it up with his flairs after the kids' performance. She outlined in no uncertain terms that the kids were not to be upstaged, since they played it as written. Derek knew better than to disregard his wife's instructions.

It was a milestone in the Davidson family's lives. Derek and Kit offered the kids the opportunity to invite as many people as they wished to their home for a graduation party. It was a good time gathering around and in the pool, and the food was plentiful. The party was catered, and Derek had insisted on professional lifeguards being on duty.

Wendy Squires visited and stayed at Ali's insistence until very late. They were pals, and Wendy seemed to fit; after all, she was just one of the family. Everyone seemed to be having a great time together. It was a one-of-a-kind evening.

The kids finally wore themselves out around three in the morning after hours of swimming, dancing, and eating. The party was nothing less than a good-time event that everyone enjoyed.

During the early hours, Wendy said, "Derek, we've come a long ways from where we began years ago. I only wish Mom and Dad were alive. They'd be so happy to see these kids having such a swell time in their home."

"Wendy, I've thought about the Squireses, too. I've also thought of Garrett and Mary Fran, in addition to Jay and Jan, Greg, Leigh, and Bart all evening, wishing the same thing,"

Derek said. The Squireses and Gregsons actually gave Derek his first job and were responsible for his good fortune.

The hour was very late when Rob, Ali, and others who enjoyed music gathered around the piano to play and sing. They had a wonderful time singing pop songs that Derek had no idea they knew, even the choruses of a few hymns.

When the last kid finally left, everyone was dragging with fatigue. It had been a long night, and bedtime was near.

While the caterers were cleaning up, the family gathered around the piano and had fun for a very few minutes and promptly went to bed. It had been a wonderful evening.

2

Mr. and Mrs. John Langford were mentors to Garrett and Mary Fran Gregson from the date of their marriage, because each had something the other needed. In fact, the Langford assets provided the financial support to get the Gregson Family Foundation started. Since this early beginning the Foundation had attracted more than sufficient financing through its philanthropic endeavors to continue in fine fashion. During recent years Derek had been primarily responsible for its success because of nothing more than his musical and stage talent and the chance to succeed with the assets the Gregsons had allowed him to use. Their audiences couldn't get enough of his performances, and yet he was such a common person, without pretense and he sought no accolades. Derek was hilariously funny though totally indebted to the Gregsons' generosity, and of course, their full-blown need for someone just like him.

When a place was needed to train master gardeners, and for others to teach the various educational pursuits in which the Foundation was involved, the Gregson Foundation in tandem with the Productive Life Foundation—headed by Gus Squires, Wendy's father, and Jay Gregson—bought an old hotel in town and remodeled it to fulfill their needs. This structure had since been demolished.

Since the Langfords' mission was to assist as many people as possible, and since education had always been foremost for all the families involved, the Gregson Foundation determined that the hotel must be demolished and a new educational center developed. To house those who came from across the country to be taught their jobs at the Foundation's facility, a nearby motel was purchased and enlarged. Students were housed in the motel and received the education to qualify for their licenses at the Foundation's facility.

The Langford Academy and the Foundation's teaching facilities had now built one very large structure adjoining other structures owned by the foundations. The one-story building covered an entire city block. A soundproof firewall ran down the middle—separating the children's academy, beginning in the sixth grade, from the adult students using the other side. Each side had its own auditorium for mass meetings. When larger meetings were held, rooms in the Performing Arts Center were secured.

The Academy itself was a state-of-the-art teaching facility and had a waiting list of qualified, tuition-paying students who wanted to attend. The Academy boasted of only the finest instructors. Should a student without funds apply yet who possessed unusual talents worthy of polishing, the foundations stepped in. The headmaster and all the instructors were top of the line.

Carter Associates in Chicago provided all the instructors for the adult programs—trained to teach in such career fields as the master gardener program, as well as provide instruction to those attempting to earn their GED and then become licensed in various occupations to better themselves. Those struggling to become executive assistants, master plumbers, electricians, contractors, and so on were also ably assisted to achieve their goals.

People who wanted to become nurses and medical assistants were taught in the hospital. Dr. Casey Cagle was initially in charge of this program, but age and the sheer numbers of students ultimately made this task unmanageable for him. Also, Dr. Cagle was actually in charge of a number of hospitals around the United States whose administrators answered to him. Another educator was hired to handle the instruction in the nursing area. Associated teaching facilities were strategically scattered across the United States, so each quadrant of the United States had its own general administrator who answered to Derek. Because of the need for all the instructional personnel,

Carter Associates' people moved into the communities in which they taught and became model citizens.

The Gregson Family Foundation and the Productive Life Foundation were already into teaching as well as constructing all sorts of specialty hospitals and assisted-living facilities. The old hotel that the foundations were originally using locally for teaching would no longer accommodate those applying, so replacing it made perfect sense. Erecting a facility that taught various career enhancement subjects was only logical. Since the foundations' faculty lived in the area, and since the local schools were not up to the foundations' standards, they decided to double the size of the building and add a prep school that covered sixth grade through high school, the Langford Academy.

While the Academy was being constructed, it was determined that a children's hospital should be erected also in the same general area. The Foundation's children's hospital specialized in several areas and was a substantial asset to the medical outreach mission of the Foundation. In fact, due to the large number of buildings that the Foundation required, most of the buildings in the community were new and owned for their specific purposes. The settlement was now made up largely of Foundation buildings.

Because the Gregsons' benefactors were Mr. and Mrs. John Langford, both deceased, the Gregsons felt it only right and proper to name the academy in the Langfords' honor. The Academy had the distinction of teaching every area of mathematics and science possible and included as many honors and Advanced Placement courses as any high school in the country. The school hired only the finest instructors available and required much, much more from students than an ordinary public school.

3

The Davidson family was slow getting out of bed the morning after graduation. It felt as if it had been a short night! Everyone was up around lunchtime and having a bite to eat and a fun conversation around the pool.

"Well, folks, what is the next step?" Derek asked.

No one spoke up quickly. Kit finally said, "I've got a decorator coming in a few days, and I will be in over my head with a few home repairs and some new decorations. Maybe you ought to go back to work, Dad?"

"Dad, if I had my wish I'd like the two of us to go to the ranch," Rob said. "I think a few days at the cabin would be a fine way to slow down and take inventory before thinking about more school in the fall."

"What about you, Ali?" Derek asked.

"I'd like to go back to Boston with Wendy, but I don't want to unless she invites me."

Kit asked, "Are you really serious about medicine, Ali?"

She said, "I want four years of keyboard and voice. I do have a yearning to be a pediatric surgeon, but I'm not sure enough to jump right into it. I think music first."

"Are both of you still satisfied with the University of Florida?" Derek asked. Both answered affirmatively.

"Well, I have no problem with either of your requests. How about you, Mom?" Derek asked.

"No, sounds good to me," Kit replied.

"Okay, if that's what each of you want to do, that settles it," Derek said. "Ali, why don't you visit Wendy this afternoon, and if it sounds good to her why not talk about a week's visit? If that will work, I need to go first to Minneapolis and assist the Bishop, and we'll just drop the two of you off on the way."

Kit piped up. "Nothing doing. You are breaking company

rules, and I don't want both my kids and my husband all on one plane. You need to make other arrangements."

"You're right, Kit. I should be on a separate plane from Rob even."

Since it was Saturday and everyone was tired, no one left home that day. Later some friends came over to visit Rob and Ali. Derek and Kit sat around the pool all afternoon with the kids and enjoyed them. Derek later excused himself and from his study talked to the office and tied up a few loose ends for Monday.

Wendy was all for Ali visiting for a few days, and Derek sent them to Boston late Sunday afternoon on the company plane. Though vastly different in ages, the pair had always been great friends, and visiting together had the benefit of perhaps helping with some conclusive decisions in Ali's mind regarding her education. On the way home the jet dropped off some supplies for an assisted-living retreat coming up soon in the Washington area. The area supervisor had requested the materials.

Derek had always wanted both kids to know and enjoy music. He did not, however, encourage either to do what he was so talented at doing. Yet in his mind, between the two, Rob was the one more likely to follow a musical career.

4

The plane was waiting at the company strip at 1 p.m., Monday, for the trip to Minneapolis. Derek boarded alone. Rob was already in the air aboard a commercial airliner. They would meet at about the same time. The company rule was still centered on the agreement that the family would not travel together. This had been the rule since Jay and Jan Gregson's untimely deaths on a runway in Salt Lake City.

The purpose for the Minneapolis trip was a commencement exercise for some graduates from the Foundation's adult education activities. These events occurred only annually now by region, and people finishing the requirements during the year were encouraged to attend even if it was at a later date.

Derek had Rob fitted for a couple of suits, some blazers with appropriate pants and shirts, and two tuxedos. Rob was about Derek's size and shape, and he bore a striking resemblance to his father. This would be Rob's first appearance with his dad, yet Rob was unaware of it at this point. This was one of Derek's devilish traits: one could never assume what he would do next, particularly during a live performance.

They arrived separately in Minneapolis around 3 p.m. A car was waiting on them for transportation to the hotel. The Carter folks had the ceremony all planned, and the Foundation's musicians were on hand also for the dinner and dance that would follow the graduation ceremony. Derek would get the evening off to a good start by offering a few words of appreciation to everyone involved as well as sincere congratulations to the graduates, and asking for their continued efforts in assisting others through the foundations. Graduates helped not only with their work but also with direct financial contributions to the foundations once they began working. Contributions from graduates were kept separately for accounting purposes and were intended to indicate some measure of their success in the workaday world. Such contributions were a source of pride for the foundations, and also served to motivate present students as well as graduates.

Arriving at the hotel, Rob and Derek's luggage was taken to the room. Derek took Rob down to the Grand Ballroom and tried out the piano and the keyboard. The other band members were setting up their instruments. Derek carefully checked every speaker in the room with Rob playing the piano. Derek and the band leader decided to use the Foundation's sound system and not bother with the in-house equipment.

Much to Rob's amazement, Derek took him to the hotel room and both went to bed for a nap. Rob couldn't believe it. Derek was immediately asleep. Rob lingered for a few minutes and dropped off himself.

Derek seldom did these kinds of performances anymore since there were musicians and others hired to take care of them. On this occasion Rob was with him, and Derek decided that both of them would participate. How, he had not yet decided, and Rob was still in the dark about what his father had in mind.

They walked to the rear of the dining room after showering and dressing. Derek had already told Rob that, to keep from wrinkling his trousers, he could not sit down. Rob already knew this regimen from some of the others in the company, yet he was excited about the possibility of being a part of the evening performance but still didn't know what it might be like.

The dinner was concluding, and the Carter folks were in the midst of the graduation ceremony. When the finish finally came, the master of ceremonies knew Derek was in the back of the room and introduced him.

"You stay here, Rob," Derek instructed.

Rob nodded and said, "Yes, sir."

Derek approached the microphone on stage and offered a few words of congratulations to the graduates and some general good-time banter. He received lots of laughs, and that most of the graduates already knew they were in for a good time made it all the more sweet for Derek.

"Ladies and gentlemen, I've a surprise for you tonight. My son is with me, and I want you to know him. This is his first time out with me, and I know he will have a big time just like you are expecting. My son, Rob Davidson . . . would you welcome him, please?" Derek said.

Rob was dumbfounded. He just stood there and grinned until it finally dawned on him that his dad wanted him on stage since the entire audience was applauding.

Arriving on stage he received a rousing welcome from the crowd. Derek put his arm around him and said, "Rob can play the piano and sing much better than I, and he can also dance better."

When he was finished introducing Rob, Derek turned to the orchestra leader and motioned him to stand down for a few moments. The leader knew that with Derek, anything could happen, and it usually did.

"This isn't the manner in which we start a good-time evening, but I want to show you that I'm telling you the truth about my son," Derek said. "We will begin the evening's entertainment."

Now Rob was completely speechless. They had practiced nothing, had not even talked about the two of them doing anything, but most of all he knew his dad would not embarrass him.

Walking back to the piano Derek said, "'You Raised Me Up.' You sing the first verse, and I'll accompany, I'll sing the second, and you accompany. Then you play the third, and we'll harmonize this one, okay?" Looking out over the nearly one thousand people present, Rob couldn't talk nor could he even remember the tune or words. He was totally taken aback.

Derek played the intro and mouthed the first words to Rob. Derek was aware that Rob knew it by heart and could play it from memory. By this time, Rob had his wits about him and didn't look out into the vast audience until he and his Dad were moving along, at which time he took the microphone off its stand and proceeded toward the edge of the stage. He did a bang-up job of singing but knew he had to somehow get to the piano bench to play. When the first verse was concluded he had moved back to the bench by backing up to remain facing the audience. Derek played just the appropriate notes to give Rob a chance to turn around, and he took the microphone from Rob's hand. Rob transposed a few bars to put Derek into the right place to sing. On the third verse Rob played and sang into the piano microphone. They received a standing ovation from the audience.

The orchestra leader motioned Rob to remain seated, and together they played a few dance numbers. The dance floor was filled, and a single woman even grabbed Derek to dance. Although Derek was trying to get off stage he had to dance when asked. Derek was so emotionally pleased that Rob had passed his first on-stage test that containing himself was difficult.

The regular pianist slipped over to Rob and told him he would take over when the next dance number was finished. Rob gladly obliged.

Rob tried to slip off stage and watch his dad when a younger woman grabbed him, and both were now on stage dancing. It went from number to number for Rob. When he finally relaxed, he began to have a great time with the people gathered for the celebration.

The orchestra moved from rock and roll to country to line dancing and anything else the crowd asked for. It went on for more than two hours.

Derek moved off stage at the first chance and sat down at the Carter table. He was overjoyed at the great job Rob did at adapting to the situation and had fun just watching him dance.

When they returned to their room Derek ordered dinner, and they sat and talked for a couple of hours, laughing about the evening. Rob wasn't ready for bed when the time finally came because he was already projecting himself into the future.

Rob's first question to Derek back in the room was, "Dad, is what we did tonight what you've been doing all these years?"

"Yes, it is, and I've had a fun time and some tough times." As Derek said this, the phone rang. It was Bishop Hornsby.

"Derek," said the Bishop, "I've had a new development and need some help."

"How can we help, Bishop?"

"I have a weekend with two hundred couples here in Minneapolis. The men are military and headed back to the Far East for duty. The sad thing is that they've only been home for about four months, and their kids are now with them and will continue to be tomorrow night at the banquet we are hosting for them. It is just a pick-me-up session. Kit told me that you and Rob are going west for a few days, and I'm wondering if you could postpone your trip and help me just tomorrow night?"

Derek knew he couldn't refuse since the Bishop had been such a great help to the foundations and to him personally. Derek said, "You are already in Minneapolis, you say, Bishop?"

"Yes, and I also talked earlier to Evelyn to check your schedule. She says you have the time after your conference with Carter in the morning. If you send Rob ahead to me, Evelyn and you can come over when you are finished," the Bishop concluded.

"Since you've already worked it out, can you get some dry cleaning worked out for us when Rob arrives?" The Bishop answered "Yes."

After the conversation with the Bishop, Derek turned to Rob and said, "Son, we have to stay and help the Bishop out tomorrow night here in Minneapolis prior to going to the ranch. Can you handle that?"

"Yes, sir," Rob answered.

5

For the very first time Rob was on a business trip for the foundations. He was dressed in coat and tie and excited about what the day would be like, yet he also wanted to appear as if he had his act under control.

The people who personally escorted Rob over to the Bishop knew him and were filled with questions about his mission. Rob said, "The truth is, you fellows know more than I do. I'm just going over ahead of Dad. When you get him here we'll all know what we are going to do, after he asks Evelyn," to which they all had a laugh.

The Bishop was waiting, and they were off to the hotel ballroom. The Bishop was more interested in Rob's recent graduation than what had happened the previous night.

Rob's hunch was that the Bishop would turn the stage over to his dad and then the sweating would begin for Rob—that is, if Derek acted like he did the night before.

As the evening had begun and the dry cleaning was being tended to, Rob entered the ballroom without having dressed and stood in the back listening to the Bishop talk to the service personnel, all of whom were totally distraught about such a short stay with their families. The military couples looked middle-aged, and their kids were about the same age as Rob—as best as he could determine. His plans were to dress while the group had dinner.

The big problem for Rob was that the orchestra on the Foundation's payroll was not here and would not be. The music would be up to him and his dad.

Much to his surprise, the Bishop, after pronouncing a blessing prior to their meal, told the military families that he had arranged entertainment for them while they ate. This announcement came as a complete surprise to the entertainer.

"And now I ask for a rousing round of applause to help me get a young man on stage you will enjoy knowing. Welcome, please, Rob Davidson."

The crowd went wild, just as though they had known him for years. Rob was petrified, yet he stood and in a short jog jumped up on stage as if he knew exactly what he was doing.

"Rob Davidson, ladies and gentlemen," the Bishop said and exited the stage.

Rob, still petrified, walked over to the stage microphone and looked out across an audience with every woman present having eyes that looked as if they had been on an extended drunk from grief. He assumed it was from grief for losing their husbands again to overseas duty. Some of the kids looked the same.

After a long moment, Rob said, "Ladies and gentlemen, if my dad saw me on stage with a pair of pants as wrinkled as the ones I have on, it would be the end of me. The Bishop pulled this on me, and I will be the loser when my dad finds out about it. But, I'll say this: given the circumstances of this evening's banquet I believe he'd let me off the hook if I wore my swim trunks!

"Since the Bishop is a devilish fellow, as you've just witnessed, and since I know nothing about what you like, I'll make a deal with you. I'll begin with a little dinner music, and then we'll continue into whatever you want it to be. We'll sing, we'll dance, or we'll do anything the Bishop will let us. I guess we have about thirty minutes to have fun, so I'd better begin."

The Bishop yelled from his table, "You've got as long as these folks want to stay, even if it's all night, Now have at it since you are already on stage." This remark brought a thunderous roar from the audience.

Rob diddled around a few soft dance numbers for the most of the dinner hour until someone yelled out "The Impossible Dream." Thankfully Rob knew it. He transitioned himself away from the piece he was playing and sung the song to resounding applause. He found out later it was the Bishop who requested the number because he had heard Derek sing it so many times.

When finished with the song, Rob asked from the piano, "Who among you—servicemen or family members—will have a birthday during this deployment?" Almost everyone held up their hand.

"Let's sing 'Happy Birthday' to each other and celebrate the birthdays now." He began to play, and the singing was pitiful because of the situation. Rob stopped them in mid-song and said, "I know you can sing better than that. Let's stand and try it again." On the second attempt the song was much better.

"Since there are those who will have anniversaries while deployed, here is 'The Anniversary Waltz.' I invite you to dance if you will." To his amazement the dance floor filled to capacity, and he played it until they tired of it.

While the waltz was in progress, Derek walked in, and the Bishop saw him. "I believe you've lost your job to Rob. He has handled the audience like a pro. Has he ever been out with you?"

"Only last night," Derek answered.

"Well, he is doing a whale of a job here."

When the waltz finished, Rob asked, "Young people, tell me what you'd like to dance to." All sorts of numbers were suggested. "Will you dance if I can play them?" To this question he received a resounding "yes."

The floor filled with folks in their teens and twenties, and Rob played requests for at least an hour. Lots of rock and roll, line dance numbers, and nothing slow. The parents were having fun just watching them, yet some couldn't contain themselves and joined the youngsters on the floor.

The Bishop turned to Derek and said, "I believe this has gone on long enough. These folks will be departing tomorrow, and I know they want some family time. I'll introduce you and say a word to the audience, and you figure out how to end the evening."

Now Derek was the one in a quandary. What should he do with such an occasion? What should he say?

The Bishop stopped the dancing and Rob's playing and said, "Ladies and gentlemen, we've had a great time here, and Rob Davidson deserves our sincere appreciation since he had no knowledge he would be performing here. I sort of pulled it on him." The crowd gave Rob a standing ovation, to which he responded as best he could—although he was a bit embarrassed by it all.

The Bishop then asked the audience, "Would you please stand and join Rob in a song?" The Bishop turned to Rob and asked, "Do you know 'Let There Be Peace on Earth'?" He nodded and began. When Rob started, Derek came to the stage to assist. Most of the audience helped sing the number, although some were too emotional to even attempt singing.

"Now I have another surprise for you. While you were dancing the last number, a special guest arrived. I would like to introduce Rob's father, the internationally famous Derek Davidson, ladies and gentlemen. You should also know they were in Minneapolis last night on another assignment, and I imposed upon them around midnight to come here. They are headed west for a few days of father-and-son vacation, and we should offer our sincere thanks for their coming here tonight." The crowd responded again since they knew and loved him already.

When Derek acknowledged the introduction, it was evident he had worn his clothing since very early that morning. His coat was wrinkled, and his pants were beyond help. His collar wasn't buttoned. Rob said, "Dad, do you realize how you look and all the things you've taught me about being dressed on stage?" After saying this, Rob just cackled out into the microphone with a laughter that was so infectious the crowd roared.

Derek looked down and turned to Rob with a menacing look and then back to the audience and said, "Only through the mouth of a smart-aleck, spoiled brat of a kid would you expect such a remark." This brought another tremendous laugh and applause.

Derek continued, "Rob is correct. We don't appear in wrinkled clothing. This is an absolute first for me. The Bishop asked that we come over tonight, and we had to respond because of who he is and more important who you are. We are appreciative of the sacrifice you are making in the name of our country as well as the sacrifice your family is making. We know you've had too short a break and are not looking forward to leaving again so soon. I don't know quite what we could do to ease the pain you must feel at this time. If I knew it would certainly be done. Since the hour is late and since we want to do the right thing, I want to ask you to stand and allow Rob and me to sing 'The Lord's Prayer' to close. If you would like to sing along, feel free to do so."

Rob began the introduction as the folks were standing, and at the appropriate moment both began to sing "The Lord's Prayer." To their amazement the entire crowd joined in, and it was one of the more heartwarming moments Derek had ever known. It was a moving rendition of this age-old classic, and when everyone started to sing, Derek directed them.

When the number ended, the Bishop asked the crowd to give Rob and Derek a chance to get to the hall so their appreciation could be expressed. Rob had never experienced such a thing.

Everyone was so nice and congratulatory that it all left him speechless. He did his best to respond by thanking the men for their service to the country. There were some younger, great-looking girls whom he did not mind hugging at all. A few even kissed him.

When they were all gone, Derek walked over to Rob, who was wet with perspiration. Derek gave him a bear hug and said, "The Bishop has told me how you handled the crowd. I'm very,

very proud of you and would not have subjected you to this had I known it was coming."

"Yeah, right. He set me up, didn't he, Bishop?" Rob responded.

"Rightfully, Rob, no. Your dad thought this was coming tomorrow night, and so did I until the service personnel had their orders changed. Thank goodness you were here, Rob. We may not need your dad anymore since you were totally professional. I think the two of us can handle it."

Since Rob had had nothing to eat, they went to the hotel coffee shop, which allowed Rob time for a meal. Derek had already had a sandwich earlier. While Rob was eating, Derek and the Bishop discussed the program and bragged on and encouraged Rob. He felt so much better about himself and his ability after being caught in such a predicament without Derek. He was gaining his professional footing.

"Son, I'm sorry, but the jet is waiting to take you to the ranch. Someone will be waiting up for you according to Evelyn's instructions and help you get situated. I will see you day after tomorrow. You will have a chance to rest up and think about how you could have improved on tonight."

The Bishop responded, "Rob, regardless of how your father kids you about tonight, remember it is good-natured. I'm telling you straight out you did a fabulous job, and on the spur of the moment. I know talent, and you are running over with it. It shows in your musical ability, and I know there will be a wonderful future in store for you." Saying these words, the Bishop gave him a hug.

"Thank you, sir," was about all Rob could get out since his emotions were coming to the fore and since his sense of accomplishment was beginning to surface within himself. He also considered all the mistakes he made that others knew nothing about. Those things were beginning to play heavily on his mind.

6

Azzi let Rob sleep all he wanted to. She had put him in Derek's bedroom across the pool from the main house so the noise of those working there wouldn't disturb him. When he did awaken and after he showered, he ambled over to the kitchen to see if there was any breakfast left after the pilots plowed through it.

"Hi, darlin'," Azzi said. "I hope you had a good sleep?"

"I did, thank you."

She had a man-sized breakfast awaiting him. He did his best to eat everything on the table.

Azzi, short for Azziru, asked, "Rob, what are your plans for today?"

"If the cabin is stocked, I think I would like to ride a horse there, and Dad can come whenever he decides to," Rob answered.

"It is all stocked for a week, though Pepe will have to bring more ice in a couple of days," she said. "I've already told him to have your horse saddled."

When Rob left for the paddock, Azzi offered her standard warning: "Be very careful, darlin'. Watch for snakes and wolves and anything rabid. Be very sure you have a carbine and a pistol. That's the rule, you know."

"Yes ma'am, I will," he replied.

Riding across the plain, Rob thought that it had never been more beautiful. Though he had just gotten out of school in Florida, it seemed as if it was spring here on the high plains, and it was. The wildflowers were blooming. The cattle were getting slick and losing their winter coats. After a couple of hours, he stopped on the bluff overlooking the long expanse below and saw the little cabin over by the snow-capped mountains with the little river running by, making its way though the mountains to the side. There were endless numbers of cattle grazing below. A few cowhands were doing something in the distance.

Arriving at the cabin he unsaddled his horse, looked inside, and then decided to visit the river with a fly rod and cast a few times. He caught a couple of trout and promptly threw them back. He enjoyed fishing, though he wasn't in the mood for fish to eat that night—maybe another night.

After putting the rod up he sat on one of the straight chairs out in front of the cabin and leaned back against the wall. It was so quiet and peaceful. He sat there until dusk, watching the animals come down to the river and drink. There were all sorts of animals—from antelope, deer, and elk to a host of small critters scurrying around.

Just as the sun was going behind the mountains and the weather was cooling fast, Derek rode around the corner of the cabin on his horse. "What's for dinner, Son?"

"I haven't looked in the cabin for food. I fished a little and then sat down right here and watched the animals drink from the river. This has got to be one of the most beautiful places on the face of the earth, Dad. I could live here."

"It truly is that, and it is just as Mrs. Gregson's father left it. Nothing has changed over the years, except Bart put some long-boy beds in since he was so tall. I share your affection for the place."

They enjoyed the scenery until the temperature ran them inside to fix something for their evening meal. A fire in the stove warmed the cabin, and they enjoyed each other for the evening and dinner. It was always a cherished time when they were together, and they discussed lots of subjects having to do with their future.

Evelyn and Pepe were banging on the door about daylight. "The office manager at home needs you, Derek," Evelyn yelled through the door.

"Give us a minute, and we'll get dressed. Come on, Son.

Let's go to the house, have breakfast there, clean up, and we'll come back," Derek said to Rob.

"Yes, sir," Rob replied. "I was just wondering how I was going to face the pond at the waterfall this morning as chilly as it is. Your thinking is good."

Pepe asked, "Mr. Davidson, do you want me to bring the horses home and you folks take the pickup?"

"You want to ride them back?" Derek asked Rob.

"Only if you do. It really doesn't matter," he replied.

"Yes, feed them, Pepe, and bring them in," Derek instructed.

"Yes, sir," Pepe said. "Azzi is sending a maid to clean up and bring dinner for this evening."

"Thanks. Do you know what the office wants, Evelyn?"

"Not really. The pilots talked to them and got me prior to finishing breakfast," she replied.

After a breakfast fit for a king, Derek said, "Rob, you clean up, and I'll see what the office needs." With this, he was out the door to the office.

Evelyn had the videoconferencing up and running, and the folks who needed to talk with Derek were awaiting his arrival. "Good morning," he said. After a reply and a litany of items they needed to discuss, they began one person at a time.

When Derek was finished, Evelyn said, "They are not going to let you alone, Derek. With Bart out of the picture you are all they have to rely on. It will be this way every morning."

"What do you suggest? I've promised Rob some time," he said.

"Could you take the horses back, ask Pepe to leave you a pickup there, and the two of you come in for breakfast and a shower? I'll have the items ready, and we'll take care of them first thing every morning. Since we are three hours behind, it is now lunch at home."

Derek replied, "That's a good idea, except it will get you up earlier than planned."

"What's the difference in that and traveling all night?"

"Okay, that's the way we'll handle it for a few days," and he was up and out of the office.

After a shower, Derek said to Rob, "Son, the office won't let me alone. Let's ride the horses back to the cabin. Pepe will leave a pickup at the cabin, and we will come in for breakfast. I can check in, and then we'll go back to the cabin for the remainder of the day."

"We can also shower and shave here," Rob replied.

"Let's plan on this idea. Is that suitable?"

"Yes, sir."

Later that night and back at the cabin, Rob asked, "Dad, does this place show a profit?"

"The best I can say is that it just about pays its own way. Why do you ask?"

"If the beef that is grown here could be channeled in such a manner as to feed the homeless, would the foundations buy it?"

"I suppose that's a possibility," Derek replied.

This ended the discussion of that subject for that night. When they arrived back at the cabin the next day, Rob asked, "Dad, have you ever followed that river through the mountains for any distance?"

"No, I've never crossed the river even," Derek replied. "Would you like to?"

"I sure would, and do it on horseback."

They saddled the horses and followed the river west between two gigantic mountains. On the opposite side of the mountain they also found a very large plain that was filled with cattle and standing in grass knee high. There were antelope, deer, and smaller animals dispersed among the herd that quickly made their way to safety. Several carcasses were strewn occasionally that wolves had apparently eaten, but not enough to be alarmed about. Just as they were about to turn around for the trip home and while looking at the far mountain at a much higher altitude, they saw a grizzly making its slow way toward the top.

"Dad, does the ranch own this property?"

"I guess so. We own all the way into and most of the next county. These must be our cattle since our brands are on most of them, and they are apparently in good shape. They probably enter this area from another entrance than by the cabin since there were no tracks by the river except ours."

Rob and Derek managed to remain on the same schedule for the next week, but so much had piled up at home they had to return. But for them it was the trip of a lifetime just to have the opportunity to be together for an extended period. They did make it a practice that even though they shaved and showered back at the main house, late every evening they took a frosty dip in the pool by the waterfall that formed the river running by the little cabin.

7

Derek and Rob got home from the ranch considerably after midnight. Azzi had cooked a special dinner for Rob earlier in the evening since he was going away to school, and the ranch hands had to have a little sing-along with him prior to leaving. Rob flew into the night, arriving very late. Derek followed along using a commercial airliner.

Derek picked up the phone by his bed before daylight. "Derek, are you awake?" Casey said.

"I am now. What's up, Case?" Derek asked.

"Bart just died. We need you at the hospital to take Anna home. She came in the ambulance with Bart earlier tonight."

"What happened?" Derek asked.

"We are still trying to determine that. Can you come now to the Foundation Suite?"

"Sure, I'll be there as quickly as possible," said Derek. Hanging up the phone he awakened Kit and asked her to go with him.

Anna was totally distraught when they arrived, and Casey was with her. Derek offered his condolences—as pitiful as they were under the circumstances—and she immediately asked, "Derek, can you get Evelyn to get our kids home from camp?"

"Anna, your mother is with you now. Let me get your kids. Don't you think they will be more comfortable with me, given the circumstances?" Kit asked. When asked this question Anna simply nodded in the affirmative, and Kit was out the door.

Casey was back in the room asking permission from Anna to have an autopsy performed to determine the exact cause of death. She, of course, agreed, and since Bart was an organ donor it wouldn't interfere with their work to a great extent.

Derek called Evelyn and asked her to be sure that word of Bart's death didn't leak from the office. He told her he was bringing Anna home and asked her to walk over to their residence and alert their staff to prepare for a crowd and their homecoming.

Walking down the hall toward Derek's car, Anna said, "Derek, Bart had suffered so long and so hard, yet there were times when everything looked up and we thought he would overcome his physical difficulties. He hasn't been the same since Chicago and the automobile accident. He said he'd never felt the same. Though I can hardly stand the thought that he won't be around any longer, at least his suffering has come to an end. That's the one thing I'm thankful for."

They talked about Bart all the way home—the good and the bad times. Painfully they had to discuss the funeral arrangements.

"Bart also asked that a portion of his ashes be spread in Bath Pond with everyone who had predeceased him. He wanted the balance buried in the family plot at the little cemetery where all the other family members were buried and in the same family tradition," Anna offered.

The decision was made to hold the service itself in the Langford Academy auditorium with a reception following. The burial itself would be at sunrise the following day just for the family, close friends, and employees. A breakfast followed the service at the Gregson home.

The family met at sundown the day following the funeral, and Anna deposited the ashes in the water. She also asked Rob and Ali to sing "I'll Fly Away," with Derek accompanying them. A standing-room-only crowd attended the service at Bath Pond.

Since Bart was such a vital part of the organization, all the Carter folks were in attendance, including all the area managers for the foundations. Since the Foundation owned the motel that had been made into lodging for conferences, there was plenty of room for everyone.

The day following Bart's service, Derek asked everyone who was vital to the organization and its ongoing activities to remain and meet with him for lunch, and after a short meeting they would adjourn. Since all this had happened so fast and since Derek now had no one with whom to consult, the meeting simply consisted of his stating that changes were surely coming, but he was unable at the moment to conduct any sort of a strategy meeting. The meeting adjourned, and Derek went home mid-afternoon.

Sadly, of all the original board members, Dan Hunter was the only survivor, and old age had taken a terrific toll on him. He was a director in name only. Derek was facing some drastic changes. Because of the foundations' closely held nature through the years. he felt it prudent to include Wendy, Kit, Anna, Dr. Casey Cagle, Ron Anderson (the chief comptroller), and Dan Hunter.

Derek had no choice but to curtail some of his activities and move into Bart's office. Evelyn and Bart's assistant developed a summary of those things Bart was engaged in and presented them to Derek. Added to the items he was working on, there was simply no way he could accomplish everything necessary without assistance.

While he was describing the problem to Dan, Derek make his decision. He felt that if the right management person in all four quadrants of the United States was found and answered just to him, he might be able to handle all the balls that were in the air. Derek was so overcome with the enormity of it all that he took Kit down to Marco to the fish camp for a few days and tried to get his mind around all that was happening.

He really had several severe problems. One was the size of the foundations and all the different arms of each. He had good management in all areas now, but he needed some highly intelligent folks answering only to him, and he didn't have them. He couldn't drop the ball on his family. More important, he couldn't drop the ball on all the items he faced that would be a personal physical burden, and he couldn't forget Dr. Spurgeon's advice regarding his health.

After he and Kit returned home from Marco, Evelyn had Dr. Spurgeon's nurse work Derek into his schedule, and he flew to Shands Medical Center. It was like old-home week for about thirty minutes—just good ol' boy talk. Dr. Spurgeon had saved Derek from total disaster earlier in his life, and they had become close friends, even though the foundations had all sorts of doctors, plus Casey Cagle. Casey knew of the friendship with Dr. Spurgeon. Since Casey and Derek were such good friends, he felt it much better that Dr. Spurgeon remain Derek's physician, for nothing more than the solace of having two opinions since Derek now had a mammoth load.

"What's the problem, Derek?" the doctor asked abruptly.

Derek then carefully outlined what he was facing and wanted to lay out his agenda in a manner he could handle it. He was really asking for Dr. Spurgeon's advice.

Dr. Spurgeon didn't answer him for several minutes. After contemplating the question, he said, "Derek, I reserve the right to change what I'm about to tell you, and I want you to agree that I can do it, okay?" Derek nodded his head in the affirmative.

"You like to entertain people, and it's fun for you, yet it isn't the same kind of work as wrestling with a business problem that seemingly has no solution. Business problems can become increasingly irritating. Or it's like doing a stand-up presentation that lasts about an hour and leaves you all washed out when you are finished. Yet it is a good feeling of being washed out because you like to do them. Am I right? Yet the same washed-out feeling after doing something you had rather not do isn't the same, is it?" Derek nodded again.

"After you continue to consider the situation thoroughly you'll find that there is no other choice but to hire some high-powered managers. These managers are actually highly trained executives who are extremely intelligent and possessed with the degree of honesty necessary and answer only to you. Consider me, if you will. I have no problem handling serious illnesses even though I don't always win. But remember this: I diagnose, and while I keep track of the progress, all those other items like blood tests and all sorts of other tests I don't have time to do have to be completed. If I did all the ancillary tests, there wouldn't be but a couple of patients a day for me. It is the same with you. You need good people to do all your follow-through to preserve your time for what you're best at. You diagnose, lay out the long-range planning, and manage just like Greg did. No one ever thought he was under the stress that would kill him. I examined him, and you can count on it, he wasn't. He'd found a way to handle it. You find just the right executives to answer to you and to you alone, and that can be your private executive committee. That is how you run an organization the size of yours, and you already know it is tremendous."

The two talked another hour, and Derek left knowing that Dr. Spurgeon was correct. The bombshell was that Dr. Spurgeon was retiring, and the doctor introduced Derek to the young man who would be his new internist, Dr. John Miller, who had studied under Dr. Spurgeon and was indeed a Gator himself. Dr. Spurgeon took Derek up on the offer to go fishing at Marco sometime in the near future.

Arriving back at the office, Derek called the Carter office in Chicago and asked the name of the best executive recruiting office in the nation. They were able to assist him.

Casey walked into Derek's office just as he finished the Carter conversation. "I've had a talk with Dr. Spurgeon. He told me what the conversation was about and what his recommendations were to you. He's right!"

"Oh, no, Case. You weren't supposed to know about that."

"I do, though, and I know John Miller personally. Together, we can keep you straight. Plus, I'm going to take off and go fishing with Dr. Spurgeon. Thanks for setting the fish camp up in first-class style and having only the finest fishing equipment and the best guide on Florida's west coast. Can I count on you to do what you promised Dr. Spurgeon and keep the fish camp in good shape for us?"

"Yes, as long as you keep your slimy mouth locked tight to Kit," Derek replied.

"I consider this doctor/patient privileged information—that is, as long as you mind him. If I catch you not following instructions, I'm going straight to Kit. I know you too well," Casey laughed.

8

Derek also hired a corporate consultant who worked only with him, on an as-needed basis. The consultant told him the same thing Dr. Spurgeon had outlined. But having the consultant to call on was comforting, and he did come in handy under the strangest circumstances and at the oddest times. His name was Dr. George Hinton.

After completing the hiring of district representatives, each began to get his program together and managing the foundations became easier. Each slowly became acquainted and realized how the others worked, and everyone now had the opportunity to begin relaxing. All this emerged from meeting with Derek once every other week for half a day at some place convenient to all. Videoconferencing became invaluable after all four were set up with the necessary equipment.

While Derek maintained an office in the executive suite, the Bath Pond office was his favorite. Mae was still in charge, except she had a helper who did the work. Mae was just too infirmed for anything to be expected of her. Derek's visitors—Bishop Hornsby and now Dr. Spurgeon—from time to time used the bedrooms there. Of course, everyone still took advantage of a swim at every opportunity. Dr. Spurgeon actually thought everyone was kidding about skinny-dipping there until Rob came driving up one day, located the whereabouts of the women, dove in without a swimsuit, and the Bishop quickly followed.

Dr. Spurgeon had become like family. Shortly after his retirement, Mrs. Spurgeon passed away. To accommodate Dr. Spurgeon, Derek took Rob, Ali, and a selected few of the musicians from the band and provided the music for her funeral and reception. They performed according to instructions, and it went off well. By predetermined agreement, no mention was made of who they were. Dr. Spurgeon and his wife had no children, and he was perfectly at home at Bath Pond at every chance he had to visit.

Since the Bishop was beginning to slow down, he and Dr. Spurgeon became great friends, meeting at every opportunity at Bath Pond. With the accommodations and quality of food it was the perfect place to hang out. With Casey slowing his pace as well, the fish camp was also a great place to visit, and the threesome fished often. More important, they liked each other and had a great deal in common.

9

After six years in the driver's seat alone with the foundations, Derek was beginning to feel the strain again. Because he had felt this way before and did nothing about it, the prescription was a year off to get back on his feet. He really didn't want this now.

Having Casey, the Bishop, and Dr. Spurgeon around helped him keep his perspective, because when they were aware by mere observation that he was overdoing his travel or work they chastised him severely. They kept him in line, and he always respected their advice because of who they were. When they were all at Bath Pond they continued to swim together and sit around on the dock and kibitz about various subjects of interest.

Unfortunately the Bishop and Dr. Spurgeon were forced to move into one of the assisted-living facilities. When they were up to it, a swim at Bath Pond was always a welcomed few moments.

Derek had decided that Gus and Greg's units in the facility were not to be rented to anyone but an executive of one of the foundations. Casey and Janet got Gus's unit. Greg's unit was standing empty but still cleaned weekly.

Ali finished her college early. She was studying medicine in Boston and had an apartment close to Wendy's. Wendy was very close to retirement. Even so, the two of them remained as family and visited every chance they could. They would catch the jet coming south, knowing full well Derek would send them back home. Ali had another couple of years before internship.

Rob had problems in college before they both graduated. The music department didn't appreciate his style of playing the piano. They ran into differences that couldn't be resolved. His voice teacher offered great training during the first two years and left the university.

Rob called Derek. "Dad, I really need to see you in person. There are some problems we need to discuss. Is that possible?"

"Sure, Son," Derek replied. "You want me to stop by, or do you want to come home? My schedule is in decent shape next week."

"Can you meet me at Bath Pond late Friday afternoon, and let's stay through the weekend? And, also, since Ali is at home this weekend, bring Mom and her also," he requested.

Friday afternoon found Rob on the dock alone. The cook was fixing dinner for the four of them under Kit's instructions.

When Derek drove up, he said, "You had a swim yet?" Finding that he hadn't, they both began to undress on the dock and hit the water. Meanwhile, Kit was picking Ali up at the airport.

Kit and Ali drove up in time for dinner and found them sitting on the dock drying off. "Aren't the two of you ever going to learn to wear clothing when you are together?" Kit asked.

"Can't have as much fun, Mom," Rob replied as he hugged and kissed his mother trying to keep his towel in place.

Kit backed up and looked at both of them. She felt Rob's biceps and abdomen, and then felt Derek's and said, "Hmm," and walked off. Walking away she said, "Derek, you need to get back to where Rob is physically." Joking followed, with all sorts of excuses from Derek as to why Rob was in better physical shape, as well as why Rob now weighed more and looked as if he weighed less.

The four joked around the table and had a great dinner together. School activities and Derek's schedule kept them apart much more than they would like to be.

When dinner was over, Derek said, "Okay, Son, what's the subject of this conversation?"

"You know, Dad," Rob began, "my voice teacher has been offered a better position elsewhere."

Derek acknowledged he was aware of that.

"You know that my piano instructor and I don't see eye to

eye on my style of playing, yet for all practical purposes my playing is much more pleasing to the ear than his. I play as you taught me and really don't want to play in the stilted or stiff style they teach. You remember we filled in time between verses for the benefit of the singer, and we did runs to fill time. We even transposed a bit to get everyone in place. The truth is that I'm more at ease with the fluid motions we play," Rob said. "We don't have any problem with me practicing or learning the music. In fact, most of the music I've been given at the university I can sight read. If it is in any way close to the time frame that we play, I can already play it probably. This blows their mind that I've had this experience."

"What's the solution, Son?"

"I have a bit under a year until graduation. I assume Ali will continue in Boston studying medicine, and I think I need an MBA."

Kit said, "You are right. An MBA is necessary, and I insist on it if at all possible."

"The question is still the same: what's the solution?"

"I would like to have a private tutor in keyboard and voice and spend the rest of the time at the university in the school of finance and business."

"Do you have someone in mind for the tutor?" Derek asked.

"I'd like that person to be you, but I know it can't be. I believe I can find just the right person though, if you agree with my assessment. It's doubtful I can find both in one person. If not, maybe two people," Rob concluded.

"Oh, also," Rob continued, "I would like very much for the two of us to go out occasionally on weekends and perform together again. We could be Papa & Son. How does that sound?"

"Rob, there is nothing I'd rather do than the two of us have fun before an audience, but this I can't promise. My duties are not the same as when you left for school. I'm more office bound by necessity, though I'd like to change this."

Derek looked over at Kit and asked, "Mom, what do you think of Rob's request?"

"If the right instructor or instructors can be located, I have no problem. The only thing I have a problem with is you and Rob becoming overloaded with this Papa & Son thing that will take needed energy away from other more important things. Having fun playing and singing can come later. The one thing I must insist on is both Ali and Rob finishing their education. And by the way, why is Ali not having the same trouble? You have been pursuing the same major, at least up to now?"

Ali said, "The answer to that question is simple. I simply want to further my musical education by learning all I can about the keyboard and voice. There is no problem with my instructors, though different from Rob's. I can understand his problem by knowing those who are working with him. He's right about what he's telling you."

"That answer is simple. I played with Dad enough that my style is not like Ali's. She does exactly as the instructor asks her to. She plays by the music and I play in the same fashion, but without thinking I add my own flourishes and this blows my instructor's mind.

"One other thing, Mom and Dad, I plan on music being a big part of my life. I'm sure music will be a big part of Ali's life, but she wants to be a doctor primarily and really will probably never develop the same style that Dad and I already have," Rob concluded. "I don't want to take a chance on losing my present style."

Kit looked over at Derek, who grinned and looked away. Rob noticed the glance and knew he was correct and connecting.

PART TWO

Papa & Son

10

The foursome went home for the night. They had breakfast at home, after which Derek and Rob went back to the Bath Pond office.

Derek pulled up Evelyn on the teleconferencing equipment, and they worked for an hour. She joked with Rob a bit, and they signed off the videoconferencing unit.

Derek walked over to the piano and began to play scales and had Rob sing them. Rob's range was much better than his father's. The quality of his voice was changing for the better. He sounded as if he was singing from all the way down to his toenails, nothing nasal. Derek's voice was getting lower, if anything. They sang duets and solos. They played for each other and had a great time until lunch.

Casey came over from the assisted-living facility and had lunch with them, and it was a great social occasion with no business involved at all. Before he left they all went swimming.

After Casey was gone, Derek and Rob walked out into the pasture among the cattle and looked at the grove a bit and talked about everything in general. Not busy talk, but enjoying each other in the way they always could. Then Derek said, "Rob, with your promise that you will suck all the knowledge and increased ability out of private tutors and that you will be one of the most accomplished MBAs coming out of the university, your plan has my blessing. Have at it!"

Rob had tears well up in his eyes and said, "Dad, you know I won't let you down. What you do is what I want to do, and also increase my knowledge in a book sense of the activities of the ranch out west. Thanks for seeing my way of thinking."

Derek hugged Rob as he always had in a long embrace and told Rob that he loved him and that he was a special person. For the first time since Rob was a little boy, Derek kissed him. Rob told his dad the same and kissed him.

11

After the weekend with Rob, Derek began to get excited again about music, thinking of nothing more than playing sometime for his relaxation at their local assisted-living facilities and the hospitals. He felt he was missing out on some fun, yet lack of extra energy and too much work was preventing him from keeping that aspect of his life exercised. In addition, he was operating a gigantic business and had just gotten into the position where he could rest a bit easier. The operation was so huge, it was difficult to keep up with. However, he had come to the realization that the corporate consultant who led him to the managers for each of the four quadrants had the right answers.

The managers answered to Derek, and while he had had the unpleasant duty of relieving a few of them, now he had the right group of managers all aware of their duties and producing at a high level for the foundations. Their production was due in no small measure to the productivity of their staffs.

Evelyn asked Derek, "You know the quarterly meeting with the four division managers is coming up shortly. When and where do you want to do this?" She said this while placing only that mail Derek should see on his conference table. She also plugged in a new pot of coffee on the credenza.

"Haven't given it any thought since we've been bringing them here and putting them up at Bath Pond," he said. "What do you think?"

"What about the ranch? This would be a change of pace, and they could bring their wives. And it would be a different flavor. Maybe we could have some fun if their wives were there."

"Can we put them all up there?" Derek asked.

"Well, the Davidson wing is across the pool. My bedroom is in the main house, and there are four extra bedrooms there. Seems to me that would do it," Evelyn concluded.

"Okay, talk to Azzi and get her approval with the provision she can hire all the help she needs. Talk to Rob and Ali, and be sure both can come for the weekend beginning Friday night. Fully apprise Kit as to what is happening, and have everyone but you, Kit, and me fly into Salt Lake. Set up charters to bring them to the ranch, with the reminder my kids never fly together. Also, tell the band leader to call me. Does that cover it?"

"It covers everyone but Ron Anderson. What will we do with him?"

"His wife can't be there because of illness, so Ron can stay with the pilots in the bunkhouse. That'll work."

Since the western operation had grown so significantly, a large meeting room that seated about one hundred people had been built adjacent to the bunkhouse. In true Gregson fashion, the meeting room was well furnished, with comfortable accommodations.

Evelyn buzzed Derek. "The band leader is on line four."

"Hi, Chip," Derek began. "I want to ask a favor." He told him of the upcoming weekend conference and asked for a drummer, a guitarist, and a bass player to be flown in, not the entire musical ensemble.

On late Friday afternoon everyone began to arrive. Dinner was served around the Olympic-sized pool. The Davidson wing across the pool had a twenty-foot overhang toward the pool. The house had an identical overhang. The side adjacent to the airstrip had a stone wall twelve feet tall of the same stone from which the house was built. The other side of the pool had a twenty-foot-wide hallway—fully enclosed and tastefully furnished, built from the same stone, and with windows on the pool side—that allowed those in the Davidson wing to walk to the rest of the home during inclement weather. It was also decorated in classic Gregson style.

Azzi had the pool area decorated with fresh flowers and potted palms. Individual tables were scattered around under the overhangs, and a buffet was set up next to the kitchen entrance.

Dinner was at 7 p.m. Everyone began to gather just a bit earlier to become better acquainted with each other. Some of the wives already had strong friendships from other occasions. The dress was casual.

Derek walked over to where Rob was standing with some of the ranch folks and ask him to find the band members and take them to the raised platform and play a little dinner music. "Yes, sir," he answered. "Should I use all of them?"

"We hauled them here for that purpose. Let's get our money out of them."

Rob told the musicians to start with dinner music, and if a song came to mind to suggest it and they would move into it. They were playing so softly that the guests didn't pay a great deal of attention, but the music added an unusual atmosphere to a place so far removed from the rest of society.

When 7 p.m. came, Rob played a little fanfare and Derek stepped up on the platform. Derek welcomed the group and asked those gathered how they liked their little place in the West. A rousing round of applause followed. Following the applause Derek offered the invocation, and everyone found their seats after passing by the buffet. Rob continued to play. When Ali finished eating, she relieved Rob so that he could eat.

The farmhands from miles around began to gather, sitting all over farm equipment and the board fences, listening to the music. Derek knew they would attend and fully expected them to have some fun as well. They always looked forward to Derek coming. They already knew, as did the company employees, that nothing alcoholic would be served or consumed on Gregson property—nor drugs of any kind. This rule they obeyed.

Somewhere around 8 p.m. Derek stopped the combo and announced that no program had been planned for the evening except to have a little fun singing and dancing. "Those of you outside the pool enclosure should come in and join us. We counted on your being here to help us have a good time. What would you like to hear first?"

Someone from outside the fence yelled, "Rocky Top." Ali was seated at the piano. Before Derek could turn to nod approval, she had already begun to play. The farm laborers were clean and came in dancing. Of course, the division managers and the pilots thought they should dance as well.

Derek stepped off the platform, and Kit was waiting to dance, too. About thirty seconds into the dance, someone tapped Derek on the shoulder. The largest Hispanic woman at the gathering was waiting her chance to dance with him. Kit gladly obliged. Turning to walk away, Rob walked up and finished the dance with Kit.

Ali played a few requests and asked Rob to take the piano for a while. She wanted to dance, too!

The little combo was perfect for the setting. The division managers and their wives were mixed in, dancing with the farm employees and having the time of their lives. The pilots always expected music when they visited the ranch, and they joined in as well.

Quite out of order for the music of the evening, Rob moved into "The Blue Danube" waltz. The beautiful sight of those Hispanic cowboys and their wives waltzing put everyone in the mood. One of the pilots danced with Kit, and Derek snagged Azzi.

Somewhere around 9:30 p.m., Derek knew the group was tiring and stopped the dancing. "Since the hour is getting late and we all have a full day tomorrow, why not sing a few songs before we call it a night?" Everyone agreed.

In the past, Derek had introduced them to the old hymn "Beautiful Isle of Somewhere." Rob moved into the introduction, and Derek and Ali stepped up on the platform. Derek said, "We will sing the verses, and you folks join in the chorus. In fact, we will do that with every song we can."

Derek, Rob, and Ali sang the first verse, and the group

joined in the chorus. It was beautiful music since the Hispanics could sing very well.

Rob moved from hymn to hymn and followed the same procedure. Derek was very proud of the job Rob and Ali did that evening. Their training was showing.

"We are coming up on the close, which is 'I'll Fly Away,'" Derek said.

One of the laborers asked, "Mr. Davidson, would you first sing 'The Impossible Dream,' please, sir?"

"I guess that's possible, if Ali and Rob will help me," Derek said.

Rob said, "Here, Dad, you play." The three harmonized the great song, which had developed into a real showstopper.

Finishing the song, Derek segued right into "I'll Fly Away." This ended the evening, and everyone slowly moved out from around the pool. The workers' wives generously stayed and helped Azzi clean up around the pool.

When Rob was thanking the musicians and giving them directions to the motel in town, four young men came up to him. When Rob finished with the musicians, he turned to them and said, "Hi, I hope you had a good time tonight."

They unanimously agreed that they had a great time. One said, "Sometime tomorrow, when you have a moment, we'd like to talk to you if we could."

"Sure," Rob said. "Tell me what we are going to talk about."

"We've been studying music and more specifically vocalizing since your dad first came here. He has actually been our idol, and we've tried to learn from watching and listening to him. Our aim is to talk to you and see if there is some way we can polish our ability and maybe sing with the group sometime?" one asked.

"Sure. Let's say 10 a.m. tomorrow?"

They agreed and left laughing and talking among themselves. Of course, they thanked Rob for agreeing to their request. They were impressive young men—all about six feet tall, very well groomed and handsome. They wore western garments and were well muscled.

Rob was a bit baffled by the request to meet with him, but he understood another's like for music since that was his first love. Music was his life at the moment, and he could think of little else.

The next morning the Foundation meeting started at 9:00 sharp in the meeting room behind the bunkhouse. Rob slipped out at 10:00 and started his walk across to the main house. The four young men were awaiting him at the kitchen steps.

Rob greeted them. "Hi, fellas. What can I do for you?"

The spokesman of the group said, "We've watched and admired your dad since we were little kids. He is a real professional, and his work has inspired us to get all the musical training we could in high school, and we even received extra free lessons from the chorus director and the choir director at church. We are learning, and our hope is that you can find a way to work us into singing with you at some time in the future."

Rob said, "Before we get into that, maybe you should tell me your names?"

The spokesman said, "I'm sorry. I failed to introduce you to our group. My name is actually George. This is Bill, this is Bob—we call him Butch—and finally Bang."

"Who sings what part?" Rob asked.

"Butch is our bass, I am the baritone, Bang is lead, and Bill sings tenor,"

Rob said, "Have you sung anywhere in public, or do you just sing for fun?"

"We've sung in church a few times, and others have invited us. While we have sung in front of an audience, we know we need lots of work," George said.

"Let's go into the living room." The four followed Rob.

"Azzi, is anyone else in the house but you this morning?" Rob asked.

"Did you boys wipe your feet before you came into the home?" she asked gruffly.

"Yes, ma'am," they said almost in unison.

"Why do you ask that?" Azzi asked.

"Because we want to use the piano in the living room, and we aren't interested in everyone hearing us," Rob declared.

She said, "All the ladies have gone shopping. I'm the only one in the house. The rest are in the Davidson wing and around the pool getting ready for tonight."

Rob sat down at the piano and played four notes, one for each of the boys. "Here's the drill. Butch, you are bass and you sing this note, and each of you should just hum the note suited to your voice." They did, blending remarkably well. "Now," Rob said, "continue to hum, but soften your voice so that you can hear the fellow on either side of you but not yourself. You are not supposed to hear yourself." They did, and it was perfect. Rob then said, "We'll move up a half step now." It continued perfectly. By doing this, Rob was trying to find their ranges individually. Theirs were about as good as his.

Rob said, "You boys are good, and I wanted to see how well you blend and what your ranges are. You've practiced a great deal apparently."

Bang said, "We have, but it is without instruments. We can't play any sort of an instrument. All we can do is sing. We started with 'I'll Fly Away' because you always end with it, and it made the song special for us."

"Bang, since you are the lead singer, sing the first verse, and all of you sing the chorus. George, you sing the second," Rob instructed.

They sang the hymn as if they were professionals. "You boys set me up, didn't you? You've had lots of experience, haven't you?"

"Not unless you call working cattle or building fence as singing experience. We did it to pass the time and liked it to the point that we wanted to get better," George replied.

Rob said, "Tell you what. You get four chairs and arrange them behind the piano tonight. Remain seated, and sing every song you know and harmonize it."

"Some of the songs we know we can't harmonize since we don't know how. We know the one we sung since we've heard it most all our lives and followed your father closely," Bob said.

That night when Rob went out to the piano and sat down, the four boys were seated as he had instructed. They were dressed alike in new jeans, western-cut shirts, and boots. They also didn't wear hats, which Rob had expected. They were very well groomed.

"Now, fellows, when I sing a number, you sing very softly with me as background. If you can harmonize it, do so. If not, sing the melody, but never hear your voice unless you are singing solo. Be sure you are hearing the one on either side. If I play a dance number and you know the words, sing that as well, even when I'm not singing."

Rob conducted the dinner music around the pool that night much the same as the previous night. He did the usual fanfare for Derek, trying to embarrass him, and after the invocation Rob played some dinner music, occasionally singing along. When he did, the quality of the four boys singing with him was amazing.

About 10 p.m. Derek stepped up on the platform to close out the evening. He noticed the four boys but thought they were just ranch kids interested in watching Rob play and not participating. He had no earthly idea Rob was behind their being there.

"Folks, we need to bring our weekend to a close. We've accomplished a great deal business-wise, and I know bankruptcy is lurking nearby for me when I see all the items Kit's purchased, so it's necessary to get back to work. You fellows might be in the same shape. After breakfast tomorrow, everyone will head home and hit it again on Monday. It has been great just being with you and your wives. We wish you safety while traveling. Those plans that we made here this weekend will be developed further, and we will be communicating with each of you. And now, Rob and the musicians will handle the closing."

Rob stood at the piano and said, "I've found right here on the ranch what I believe will be a real treat. Here are four young men who want to sing, and no better song than our closing number for their performing debut. They will sing the verses, and you help with the chorus." While Rob was speaking to the managers and farm workers, the four boys came to center stage and presented their song using one microphone. The farm workers gave them a rousing round of applause.

Rob played the usual introduction to the age-old hymn. The boys hit the first note right on target and sung the verse as professionals. Rob put more volume to his playing to get the crowd to sing the chorus louder, and he was singing from the piano into the microphone.

Rob looked at Derek, who was visibly astounded at what he was hearing. When they were finished, Derek stood—as did everyone—and gave them a standing ovation, which really made the boys' evening one to remember.

All the managers came up to congratulate the boys when they were leaving, which made a tremendous hit with them. Derek stood around until everyone else had spoken to the kids and asked, "Do you boys work here?"

To which they all answered, "Yes, sir."

Derek then asked, "Have you had any musical training?"

George said, "Only at school and in church. We really were taught what we know by listening to you."

Derek talked to Rob about the boys until late into the night, discussing their future. The next day he was still overwhelmed at what he'd heard.

"Rob, whatever you do, don't let those boys get away from us. We can use them in better places than punching cattle," Derek concluded.

12

Ali completed her musical training and was now into the final throes of medical school, before residency. Her music consisted mainly of relaxing at the piano before, during, and after her study night. Wendy had told her that when residency rolled around, she could kiss her piano good-bye for a while, until at least the residency was finished.

Rob had just completed his MBA, and thankfully school was over for him. Now it was time for his work to begin.

One of the first visits Rob made was to the Bishop and Dr. Spurgeon at the assisted-living facility. They were becoming a bit infirmed because of their age. Both had a great attitude and both wanted to talk to someone, but Rob found it difficult to get away from them.

While they were discussing what Rob might do now that his formal education was complete, Dr. Spurgeon said he had been reading all sorts of books and periodicals, and he had an article for Rob.

"Rob, since your office has videoconferencing capabilities, there is now the technology available to do most of your entertaining and speaking to groups this way and never leave the office. Did you know that?"

"No, sir, not to that degree," Rob said. "I have heard of piping a speech to an auditorium. The problem I can't overcome in my mind is that I have to see the crowd's reaction in order to know how to change up."

The Bishop said, "Rob, you had better bone up on what the Doc has said. I think the possibility exists for you to actually see the crowd by reverse flow via satellite. You can probably see the crowd's reaction. Plus, I think there is such a thing as interaction."

Rob left confused about the possibility of a satellite feed to various places and walked into his dad's office and told him about the conversation.

Derek said, "Son, I've heard about such a thing and think it is something we might take advantage of. At the very least, it would circumvent a new jet every few years. If we could park that jet, it would probably free up enough money to handle it without a great expenditure. Look into it."

"Yes, sir," Rob replied. "Oh, Dad, since you are sequestered here in the main office, where did you have in mind for me to work from?"

"Son, we haven't really outlined your duties yet. For the time being, I've asked Evelyn to clean my belongings from the Bath Pond office and initially that can be yours, although with the understanding that you will have to spend more and more time here as you grow older and begin to learn some of my duties."

"Can I live at Bath Pond?" Rob asked.

"That's fine with me, but you need to run that by your mother."

"Yes, sir," and with this Rob was off to Bath Pond.

He walked into the kitchen and found Mae sitting at the table with a cup of coffee. "Any more coffee?" he asked.

"Help yourself," Mae said.

He did and sat back down at the table with Mae. "I've got an announcement. From this point forward I am the new boss at Bath Pond. How do you like that?"

"Yeah, you and whose army?" Mae rebutted.

"Well, I just found out my office will be here, and if Mom will let me, I'll be staying here permanently."

"Can you cook?"

"No, that's what your helper is for," he replied.

"You need to understand and get this straight. I run this place and don't intend to let the likes of you shove an old lady out," Mae replied.

"Yes, ma'am," Rob answered, and went into the office

where Evelyn was working. He saw her talking to Derek, and as he sat down Mae came in, sat down in Rob's lap, and began to wail. Evelyn looked away to see what was happening, and Derek immediately knew something was wrong.

Mae said, "Oh, honey, I wouldn't have hurt your feelings for anything in the world. I hope you are not mad at me. The only folks I boss are Derek, the Bishop, and Doc."

Mae didn't realize Derek was sitting there and heard the whole conversation. "When did you start bossing me?" Derek asked.

Frozen in her tracks, Mae immediately knew Derek must be on the videoconferencing machine and said, "Oh, Derek, I was just breaking Rob in and had to talk rough to him like I did you when you first came. You know I don't boss you. Evelyn and Kit do."

"I'd hate to read the headlines tomorrow and find them saying, 'Old Woman Drowns.'"

"Come on over, Buster. I can still throw you in the lake," she gruffly replied, and Rob was laughing out loud.

Derek couldn't hold his composure any longer. He grinned and said, "I'll tend to you later in the day. You can be scarce, because Rob and I might take a dip."

13

After Evelyn left and Rob was fairly well updated on how to work everything in the office, he began tinkering around with the piano. He was thinking about the four boys out west and what he should do with them. He was also wondering about his future, and what his dad would have him do.

The Bishop and Doc drove up and entered through the kitchen. "I guess you old men want a snack or a cup of coffee?" Mae asked.

"Coffee would be nice, thank you, Mae," the Bishop said. "We've just had a nice lunch. A mid-afternoon snack might be nice."

"How long are you planning on staying, for crying out loud?" she inquired.

"We have a new buddy here now," Doc said. "We have someone to visit now since Derek is too busy to bother a whole lot with the likes of us."

When the pair walked into Rob's office they both spoke, and Rob said, "Hey, now that I'm close by we can visit often."

"That's what we thought, but Mae thinks differently. She's okay with an occasional coffee, but a mid-afternoon snack might be out of the question," Doc said.

"She's not nearly as tough as she makes out like. She made a fool out of herself a few minutes ago, and Dad heard her over the videoconferencing machine," Rob laughed.

Doc said, "Rob, I was reading earlier today and ran across another article I thought you'd like to know about. There is a satellite of some kind you can purchase that can set up your conferencing so that you can do most of your work from here. I don't know the details of it, but I can tell you we used to conference with medical specialists worldwide. They spoke to us and saw our reaction to their remarks. We responded to their assessments and that sort of thing. If you had something like this, it would park that jet for the most part."

"If you think about it just a little bit," the Bishop interjected, "you could use it in every area of your outreach. For example, you could teach the gardeners around the country, you could entertain the assisted-living facilities periodically, you could develop a prison project like you had projected, the couple's idea you wanted to pursue would work this way, and all sorts of other ideas would come to the forefront. But I want to caution you not to mention this to your dad until you know all there is to know about how it works, and every detail of its cost of operation. That way he'll know you have done your homework."

"You know, Bishop, you could do a short devotional for the prisoners and the assisted-living facilities," Doc said.

"Well, Doc, if you are looking for jobs for others, why not have a 'Medical Moment' for everyone? That way you wouldn't go stale on us," the Bishop responded. "We may need you, and you need to keep your abilities polished. We could use Casey for this, too."

"You fellows are filled with great ideas," Rob said. "You can be my board of directors."

Just as Rob said this, Derek's car door slammed, and he walked in the back door to enter Rob's office. "You fellows taking up residence over here and keeping my employee from work?"

"No, actually we've just been hired as Rob's board of directors," the Bishop said.

"That's right, and we are just about to discuss compensation. Would you like to be seated and listen to our proceedings?" Doc asked Derek.

"If Mae's telling me the truth, there will be no compensation since you eat so much over here. I can already see it was a mistake letting Rob use this office," Derek said.

Doc replied, "Don't believe Mae. The Bishop and I are both dieting, and we only drink coffee when Mae invites us."

When Doc said this, Mae was coming in with about half a cake and said, "I ought to throw this cake in the trash can. You old buzzards come over here and mean-mouth me to the boss, and then expect me to be nice to you."

"Now, Mae, you know Doc is a big kidder, and he didn't mean what he said. In fact, he saw you coming down the hall from the kitchen—didn't you, Doc?—and said it to get you riled."

"Yeah, that's right, Bishop. I was just kidding because I knew she was listening."

"I'm going to take your word for it this time. Truth is, I believe both of you were lying—a doctor who has taken the oath and a man of the cloth lying to an elderly slave woman." She then set the cake on the conference table and returned with a fresh pot of coffee.

After she had safely returned to the kitchen, Rob said, "Dad, you need to watch these men. They are professionally slick. Mae had both of them dead to rights, and they weaseled out of it. That's why I've chosen them as private advisors and members of my board."

"They'll do the same to you, Son. You need to watch them very closely, too," Derek said, and everyone had a good laugh.

"Sure, I can do that," Rob said.

After coffee and cake, Derek said, "You fellows want to take a dip? That's my mission." Of course, all of them joined in.

"Turn your head, Mae. We are going to take a dip," Derek said on the way out the door to the patio.

"That's all I need. Two naked old men, one kid, and one ball of flab," she said.

Rob stuck his head into the kitchen and said, "You'd better watch what you say about Dad's weight. He thinks he's muscled up!"

"Huh, he's gaining every day."

14

When he arrived home for dinner, Derek was careful not to mention Rob wanting to move to Bath Pond. He usually helped Kit with dinner, and tonight was no different. While Kit had house help, the person who assisted in the kitchen only worked on special occasions for their private evening meal. Kit liked to prepare dinner and experiment with new and different recipes. Since Derek had professionally trained as a chef, it only made sense that he not let his talent lie dormant.

Midway through dinner Rob said, "Mom, don't you think it is okay for me to move to Bath Pond and live in the little apartment you and Dad used to live in? Mae and her helper are there, and it's not like I'd be out in the middle of that wide open expanse with just cows around me."

Kit didn't want to look shocked, but at the same time she didn't think Rob would want to live that way. He would then be in a situation where clothing would become an additional responsibility.

"Have you discussed this with your dad?"

"Yes, ma'am, I have," Rob replied.

"And what was his reply?"

"He said to ask you."

Kit turned and looked at Derek, who was busy eating and didn't look up. "So, you dumped this momentous decision in my lap?"

Derek looked up smiling. "I wanted you to be a part of the decision. Rob has been to college and graduate school for a number of years, and now that he is a young man it's not like he would be moving to another city. He would be with folks who are in our employ—the same place you and I lived for a few years. I think it would be fine. Plus, he would have the responsibility of keeping up with his clothing and things that sooner or later he is going to have to face."

"Rob, do you mind if I think about this for a little bit?"

"No, I just want you to be satisfied with your decision," Rob replied.

Before Rob left the next morning, Kit said, "Your dad and I discussed your moving to Bath Pond and both understand it from your side. You know I have reservations but won't stand in your way. However, you know Mae is an old, old lady. Even though she has all the help she needs, you need to watch out for her and not cause too much uproar in the household. You need to act like the gentleman that I know you are. Is that a sufficient answer?"

Rob's face lit up and said, "Mom, you know I'll be the same there as here. Also, I think my bedroom ought to be kept just for me when I'm here."

"You said you were moving," Kit replied.

Arriving at Bath Pond, Rob located Mae and said, "I'm the new man of the house."

"What house?" she replied.

"This house. Mom said I could move here."

"Look, Sonny, I run this place, and what I say is gospel. Evelyn is teaching me how to use that conferencing machine. If you give me any sass, I'll dial up Derek and let him handle yo' case fully. You got that?"

"Yes, ma'am," Rob chuckled. He thought how Mae had been around all his life and what a necessary and integral part she was of the whole operation—even at an advanced age.

"Carter Associates," the operator said when Rob dialed their home office.

"Hi, this is Rob Davidson of the Gregson Family Foundation," he said. The answer he received from the operator was very cordial, even though she knew nothing of Rob Davidson.

"Could you please allow me to speak to someone who handles your electronics purchases?" he asked.

"Sorry, sir, we have no one who does just that. Is there someone else who might help you?"

"Yes, please connect me to Mr. Carter if he isn't busy at the moment," he said.

"Is Mr. Carter acquainted with you?" she asked.

"Try him, please," Rob said.

In moments, a man came on the line and said, "Hey, Rob, how you doing since your graduation?"

"Fine, Mr. Carter, and yourself?"

"Never better. How can I help you this morning?"

"Do you have anyone who could help me with videoconferencing?" Rob asked.

"Not really, since that is a very specialized field. Take this number down and call it. It is a firm in New York we use. Tell them I told you to call them, that might help," Carter said.

"Thanks for the information, Mr. Carter. I'll tell them just that. I do appreciate your assistance."

When Rob called the office, the best information he could get was that they had a representative in Atlanta who would touch base with him in a few days.

Just as he was hanging up the phone, Derek came onto the video. "Morning, Son. Did you and Mom part on friendly terms this morning?"

"Yes, sir, we are the best of buddies. She did balk a bit when I asked her to keep my room open for the future. Realistically, I believe she is okay with the move, don't you?"

"I think so. Listen, I need you to go west and straighten out some equipment purchases and other problems in the office. Evelyn is sending one of the office personnel with you, and if you'll stop by later we'll talk about what is necessary there," Derek said. "Why don't you invite your board members to go with you? I think you could squeeze in one night at the cabin. Be sure Azzi knows you want it stocked. I'll see you later in the afternoon."

Doc and the Bishop jumped at the chance to go. While the

Bishop had been there on a number of occasions, this would be Doc's first trip. The cabin in the west was all most everyone around Bath Pond wanted to talk about. They imagined that it must be palatial.

When Rob slipped into the back door of his dad's office, Derek said, "Come in, Son. Sit at the conference table, and let's look these documents over together."

Saying this, Derek buzzed Maggie, whom everyone called Mag. "Could you come in, please, Mag?"

"Yes, sir," she said, and was in the office in minutes.

"Rob, Mag knows all the problems you will have to correct." He turned to Rob and said, "Listen to her, and she can safely guide you through." Mag was an older lady and had worked for the Foundation most of Rob's life.

"Yes, sir, we'll handle it," Rob replied.

Back at Bath Pond, Mae said, "So, you are going out on a trip with one old woman and two old men?"

"I'm a busy man, Mae, and don't have time for foolishness," he said.

"See that it stays that way, and we'll get along fine. Oh, your mom called and said when you get back your things will be here. It looks to me like she is glad to rid herself of the likes of you and dump you on me. If there is anything you have at home that is hidden from her, you'd better get it before you leave. I think she has redecorating in mind."

"What do you mean, 'hidden from her'?" Rob asked.

"You know, a Christmas present or something like that for me. And for all I know, something that you might be ashamed of if she found it."

Rob answered, "Thanks for the heads-up. I'll take care of that when I pick up my shaving supplies and a change of clothing."

The jet left the runway at 2 p.m., and they planned on being at Azzi's table for dinner. This was great news to everyone on board since they all enjoyed Mexican food—particularly

Azzi's. Doc grew excited when he saw everyone else's response.

Arriving a bit earlier than they had predicted, Mag and Rob finished the work they had to accomplish for the Foundation right away. Mag said, "There is so much here that needs catching up, but you'll still have time to show the Bishop and Doc the cabin. I've more than enough to do to last even a couple of days."

The Bishop and Doc were sitting around the pool when Rob was finished. "You fellows want to take a dip?"

"We've talked about it and know that a bathing suit is expected here, and we think we'll just pass," Doc said.

"I told him about the river at the cabin, and that will be sufficient," the Bishop said.

Rob asked, "Do you want to ride horses or go in a truck?"

"We think horses," Doc said. "I haven't been on a horse in years."

"We are an awful long way out in the country for a broken hip, Doc," the Bishop said.

"One has to be tough to live as long as I have. I've looked at the horse flesh, and there are a few out there as old as we are," Doc replied. "And there is some good horse flesh as well. I'd like to be buried by that horse out front. He must have really been something,"

"I understand that he was also a Bishop!" Rob said. "He belonged to Mrs. Gregson's father, whom everyone called Poppy because Bart called him that. Poppy's name was Bob Barton, and quite a corporate executive I've heard."

The Bishop said, "He must have been something else to amass sufficient funds to buy a place like this."

After dinner, the farmhands began to gather outside. Azzi came over to Rob and asked if he wanted her to run them off, or was he up to a sing-along?

"Doc hasn't heard this group sing. He might find a talent lying deep down inside himself that could be resurrected and polished. I'd say let them in if everyone wants to."

Getting approval from everyone, Azzi let them in—provided they pull their boots off. The last time she let them in her living room, it took a while to get the place back up to her standards, and this was all she could come up with. The farmhands knew it, and they wore clean socks after taking a bath and changing clothes.

Rob had wondered if Bill, Bang, Butch, and George would be present, and sure enough they were there. Since this group liked "Rocky Top," he put the foursome behind the piano to sing the verses and everyone else sang the chorus.

Doc was blown away by the singing—particularly the four young men he'd already heard Rob talk about. Their talents were superb.

Mag slipped out around 9:30 p.m. to her bedroom. She was older and a bit tired from the day. When Azzi saw her leave, she went to her room to determine her problem. Finding out that she was just tired, the group in the living room was immediately informed they had room for one more song and the night was ended.

The next morning, after a field hands breakfast, the threesome began their journey to the cabin. All three had a carbine and pistol and felt armed to the teeth, though neither had ever shot either type of gun. They laughed and talked all the way to their destination.

Azzi fixed a sandwich with a few trimmings for their lunch. Pepe had iced some sodas down, and there was water there. Azzi had steaks in the cooler and all the fixings for dinner and breakfast. Pepe would replenish their supplies the next day.

After lunch they were sitting outside in straight chairs, leaning back against the cabin. Doc said, "You know, fellas, a place like this is what I've dreamed of all my adult life. If I had a place like this, I'd still be practicing medicine. This has got to be the most relaxing place I've ever been. Look at the beauty of the river, and listen to the sound of the water. Listen at the birds in the trees and the sound of the eagle echo back into the mountains. This sounds like a studio. I don't know anything at all about acoustics, but listen. One can distinguish the sounds of each animal perfectly."

"You are right, Doc," the Bishop said. "I can hear what you are talking about. Can you, Rob?"

"Sure can. That might be just part of the reason why this place is so relaxing," he added.

After a nap and before dinner, they decided to take a dip in the waterfall pool. Not being used to such, the cold water was paralyzing at first, but it soon became refreshing and the threesome actually stayed in much longer than they had expected.

When dinner was finished and they were about ready for bed, the Bishop said, "Rob, I've been preoccupied all afternoon with Doc's remarks about the acoustics here. Would you do me a favor?"

"Sure," Rob said.

"Wade back across the river to the spot by that dead stump between the first two mountains, which should be midway between the mountain on your left if you were facing us and the one behind you. When you get there, turn around and sing in your best voice a deep, deep rendition of 'The Lord's Prayer.' I'd like to know what it sounds like from here. Would you do that?"

Rob positioned himself just as the Bishop had asked and began singing. The sound of his voice was echoing throughout the mountains with an unusually beautiful timbre. Neither Doc nor the Bishop could describe it adequately.

"Doc, imagine Rob dressed in a tux and doing an Easter program from here. Wouldn't it be beautiful?"

"It is breathtaking dressed as he is. His voice seems amplified and has a magnificent tone," Doc said. "His voice is perfect in any setting but beyond description here."

When he was finished, Rob asked, "Any more requests?"

The Bishop said, "Could you stand on the stump and do it again?"

With just a bit of height, it was even more beautiful. After singing this time, they brought him back across and went inside.

Doc said, "Do you know why your voice sounded as full and melodious as it did a few moments ago? It's the same voice, of course, and wonderful anywhere, but there is something sacred about singing across the river with the echo and the reverberation of the sound in the wild. I've never heard anything like it."

"I don't know why it is any different. But I can tell you I'd heard Mr. Gregson and Dad casually talking behind the mountain when I'd be sitting here, and I could make out every word. It is mystifying but real," Rob concluded.

Doc said, "Rob, could we get the four boys here tomorrow night at about this time and let them sing backup and hear what it sounds like?"

"Sure. Pepe will bring us food and ice tomorrow, and I can set it up," Rob said.

Doc was out fly-fishing when Rob and the Bishop finally got up. He had sufficient trout for the morning meal, but the Bishop talked him into bacon and eggs for breakfast. They enjoyed the fresh fish for lunch.

Pepe sent the four boys back late in the afternoon in a pickup. They brought dinner from Azzi's kitchen. Rather than eat too much, they decided to sing first and eat later.

It was a bit earlier than the day prior, and the day sounds had not begun to subside. They sang a number of songs so they would have something to compare their singing to later. Rob sang "The Lord's Prayer" again, and the four sang mostly backup until the last part.

Doc looked over at the Bishop, who was sitting there grinning at the beauty of their voices blending in such a remote place. When they stopped, it echoed far back into the mountains. The reverberation went on for a few seconds. The moment was breathtaking.

During dinner they discussed what had been discovered. No one knew. Was it the specific place? Did the same strange thing happen everywhere in the deep woods? What?

15

They arrived home too late to talk to Derek, and the next morning all three were at Bath Pond. They were cocked and primed for Derek when he arrived at their invitation for breakfast.

"Don't think all you birds are going to come marching in here for breakfast every morning just because of the quality of the food. I'm feeding you today because of my good nature, nothing else," Mae said. Of course, she had a helper who was doing the work while Mae was sitting at the counter drinking coffee.

"This is a special occasion, Mae, and we are having a board meeting. These are the members of my board, and it is an important day," Rob said. "After breakfast we'll go into closed session in the office and be out of your hair."

Mae said, "I thought you told me I was on your board of directors. That is, since I was at the White House with your dad, and the president went on all about me an' all."

"I'm saving you for greater things than the penny-ante items we'll discuss this morning," Rob said.

"Besides, Mae, since I'm a man of the cloth, I really don't believe those rusty and worn items we have to discuss would be of any interest to you at all," the Bishop said.

"Yeah—rusty and worn just about like your naked butt diving into Bath Pond, I guess," Mae responded.

"Not quite that bad, Mae," Doc said. "Since I am a man of medicine, I can attest you are correct."

"I don't know what you mean, but I hope it was respectful of an old woman," Mae replied and walked into the kitchen.

Derek said, "You shouldn't get Mae stirred up like that when you know I'm coming over here. She has ongoing issues with me since I moved in with Bart."

After breakfast they moved into the office. Everyone gathered around the conference table.

"Now," Derek began, "just what is so important that we are having an emergency meeting of such an august group?"

"Dad, we wanted to tell you what we stumbled upon while at the cabin and all the other things we have going," Rob said.

"Answer me one question first, Rob. Are you up with all your company work?"

"Yes, sir, right up to date," he said.

"Okay, who is president of this outfit?" Derek asked.

"We haven't elected officers yet," Doc said, "so the Bishop and I have appointed Rob as head spokesman. Mae also thinks she should have some sort of official authority."

Derek turned toward Rob and motioned for him to begin.

"Dad, first we were at the cabin. The Bishop asked me to cross the river real late in the afternoon and stand by the big stump between the mountains and sing 'The Lord's Prayer.' I did, and it produced a unique sound that seemed to surround the mountains. Then it echoed for a few seconds when I finished. Then I stood on the top of the stump, and it had an even more profound effect on the lingering sound," Rob said. "We were so taken with it that Pepe sent the four boys over the following afternoon at about the same time, and their harmony produced a magnificent sound that is difficult to describe."

Doc said, "Everything Rob says is true. We don't know why the sound was so enhanced, except that the sounds of the day were largely gone and their voices were virtually all that we heard."

"We think that would be the perfect spot for special religious programs that could even be televised," the Bishop said.

Derek said, "Bishop, if we put the equipment in there to televise a program, it would require motors to generate electricity, which would kill the effect, wouldn't it?"

"What if batteries were used? All we know is it is worth

your while to go there on your next trip and listen for yourself," the Bishop said.

"Dad, we've got several other things to run by you. We videoconference with each other, and Doc says they do this in medicine and can actually see the response of the groups they are talking to. There are several things we should be thinking about. why couldn't we videoconference our meetings? Think about it: this office is soundproof. We could broadcast from here. If we get rigged up where the crowd can see us and we can see them, you could come here and speak to the graduates. We could do a few numbers, and then leave the rest to the band that would be on location. You could just about stop traveling."

"This is beginning to sound like this board has done its homework," Derek said.

"We have, and we're not through," Doc said. "Rob wants to encourage incarcerated prisoners to write notes to young people who are being held in detention centers. It would be much like the original concept of using assisted-living facilities to write to bedridden patients in nursing homes that gained so much success. Get them involved in helping to straighten out kids' behavior to keep them from a life in prison. The Bishop wants to do a devotional spot, and they want me to do a medical moment. And I was thinking that since the prison officials encourage inmates to get their GED while incarcerated, why couldn't we do the same there and maybe do a graduation of some sort for them?"

"Wow, you have been at work," Derek said. "Is that it?"

"No, sir. We also want to do a whole weekend once quarterly to couples having problems with their marriage and family problems that includes Doc and the Bishop," Rob said. "The possibilities are endless."

Derek looked at his watch and said, "Fellas, I've got to go. I like where you're going. Find out the costs involved, and then let's talk again. I assume you would broadcast from here, except in the West? What I don't know is how we'd handle the other end."

"We don't either, Dad. That's why we have a person coming in to discuss the possibilities," Rob concluded.

With this, Derek was gone in a flash. "Keep me posted. and let's talk again soon."

16

"Trident Electronics in New York is calling, Rob," the office operator said.

"Thanks," Rob replied, and he picked up the phone.

"Mr. Davidson, this is Bob Johnson of Trident. I've been studying your request and those things you'd like to do in the future. I think we all understand what you are trying to accomplish and know the quality of the work you do. I've heard your dad, and he is very professional as an entertainer."

"Thank you, Mr. Johnson, for your kind words about my dad. He's top-flight, and please, my name is Rob. What can you do to help us meet our goals?"

"Two things. First, my name is Bob, and second, we need to send a sound crew from Los Angeles to the place in the West you want to broadcast from. Let's test the quality of the sound. While we have the equipment there, I would like to send our best sound technician from here to determine the extent of those things we can do for you. My problem is we need two weeks to work you into the schedule. Will that work for you?"

"Sounds okay to me, but I'll have to check with everyone else here who is affected and establish an appropriate time for all of us. I can be back with you in twenty-four hours."

"That works, and I'll expect to hear from you then, Rob. Great talking with you," Bob said.

"You, too. Thanks," Rob replied.

Rob slipped into the back door of his dad's office and said, "Dad, a fellow whose name is Bob Johnson from Trident Electronics in New York called and has studied our ideas and wants to send a crew from Los Angeles and a technician from New York to determine if they can develop what we are looking for. Are you free two weeks from today, and can you spend the day at the ranch?"

"Yes to both questions, but we need to get some things straight between the two of us. One is, no one books any performance by you except our booking office. Second, no one can pay for a performance, ever. And last, we will never do anything that a government group of any kind can put strings on the way we do them, or, for that matter, what we do. Are these things soundly understood?" Derek said with a stern look.

"Yes, sir, I understand that," Rob said.

"One other question. What are we trying to accomplish with this deal out west?"

"Dad, I wish I could lay it out in first-grade language. I can't. All I can say is the Bishop got the idea for me to sing, I guess, because of his mood and the mood of the afternoon. It was just at dark, and there wasn't a sound except an elk bugling occasionally a great distance from us. I sang for the Bishop, and the atmosphere, the altitude, the temperature, the spacing and size of the mountains, or something put a twist on my voice that I can't describe. Doc had me stand on the stump. It was better still standing on the stump with a little elevation. When we brought the four boys the next night and added volume and harmony, it was magnificent. You ask what we intended to do with it? The Bishop thought we could make a broadcast studio from it. How, I don't know. All I know is after you hear the sound—if you like it as much as we did—you'll see there has to be something special we can do with it. It is like we captured all of nature and did something else very special with it," Rob concluded. "I know it has potential. I just don't know what it might be."

"You've gotten my curiosity aroused," Derek said. "There must be some unusual and special use we can put it to that will draw contributors to the foundations. It has to carry itself financially; that's the first rule. My overriding fear is that the noise from all the sound equipment will screw it all up, as well as more people being on the scene. It is one thing for a single person to be sitting in the woods and something else for another hundred to be there as well. Let's leave it for two weeks, and we'll see what the experts say."

Bob Johnson telephoned Rob a couple of days later and said, "This project out west has really gotten our imagination in motion. Is there a possibility that I can send a sound engineer from Los Angeles and one from here sooner? If we can do this it would then determine the nature of the equipment that the recording itself would accommodate. This sounds as if it is quite a project."

Rob answered, "Bob, I think that possibility exists. However, the final answer must come from Dad. It would require a bit of schedule rearranging. Let me talk to him and get back to you today."

Derek was amenable to Bob Johnson's request. "Be sure you give the Bishop and Doc a chance to go. Also, after thinking about the whole scheme, tell the four boys at the ranch to learn 'The Impossible Dream' and anything else that is all over the musical scale. When you pitch it for them, don't mention it beforehand but raise the pitch a half-step. We need harmony, and it must be with high notes to really test it. The two of us can sing all the low notes necessary. Send from the band a flute, a bass fiddle, a harp, a trumpet, and a French horn."

17

Rob left early via commercial airliner for Denver and then Salt Lake. Derek, the Bishop, and Doc picked up two sound engineers, Bob Lineer and Sanjay Tapton, in Kansas City and transported them the rest of the way. Dropping them off at the ranch, the jet hastily picked up Rob in Salt Lake and returned.

Rob stepped out of the jet and walked the short distance to the office while Derek was talking to the home office. Rob felt bad that Derek and he could never have any free time alone, but Derek was balancing so many issues that he didn't have the time even to come over for a swim very often. Derek wrote Rob a note that everyone else was sitting around the pool waiting on him.

Arriving at the pool Rob introduced himself to Mr. Lineer and Mr. Tapton, both of whom were nice fellows. Rob said to Doc, "You ready to go?"

The Bishop spoke up first. "No, Rob, we plan to have lunch with Azzi prior to leaving. You fellows can do anything you want, but Doc and I will be along soon."

"Rob, don't let the Bishop rattle you. Your dad told us to sit here and after lunch we'd go, and that's what we are doing," Doc said.

After lunch everyone loaded into a couple of trucks and headed for the cabin.

When everyone was unloaded, Tapton asked Rob to duplicate his actions on and by the stump. Rob walked over to the stump, turned, and delivered two or three bars of a song. He then stepped up on the stump and did it all again. "How's that?"

"Great," Tapton said. "Now, Bishop and Doc, you sit exactly where you were sitting. The rest of you get around behind the building, and move the trucks there as well."

When this was completed, Tapton said, "Rob, when I get

over to where the Bishop and Doc are seated, you do the same thing again, or sing something else."

When everyone was in place, Rob did the same thing. Derek looked at Lineer and said, "Sounds different, doesn't it?

"Sure does. Tapton knows what he's doing," Lineer said.

Tapton said, "You folks behind the building come out and sit down on the ground in front of Doc and the Bishop. The quartet should come over here for a moment." He also told Rob to go sit with the group after he had given the foursome the pitch. Rob pitched it up a half-step as Derek had instructed. The sound they produced was absolutely magnificent.

When they were finished, Tapton said, "Wow, what a sound." With this he turned to Rob and asked, "Rob, do you know 'The Impossible Dream'?"

"Yes, sir," Rob answered. "My dad does as well."

"You first and then your dad. Both of you should sing it alone first and then with the group."

When they were finished, Lineer asked, "Rob, can you and your dad make a duet out of 'The Impossible Dream'?" Rob answered that they could. The pair then presented the song as a duet. Their voices didn't echo throughout the mountains as did the four boys' voices, but the quality of their voices seemed to have a surreal sound that could not be duplicated in a studio.

After that, the instruments were brought in, and everyone got in on the act trying to find the best combination. It was immediately evident that the flute, the harp, and the bass playing alone or with the group or a single produced the best quality.

Later in the afternoon all sorts of animal sounds began to come from the woods, leading to the decision that nothing further could be accomplished that day. Before they left for the ranch house, the Bishop said, "I think we should take a dip at the waterfall pool before we leave, don't you, Doc?"

Doc said, "I'm not wild about it, but if you fellows want to, fine."

The four boys and Rob struck a trot to the pool with Doc, the Bishop, and Derek following along. Lineer and Tapton had no earthly idea what was happening and asked, "What are we doing now?"

Derek said, "Come on, fellows. We'll give you the thrill of a lifetime." Before Tapton and Lineer arrived at the pool under the waterfall, they already saw what was happening and reluctantly approached the water.

"Come on in, fellows," the Bishop said. "We've got Doc with us in case you can't take it. You'll never receive a more refreshing moment."

The entire group finally talked them into the ice-cold water. The sun had been off the water for an hour, and it was freezing. The pair splashed around a bit, and Pepe was there with an armload of towels. Both Tapton and Lineer agreed they had never experienced anything like the swim. They really wanted to say they'd never do it again, but knew it could have a bearing on whether they got the job or not and decided not to say anything about it except something good.

18

The switchboard operator beeped Rob. It was Lineer on the phone from Trident in New York.

"Rob, we've finally gotten thawed from the trip west. That was a great experience. It was great in the sense that somehow nature had a role in the outcome. The bottom line is it took human voices and amplified the quality to a magnificent degree without disturbing the volume. Tapton and I are completely in the dark as to what happened, but wanted you to know we are studying it hard and will report as soon as an explanation is clear. We think our response will come in a few days. Is that okay with you folks?"

"Sure, it's okay. The role that nature plays completely dumbfounds each of us. We'll wait on your verdict," Rob replied.

"We'll be back soon." Lineer got off the phone.

Rob went to his dad's office and peeped through the hole, knocked, and walked in since no one was there but Derek. "Lineer just called and said they have no answer now for our problem at the cabin but will report in a day or two. I told him he wasn't any more dumbfounded than we were."

"Son, that is the dangdest thing I've ever known about," Derek answered. "I've been thinking maybe we shouldn't let anything else disturb the area. The sound could be coming from a combination of the mountains, the trees, and the foliage. If we disturb any of these elements it could destroy the sound there. Is that sensible?"

"Sure," Rob said. "I thought of that when we had the mob there the other day. In fact, I cautioned our boys not to stomp the weeds down, and I really don't think they did."

Derek said, "The promise we made to the assisted-living facility in San Francisco is coming up soon—in fact, next week.

Why not just you and I go and then go back to the cabin on the way home and take a closer look ourselves?"

"Suits me," Rob said. "You can't leave Evelyn."

"She'll have sufficient work to keep her busy in the office there. Maybe we can take a couple of days?"

"Great," Rob said as he went through the door.

Rob left by commercial airliner the day prior to Derek coming in the Foundation jet. Rob's job was to check out the dining room and make the final plans for their performance. He had the name of the person who was supposed to meet him at the hotel, and Rob asked for her when he walked up to the desk.

"Miss Saunders has had a bad break. Her mother passed away last week, and she is in Wyoming. However, she is headed back and should be here in a couple of hours."

Rob asked, "Could you deliver my luggage to my room and direct me to the ballroom we will be using tomorrow night?"

Entering the large room, he saw an elaborate setup. The walls were covered with expensive wallpaper. The window drapery was first-class. The room looked as if it had been recently refurbished. He walked up to the stage area, and there was what appeared to be a new concert grand piano.

Rob sat down on the bench and played a few songs to determine if a piano tuner was necessary. It was in perfect tune and a joy to play.

He played a few patriotic songs, a few country and western selections, and was thinking about going up to his room for a nap when he began playing songs from the Broadway hit *Oklahoma*. Tiring, he stood and started to put the lid down when a voice from the back of the room asked, "Do you know any songs from *The Sound of Music*?"

Startled, he quickly located a beautiful young woman sitting at a table in the rear of the room. He thought to himself, *That woman would cause a mean dog to break a chain, she is so good-looking*. Because of the question he quickly moved into the title song of the musical. About halfway through the selection he decided to see if he could make an impression on this pretty female, and he began to sing as he played.

This did impress her, and she came forward to the center of the dining room. There didn't appear to be anything bashful about her. She was in total charge personally, and she evidently was enjoying his playing and singing.

When Rob finished the song he joined her at the center table. "Hi, I'm Rob Davidson from the Gregson Foundation."

"Hi, Rob. I'm Mike Saunders, and I work for the hotel and will be in charge of tomorrow night's party for the assisted-living facility you folks work with. Are more entertainers coming?" she asked.

"That will be up to my dad, who will arrive tomorrow. I know there will be two of us, and someone has tuned the piano, for which we are grateful," he said.

"That is a new one and just delivered, and the tuner has been here just for you. I think you've probably had some instruction someplace as to how to play and sing," Mike said.

"Why Mike for a girl?" he asked.

"My name is Michele. The softball team I played on in high school gave me the nickname, and it stuck."

"Can I ask you a question?" Rob asked.

"Sure."

"Are you the person here who has just lost her mother?"

"Yes, unfortunately, I am," Mike answered, with tears beginning to stream.

"I'm so sorry. I didn't mean to hurt you, just to be sure. Can I do anything to help?"

"That is the bad part. No one can help except with kind words. Now both my mother and dad are deceased, and I have no siblings. I'm pretty much alone," she said. "I've got to go back to Wyoming soon and close up their house and dispose of a few cattle and a horse or two. There is no one left to look after them." Mike then abruptly changed the subject. "But that is not the reason I'm here, for you to listen to my troubles. What do you need me to do for you to get ready for tomorrow night?"

Thinking very quickly, Rob said, "Would you mind walking around in the dining room and listening to each loudspeaker, and tell me if they are of the same volume and all work? That is something that has to be done, or my dad won't use them."

"What will he do?"

"We'll use our own system, which we always travel with, just in case," Rob responded. He asked again, "Do you have a moment you could do that for me?" He was interested in keeping Mike with him a bit longer.

"Sure. You just want to know if each speaker is working and if all are about the same volume?"

"Right," and with this he watched her every move and played corny songs and happy songs—anything to change the mood from the gloom of her mother's death.

Returning to the piano when the test was over, she sat down on the bench with Rob. "Do you sing?" he asked.

"No, I'm a complete monotone. Never could sing, but you have a wonderful voice and seem to know how to play the piano."

"Thanks," he said. "Sure sorry about your mom. That must be a devastating loss."

"It is, but the real truth is she brought it on herself. She was an alcoholic and did nothing to protect her health. Do you drink?" she asked.

"No, that is a very strict company rule. No one in our group drinks. One of the founders was an alcoholic and was taken in by a fellow who had him cleaned up, and he would never tolerate alcohol or drugs."

"Have you ever had a drink?" Mike inquired.

"Truthfully, yes, but knowing the consequences I couldn't let it get in my blood. Those things are not a part of my life or anyone in the group of foundations we belong to."

"I already like you," Mike said.

"Thanks, I like you, too. The real question is do you like me well enough to have dinner with me tonight since this is our only night here? We'll leave after the dinner tomorrow night."

"I've not looked at my schedule since coming in. If I'm free, sure," she responded.

When Rob found out Mike was free and accepted his invitation, he immediately showered and changed clothes. He was on the way to the lobby to meet her when he ran into the meeting planner for the next evening.

"You got the message that I am here and Dad will be here tomorrow, I hope?"

"Yes, thanks," she replied. "When your dad is here, we'll get together and talk about tomorrow night."

When Rob saw Mike standing in the lobby, she appeared to have had her hair redone and was the loveliest woman he had actually ever seen. She was gorgeous.

Rob took her by the arm, walked out the door, and asked, "Which is the best restaurant in San Francisco you've never been to and not down on the wharf?"

"I've been told the best restaurant is a small restaurant located just down the street from the Fairmont," she replied.

Rob had ordered a limo, and he told the driver the same thing Mike had said. "Ah," he said, "the best restaurant in town. You'll love it."

Rob turned to Mike and said, "You look so pretty tonight, I had to look twice to make sure you were the person I was to meet. I'm sure glad you are you."

"That won't get you anywhere, Buster. All you cool-talking southerners can't come out here and sweet talk those of us who live in the West and get by with it. We are on to you. But I like your kind, so you'd better be on yo' southern manners tonight."

"Yes, ma'am, I'll certainly try to be. I thought women liked to be told they are pretty and gorgeous and all that, particularly when it's true."

"They do, but you'll have to prove that you just aren't looking for a quick date with a pretty woman and go out of my life and never show up again. There has to be some substance there. There must be some genuineness, some real manners that show that southern hospitality."

"You western women must be too tough and calloused for a southern gentleman," Rob replied.

"Show me a southern gentleman, and I'll show you what a real lady is like," Mike said.

"Yes, ma'am. I'll try."

Rob was really bearing down on his best manners as they entered the restaurant. He said and did all the right things, including slipping the maitre d' a good-sized bill to get the table he wanted.

When they were seated, the waiter asked if they would like to be served drinks before dinner with hors d'oeuvres, to which Mike said, "Bottled sparkling water with a selection of pates."

"Certainly, madam," the waiter quickly answered and was on his way.

"You've been kidding me. You've been here before, haven't you?"

Mike quickly responded, "No, I haven't. You asked me which restaurant I wanted to go to, and I told you. Now if you are too cheap, we can go to another, less expensive one."

"Naw, you've got the wrong idea," Rob said. "I like this one if you do. The money is not the object. Anyone dressed like you certainly must have sufficient money to stand this restaurant."

"You'd better get on your feet and let's dance before I remove you to the alley and give you a good dusting, Buster," she said. With this Rob was on his feet, pulling the chair out and taking her hand, leading her to the dance floor.

It was a slow number, and he took all the liberties he could get by with and pulled her up close. She felt and smelled good and seemed to enjoy the dance. When they were back at the table, the drinks and hors d'oeuvres were there.

After Rob had seated Mike, he said, "Thanks for a nice dance. There must be lots of smooth women in Wyoming."

"More than most Cracker boys can handle," she said.

"Cut me a little slack, girl. I'm trying to put on my best manners."

"You are doing pretty well, too."

"Where are you from in Wyoming?" Rob asked.

"A town called Greybull," she said. "My dad worked hard in some difficult weather and was unable to ever hit it really big."

"Did you go to college in Wyoming?"

"No, I went to the University of Colorado. What about you?" she asked.

"I went to the University of Florida as did my sister, who is now in Boston trying to become a pediatric surgeon."

"You've got a sister who wants to be a doctor?"

"Sure have."

"She must be more intelligent than you are."

"You really know how to hurt a person, don't you?"

"I work at it. But really, I didn't intend to hurt you. Just a little bit of ribbing, nothing nasty."

Rob and Mike had a wonderful dinner, with dining and dancing. Seldom did Rob have the opportunity for a leisurely date to sit and talk. It was wonderful, and she was the best-looking girl or woman he'd ever had the opportunity to be with on a date.

On the way back to the hotel, Derek called to say he was leaving first thing the next morning and would be in San Francisco in time for lunch. Rob agreed to pick him up at the airport.

"Would you let me go with you, Rob?" Mike asked. "I've never seen a private jet up close."

"Sure you can go. Dad will call when they are about to get in the air and tell me exactly what time they will land."

19

Rob and Mike were standing at the hangar when the jet rolled to a stop. Derek had brought Doc and the Bishop since they both wanted to come to San Francisco again and particularly wanted a great seafood dinner.

"Who is that girl with Rob?" Doc asked.

"Beats me," Derek said. "He didn't mention her last night."

When the noise subsided and the copilot opened the door, all three stepped out of the plane and left Evelyn to fend for herself, which she had done plenty of times before.

Doc walked over to where they were standing, and Rob introduced him simply as Doc. When the Bishop walked over, Derek did the same. They were all dressed in coat and tie, as was Rob.

"Folks, I want to introduce you to a special lady. This is Michelle Saunders, more affectionately called 'Mike.' Mike, this is Dr. Spurgeon. My dad has a bad heart, and he has to come along to take care of him. This is Bishop Hornsby. Should Dad die, we have someone authorized to bury him. Have you checked Dad out lately, Doc?"

"No, just a minute," said Doc as he checked Derek's pulse. "He's fine for the moment, but I did feel an increase when he saw Mike. He's more alive than you think."

"Mike, this is my dad, Derek Davidson. Dad, this is Mike." Derek hugged her, and Doc pulled him away and said, "I didn't know hugging was allowed," and hugged Mike himself. Then the Bishop said, "I should consecrate these hugs."

Then Rob said, "And this is Evelyn Smith. She is the person who keeps all this floating. She gives out spending money and candy and tells us each what our job is for the day. Watch her!"

Evelyn walked forward, took Mike's arm, and said, "Come on, honey. These lying old birds will tell you anything and think you believe what they say. There is no good in any of them, believe me."

"It is a mighty weird bunch," Mike said.

Derek started laughing and said, "Mike, I'm happy to meet you. You don't have to worry about Rob and me. It's Doc and the Bishop who bear watching."

Since it was close to lunchtime, they stopped at a restaurant that Mike recommended, and Doc and the Bishop had a great seafood meal. Rob and Derek ate very lightly as was their custom, while Evelyn couldn't get her phone to stop. It was a constant ring, and she just finally excused herself.

They had a great time laughing and talking all the way to the hotel. When they arrived, bellmen began taking their luggage to their rooms.

Rob and Mike took Derek to the ballroom. "I've checked it out, Dad, and I think most of the speakers work."

"Why don't all of them work?" Derek asked.

"They do, Mr. Davidson, I checked them yesterday. Why not do it again now?"

Derek said, "Good idea."

"Go back to the piano, Buster," Mike said, and she turned on the sound system.

Rob looked at Derek, and Derek chuckled when Mike called him "Buster."

Rob played long enough for them to check out the system, and everything worked. Evelyn walked up and said, "The office tells me there are 546 registered for tonight. Is that somewhere within your count, Mike?"

"That is exactly the number, and the room is complete," she said.

"Rob and I are going up now. We will see you back here dressed at exactly 7:30," Derek said. Everyone agreed to meet at the table in the center of the ballroom, and they invited Mike to sit with them.

"That's a good idea," Doc said. "I can dance with Mike for a while and then Evelyn and vice versa."

"You know I told you the last time out that you'd have to take lessons before I'd dance with you again," Evelyn retorted.

Mike noticed Rob and Derek leaving. Derek had his arm around his son, and they were laughing as they entered the elevator. Oh, how losing her parents was beginning to take its toll on Mike.

The Grand Ballroom had never been more elegant. This gala was under the direction of an assisted-living retirement center that had unlimited funds. The center placed quite a burden on the hotel, particularly in the area of floral decorations.

Derek and Rob took a nap and a shower and put on their clothing just before going down the elevator. Derek had changed his mind, and they went to the back of the stage. At the appropriate moment, Derek announced, "Ladies and gentlemen, would you welcome, please, Derek Davidson!" A standing ovation greeted Derek, much to Mike's amazement. She thought she must be in the presence of a star of some sort.

Derek walked to the center of the stage, offered an eloquent welcome, and was very well received. When his welcome was concluded, he said, "We have two visiting guests with us tonight, and I do hope some of you ladies will make them feel at home. Welcome, please, our traveling physician, Dr. Spurgeon. We need a physician since we are also traveling with an elderly clergyman. Please welcome Bishop Roger Hornsby, who has been here many times." The crowd welcomed both warmly.

Derek said, "And last, my special assistant without whom I could not operate, Evelyn Smith." Evelyn received a rousing ovation.

"Are the food and service up to the standards we require when we get together?" Derek asked the audience. The applause roared. He said, "That's because Michelle Saunders is in charge tonight." Another roar erupted from the crowd.

"I have another performer whom you've never been subjected to. If he does a poor job, it is his mother's fault. If good, then it would be my doings. Please welcome my son, Rob Davidson, ladies and gentleman." The crowd got to their feet again and did Rob proud.

"Before we begin the evening, I want to ask Bishop Hornsby to come forward and offer the invocation."

The Bishop turned to Evelyn. "Why doesn't he ever tip anyone off that something like this might happen?"

"You've got me," Evelyn said.

Mike leaned over and said, "Was the Bishop telling the truth?"

Evelyn was nodding her head in the affirmative. "No one knows what they will do here tonight, including Derek and Rob. They follow their nose."

The Bishop delivered an eloquent invocation while Derek stood there with his arm around Rob.

"While you are finishing your dessert and the waiters are getting the dishes to the kitchen, I'll ask Rob to play just a bit of dinner music." Rob went blank. Still, he turned and headed toward the piano, and he heard Derek whisper, "Tennessee Waltz."

No sooner than he had begun playing did a few beautifully dressed older couples hit the dance floor. Two ladies came over and grabbed Doc and the Bishop. Derek saw another older lady headed for him and said, "Let's dance, Mike, before I get wrapped into the arms of some eighty-year-olds. I really try to leave the older ladies to Doc and the Bishop."

Rob kept picking up the tempo, and when he finished a few dance numbers he transitioned into "I Left My Heart in San Francisco." After playing it through one time, he sang it. His voice was never better, and he went over with flying colors. The audience loved his playing and singing.

Mike knew immediately she could fall for Rob. Dressed in

that tux he looked perfect—just like the man she had envisioned in her dreams. His singing voice sounded perfect as well.

Derek let Rob have the spotlight for ninety minutes, and he took the last ninety. Of course, everyone who could dance wanted to dance with Rob, but Rob's interest was in Mike.

Derek had played three numbers, and Rob couldn't get near Mike. Under false pretenses Derek called Rob up to the stage and asked him to sing a number, which he did. Then he motioned Rob to the stool behind the keyboard, and they played a number together.

When the song was finished, Derek said, "Step down the side and maybe you can get to Mike."

The ploy worked, and he had his first dance of the evening with her. Of course, Doc and the Bishop kept cutting in on him. When this happened, Derek just picked up the tempo and they soon tired.

The crowd was tiring, too, and the meeting planner motioned to Derek to begin closing shop. While the crowd was older, and even though the hour was late for them, they were still having a great time.

They closed out the evening with their regular "I'll Fly Away." Mike turned to Evelyn and said, "What an odd manner to close out such an evening."

Evelyn said, "It happens at every performance they do."

When the group finally dispersed, the Bishop said, "Okay, now, where are we going to eat?"

"Why not up in our suite?" Derek asked.

"Well, I guess that would be okay since I'm a minister of the gospel and we have an unattached young lady with us who hasn't eaten either," the Bishop said.

Doc piped up. "She should fear you the worst. Ministers bear watching in strange towns. Haven't you read all the scandals they create? And, I guess, Evelyn isn't a woman who needs protection."

Derek said, "Mike, can you get some top-of-the-line seafood delivered to our suite and do us the honor of joining us?"

"I can do that," Mike said. "Any favorite items you want included?"

"No," Derek said. "We'll leave it to you."

Derek and Rob showered and changed into casual clothing since they were drenched with perspiration. "It's a good thing you two weren't plow horses," the Bishop said.

"Why is that, Bishop?" Rob asked.

"You'd stay at the water trough all the time. In fact, I don't believe a plow horse would sweat as much as you two do with the little amount of physical work you do."

"Well, at least, Bishop," Mike said, "they have showered and smell much better. Those tuxedos might have to be discarded. They were just a bit fragrant, don't you think?"

"Derek won't do that," Doc said. "He's too tight to throw away a tailored tux."

"Where'd you get yours, Doc?" Rob asked.

"Well, the Bishop and I felt out of place traveling occasionally with you, and your tailor made them for us. To date he hasn't sent us a bill. When he does, it will be paid. We'll work out some time payments with him."

"They are tight, Mike," Derek said.

"Now, Derek, you know you don't want us with you in our old rags," the Bishop said.

The food came, and everyone gathered around the table while the Bishop graced the food. It was a fun evening and went into the wee hours before concluding.

Rob walked Mike back to her car. "When will you be leaving?" Mike asked.

"Tomorrow morning. When Doc and the Bishop travel with us, it takes awhile to get them up, packed, and ready. Listen, Mike, I want to see you again soon," and with this he took her into his arms and kissed her. They lingered a spell at her car.

The hotel van took everyone to the executive airport first. It took awhile for everyone to say good-bye to Mike.

"Rob, you are going to Salt Lake City and down to the ranch?" Derek asked.

"Yes, sir."

"Evelyn and I will go to Denver and come back. We'll see you for dinner. The jet will take Doc and the Bishop home. I'll ask Evelyn to let Azzi know to expect us for dinner. Be safe, son," and with this he not only hugged Rob and kissed him, he did the same to Mike. "It was very nice having you in our party here," Derek told Mike. "We hope to see you again very soon."

"Thanks, Mr. Davidson. You made me feel right at home with your group. I do appreciate it."

The municipal airport was crowded, and Mike went as far as she could with Rob. "You have a wonderful group to travel with. I'm sure you have fun," Mike said.

"We do have fun. My dad is a fun guy to be with and a natural on-stage. But time is short, and I want you to know I never expected to see someone like you in San Francisco. Now I'll spend all my time trying to see you again soon."

"Would that be so bad?" Mike asked.

"That's the point. I don't want to leave you now," Rob said. He kissed her good-bye and had to leave.

Both had tears welling in their eyes as he turned away.

20

Rob and Derek rode over to the cabin later in the morning of the first day at the ranch. Evelyn was busy in the office and was glad to get Derek out of her hair. The older he got, the more he picked at details.

They talked about everything but what was on Rob's mind. That was Mike. He'd fallen for her from the very beginning.

Derek suspected as much but didn't bring up her name. Since he had already talked to the office, there was no reason to believe Evelyn would come for him again, and she didn't.

After putting the horses up, Rob walked down to the water and said, "Dad, I want to try something. I want to sing from the stump and then go between the two mountains there and sing the same thing. You listen from here, and let me know if there is a difference, okay?"

"Okay," Derek said.

Because of the native beauty of the place, Rob thought a hymn would be best. He sang, "Softy and Tenderly Jesus is Calling." Then he walked a long distance between the mountains without making any noise like breaking limbs and found a large flat rock with about twenty feet higher in elevation. He climbed onto the rock and sang the same song.

Derek couldn't believe what he was hearing. From the flat rock it was twice as good as from the other side of the little river.

When Rob returned and Derek told him what he heard, Rob said, "You do the same and let me listen." When Derek returned, Rob was stunned at the difference in the sound of the two places.

"Son, I don't know what we've discovered, but I've never heard anything like it," Derek said.

"Neither have I, but something like 'The Tennessee Waltz' or 'Rocky Top' wouldn't work to me. What do you think, Dad?"

"You're right. This is almost a cathedral-like setting, and it shouldn't be desecrated," Derek replied.

Derek said, "I want to try one more, and then we need to talk." He walked to the flat rock, positioning himself in the center. After getting his pitch, he sang "Beautiful Isle of Somewhere." This, of course, was his mother's favorite song. The majesty of the setting and the acoustics of the mountains reduced him to tears, and he couldn't finish. He stopped singing, sat down on the rock, and sobbed.

Rob was mesmerized by the sound, and when his dad quit singing Rob could hear Derek sobbing. Without knowing what was happening, he ran to the rock and found him in this condition.

"Dad, what's wrong?"

"Son, I sang my mother's favorite song at her funeral, and I can't sing it here. There is something of a mountain cathedral here—and what it does to one's voice is beyond description. A soundproof studio brings out the flaws, and they can be corrected. This sounds as if the flaws are never there, but I know they are. Sing the song when I get back across the river, will you?"

"Sure, Dad, I'll sing it," Rob said.

Hearing Rob sing it reduced Derek to tears again. This experience was as close to the true definition of the word "magnificent" as Derek had ever heard. There was a beauty that turned into majesty with the sun in the background shining through the foliage. Even animals like antelope began to gather. Larger animals congregated in the far background.

Evelyn and Pepe drove up in the pickup, finding Derek in tears. They heard Rob sing the last verse of the great old hymn and understood why someone could be so moved.

"Isn't that beautiful?" Derek asked.

"I could listen all day," Evelyn said, "but the truth is that I can't stay all day. Execute these documents so they can be sent back to the office, and I can get them off my back."

Rob walked back across the river, saw Evelyn and Pepe, and said, "Now I guess we've got to go home?"

"No, nothing like that, Son, but I would like to hear Doc and the Bishop's opinions of what we just discovered, wouldn't you?" Derek asked.

"Yes, I would," Rob said. "Since we've got to leave day after tomorrow, why not turn them around this afternoon and they can be here in time for dinner?"

"Can you handle that, Evelyn?" Derek asked.

"Yes, but you do know that these are two older men who need rest. We may have to leave them here for a few days," Evelyn replied.

21

"Doc, Derek and Rob want us back at the ranch. They think they've struck gold. Are you up to it?" the Bishop asked.

"How can I say no? There could be more good-looking women in our future."

"You old fool, what do you need a woman for?"

"I dance with them, eat their cooking and brag on them and buy them presents, and then I come home."

"So, tell them we'll come?"

"I guess so. How can we refuse?" Doc asked.

During the afternoon Rob had the four farmhands practicing hymns in harmony. They worked hard all afternoon on various songs.

Everyone was waiting on Doc and the Bishop when they arrived. Pepe quickly took them by truck to the cabin and the newly named Little River Mountain Cathedral.

"Well, it took you two long enough to get here," Derek said in a very smart manner.

"We've both got such a bad case of jet lag, I doubt we'll be any good to the group. By the way, we've never found out what our pay is. Have we, Doc?"

Doc said, "Not to my knowledge. The bad thing is that quitting time never comes. We dance with every woman in San Francisco, fly home and then right back, and all the while Mike is calling wondering when the Bishop and I will be back? We're too old to do a whole lot of partying."

"Well, Doc and Bishop, we need you," Rob said. "We're ready to let you hear something few people in the entire world have ever heard. And by the way, what did Mike want?"

The Bishop said, "I didn't want to have to tell you, but she has a thing for Doc. He always was a ladies man. He has the hands of a doctor, and they know just where the spots are. He must have found them."

"Rob, whatever you do, don't let these two old geezers hassle you. They slept all the way home and back according to the pilots," Evelyn said. "They wouldn't miss coming back."

Both agreed Evelyn was right. They were just happy to be needed in some small way.

Rob sang "Softy and Tenderly Jesus Is Calling," then 'Beautiful Isle of Somewhere." The quartet sang several songs they had worked up. Derek sang, and everyone sang from atop the flat rock. The onlookers sat on the ground around the cabin, and no one tromped around in the bushes.

When they were finished, the entire group listening was speechless. They'd never heard anything like it and were simply dumbfounded. The voices each knew so well had been transformed into something more. What the "more" was, no one could explain.

Derek said, "Bishop, use your best funeral voice and pitch it low, then bring it up a bit in pitch and then higher. Use the same words each time, please."

The Bishop needed some assistance scaling to the top of the flat rock, and he waited until people were back behind the cabin before beginning. He recited a poem pitched in the manner Derek had asked. He then did the same in a soft voice and a loud one. It was dusk when he finished, and he had to be helped off the rock. The acoustics did the same for his voice that it did for the singing voice of everyone who had tried.

When everyone was finished discussing the Bishop's performance, Doc said, "Derek, someone needs to build some sort of a walkway around to the rock and insist that everyone use it getting to the flat rock. If not, all the vegetation will be tromped down, and it may play a significant role in the acoustics of a person's voice."

"You are right, Doc," Rob said. "We'll get that handled before anyone else comes onto the rock."

After dinner, Doc, the Bishop, Derek, and Rob were sitting in the living area of the Davidson quarters. Doc said, "Fellows, I need to say something, and I think I need to say it to Rob."

The Bishop piped up and said, "Doc, get off Rob about Mike. An old coot like you hasn't got a chance with her. Besides you'd be like a dog chasing a car. What would you do with her if you were to catch her?" This provided the hilarity the moment needed.

Doc's face turned deadly serious. He turned to Rob and said, "Rob, listen at what I'm going to tell you."

"Yes, sir, Doc. I'm listening," Rob said.

"When you were a little fellow, I was called to the hospital very late at night for an emergency few physicians ever witness. When I walked up to the stretcher, there lay a young man who looked in perfect health, yet every doctor in the emergency room couldn't diagnose him. Truthfully, I really didn't know what was wrong with him, so I examined every inch of the young man. Then I took his tests and sat down at a table and started to study them. I was told he had passed out on a private jet overhead. The pilot landed, and he was brought to us on the instructions of his boss. One of his associates remained with him. I questioned this young man thoroughly about the sick person's activities. The man was out. We could arouse him, but he'd go right back out. I asked the young man what sort of a room the company would want for him, and his answer was a suite. We had one available. I instructed a bath since he smelled as though he needed one and that he be put to bed in the suite. When I went home, the receptionist said the man's wife and boss were on the plane headed back to the hospital. They would arrive before daylight. I went home and left instructions for them to see me the next morning, as I recall.

"The next morning there sat a beautiful lady and a tall older man awaiting me in my conference room, who turned out to be the patient's wife and another person. I found out the man was his boss. Both were very, very concerned about the young man. Truthfully, I had already been to the room and checked on the young man first and found him sound asleep, and his vital signs were within an acceptable range.

"Rather than try to explain his tests and what I thought, I said, 'Come with me.' I took them to the suite.

"He was sound asleep. 'What's his trouble, doctor?' the lady asked.

"I think he is totally exhausted, and according to the night nurse his vital signs are coming more into the range of what they should be. I have already checked him out again this morning and agree. He will have a lengthy period before he can return to the same schedule he was on.

"Rob, that man was your dad. I've never seen a man more fatigued from overwork doing those things he loved to do. He was totally exhausted, yet physically he was as hard as a rock."

Rob looked puzzled and asked, "Doc, what are you saying?"

"I'm saying I see a young man in you with exactly the same interests and drive as the young man I examined many years ago who was worn completely down. Unless you can find a way to work all these new interests in, in a manner you can handle them, you will be in the same fix one day."

Derek said, "Thanks, Doc, not only for being a friend over the years but putting this whole thing in perspective. Of course, I remember only too well those days. Rob knows I was hospitalized, but he'd never heard about it as profoundly as you put it."

Derek continued, "Rob, I believe we should determine those things that are most important to us and prioritize them. Then we should pursue what we can handle, with all the vigor we can muster. Those things that are less important and with less returns to the foundations, we can let them slip unless we can find the proper talent to take care of them. My schedule today would be the same backbreaking schedule I had when Doc first examined me, maybe worse if I'd let it be. I outsmarted most of it and got area managers to do those things that at one time required me to wear out a jet each year. Now, like Doc says, nurses and aides carry out many of the orders for patients that doctors see. He couldn't do it all, but he had to diagnose the patients, which became a load with tremendous responsibility, I'm sure."

"Your dad's correct, Rob. Just diagnosing a patient required brain work, which is the hardest work of all—something the Bishop wouldn't know anything about since all the church sisters bring him casseroles and cakes and the like, and he buys books filled with sample sermons. You know I'm kidding him, but the point is you can circumvent severe illness with thinking everything through with your dad, remaining in top physical shape, and eating like I've normally seen you eat. And I think an occasional date might be in order," Doc said.

This created a laugh and lightened the mood, allowing the Bishop to say, "Doc didn't say the date always had to be Mike. It could be someone your mom might select for you."

"One other item," Doc said. "If Derek had not remained in good physical shape during his entire life and eaten close to properly, he wouldn't have lasted this long. He and Kit do eat well, and he is in good shape. You are in much better physical shape because of your age. If you let it slip, it will be awfully difficult to regain."

"I want you to know, Doc, that I do appreciate what you are saying. In a sense it is what Dad has been counseling me about since I've been with the foundations. Know that I will take care of myself, and I will see Mike whenever the opportunity presents itself." This statement created a little lighter mood.

"Now we are getting down to the nitty-gritty of the conversation. So many times over the years, everyone in your organization made hard-and-fast plans not to be on the road more than four days a week—and I believe it was a week off every quarter and three months in the summer. It worked for a while, then everyone was running full blast again mostly because of sickness and tragedy. Had your dad not taken care of himself like he has, he might have been one of those casualties. Everyone has great plans, and no one sticks to them for a very long period of time," Doc concluded.

"Doc is right, Rob. We did make all these grandiose plans with orders from Mr. Gregson not to do this and not to do that, and within a short period of time we were full blast again. If we have a fault, sticking to a schedule is among our worst," Derek explained.

"Oh, well," the Bishop said. "I think I'll go to bed. This conversation has slipped off into a subject that a man of the cloth shouldn't be a part of. This is a father-and-son kind of conversation. Are you going to bed or are you going to sit and try to talk sense into this pair, Doc?"

"I think so. Goodnight, fellows," and with this Doc and the Bishop were off to bed.

"Doc is right, Son. So many times we made plans that were supposed to be written in blood, mostly about scheduling, and just as soon as a good opportunity came along we took advantage of it. This is one of the reasons that we must always go through our scheduling office since they are supposed to be operating on our plan of action. Unless a deviation from the plan presents itself that we should attend to, it is a rule not broken, ever," Derek said. "We've got to watch it if we want to stay whole. Even more unexplainable, as tough as Greg was, he would let the schedule for everyone, including himself, slip from time to time when a good opportunity for the foundations came along. This is human nature, I suppose."

"So, where are we, Dad?" Rob asked.

"Since the two of us are the ones we have to watch out for, we've just got to hunker down and do the best we can. The scheduling office does a fair job, but you know we overrule them at times. This is our downfall," Derek said.

Rob's cell phone rang. It was Mike. "What's the possibility you can go with me to Greybull to dispose of my family's estate? My family's attorney is riding me pretty hard."

"Hang on, Mike. Dad's sitting right here, and I'll ask him."

Rob didn't have to beg Derek to let him go. They were through anyway and had to go home in the morning, so Derek told Rob to help her out.

"Dad says we are through here, and instead of going home tomorrow, I guess I could come there tomorrow. How's that?"

"That's fine, but I have a question. Do you have any western-cut clothing or just a tux?"

"You making fun of my clothes, girl?"

"No, but folks where I live wear jeans and overalls. Do you have any?"

"I can dig up just the right clothing. I'm good at that," Rob said. "Do you want me to come to San Francisco?"

"No, I'll fly a commuter into Worland and rent a car. Can you do that?"

"When will you arrive?" Rob asked.

"I'll be there when you arrive. Will you come in the company jet?"

"I don't know since we haven't made any arrangements yet for travel home," Rob said.

When Rob finished the conversation with Mike, he and Derek decided the jet would take him to Worland first and then pick them up and head home. Worland actually wasn't very far from where they were already.

22

When the jet rolled to a stop and the copilot opened the door, Rob stepped out dressed in faded Levi's and a western-cut white shirt. He was also wearing a wrinkled Stetson. Mike was in his arms when his feet hit the ground.

After the initial hello, the copilot was so dumbstruck he just stood there and observed the welcoming ceremony. Mike saw the copilot, reached up and grabbed his shirt, and pulled him toward her, saying, "If I hear that a word of this gets back to Mr. Davidson, I'll deal with you later, Indian style."

"What's Indian style?" he asked.

"You really don't want to know at this point. You are better advised to keep you mouth closed."

"Yes, ma'am," the copilot said.

Rob fell out laughing. The copilot's face was crimson. The pilot was standing in the doorway of the plane watching the whole thing, and he had to sit down he was laughing so hard.

When the pilot stopped laughing, he said, "Rob has run into a killer woman. You'd better mind her."

"I intend to. Let's go," the copilot said.

The Florida group had a laugh all the way home from the pilots. Doc and the Bishop were building a story to tell Kit when they arrived. It was all out of proportion, but they were working hard.

"Where is your tux, Cracker boy?" Mike asked.

"There are two hanging in the closet of the plane, just in case I go someplace else instead of home. Besides, you told me to wear jeans and western wear."

"I did, and you fill them out pretty well. I'll feel safe with you now," Mike said.

"Why is that?" Rob asked.

"Everyone can see all those muscles. That tux covers them up."

Mike had Rob by the arm as she led him to a four-wheel-drive pickup truck. "You want to drive?" she asked.

"Sure. I'll drive, and you show me the way."

The ranch house and outbuildings were located at the end of a long valley about halfway up the side of a mountain. Rob stopped and said, "Wow, you want to sell this place? It's beautiful."

"I know it is. What you don't know is I borrowed more on it than I can pay back because of my parents' illnesses and burial. My parents spent their savings on me and schooling. I don't want to sell it, but I really have no choice," she replied.

The home and outbuildings were the type of buildings one sees in travel brochures. The setting was perfect, but their condition had been sort of let go since no one lived there.

The horses saw Mike and came to her. They were good-blooded cow horses, as Rob could tell. All the farm machinery was there to run such an operation, and Rob could see that Mike's property could be a showplace.

"How many acres do you own?" Rob asked.

"Total, fifteen hundred. We go up and over the mountain. When we walk up there, you can see almost the entire place. We have several springs that we have piped to strategic places for the livestock, and they have never been dry. One even supplies the house."

The home was not plush on the inside, but it had evidence of being lived in. It also needed a paint job on the outside. The bunkhouse was natural wood and looked like all bunkhouses do.

"Do you have any idea how many cows the land will handle?" Rob asked.

"Tops, somewhere around four hundred, according to my dad," Mike said. "There are now close to three hundred somewhere on the place, and it is all under fence."

The house smelled a bit musky, and they opened all the windows to air it out. They did not open the doors to the outside since they planned to walk to the top.

Taking a Winchester rifle from the gun case, they started their trek to the top of the mountain. Looking down that long valley back to the south and over the house was a beautiful sight. The cattle were grazing in a slight depression on top of the ridge of the mountain. They were fat and in good shape. More, they were gentle. Rob and Mike walked among them.

Mike said, "My dad always wanted his cattle to calve in the spring. The cattle numbers will almost double in the next month or so, and shortly we won't have enough space to care for them."

Rob asked, "If you sold all or most of the livestock, would it get you off the hook with whomever you owe money?"

"I'd have to get someone who knows a lot more than I do to determine that."

Rob took his cell phone and called Derek. "Dad, Mike has a little less than three hundred head of cattle, heavy with calf, on her place. She doesn't know whether it is sufficient to satisfy her money requirements. Do we have someone who could estimate this for her?"

"I'll call you back in a few hours. We've just landed, and I'm headed to the office."

"Dad just arrived home. He'll call us back when he knows the answer to my question," Rob said. "Do we have groceries, lights, and so on out here?"

"No, everything is shut off. We'll have to go to Greybull to eat."

It was rather easy for Rob to find his way back to town since he'd only just left a few hours prior. They decided to buy a few groceries before eating.

When they entered the local café, a few diners knew Mike and gave Rob a strange look. She introduced him around to a few of her friends.

"I'll order since you've never been here before." She ordered a cup of chili and a filet for her and a porterhouse for him, both with beans.

"I can't eat that much, Mike," Rob protested.

"You'll have to since it has been ordered. These folks will think you are some kind of wuss if you don't. You've already pulled your hat off, and no one else has."

"Look, sister, I don't usually wear a hat, and it's poor manners to eat with a hat on one's head."

"Okay, Buster. Be from the South, and you may have to bang some of these heads together for us to get out of this joint. Folks out here are tough. Don't forget that either," she said.

"We might have to have an old-fashioned head banging, then," he said.

The chili came. Rob allowed Mike to take the first bite, and she ordered some hot sauce. Rob tasted his, and it was as close to liquid fire as it could get already.

"Why did you order hot sauce for this stuff?"

"If I'd known you were going to complain about our food, we just should have bought some hot dogs and had a roast at home," Mike replied.

Rob ate a few of the beans and the entire steak. It was a wonderful steak, and it helped to put out the fire the chili started.

Rob had a text message from Derek when dinner was finished that read, "Our ranch manager is sending a person out to estimate the worth of Mike's cattle tomorrow. Try to be at home at 10 a.m. your time."

Rob texted right back, "Will do." He signed it "Buster."

Mike and Rob sat on the porch and talked about Mike's childhood on the ranch. From the conversation it was obvious that she did not want to sell it, but it was the only way out. Rob observed no expensive items in the house. It was an ordinary working ranch in a beautiful setting.

More than that, it was peaceful beyond description.

Two men drove up promptly at 10 a.m. the next day. They closely looked at each cow and held a private conversation when the inspection was concluded. One wrote a figure on a piece of paper and handed it to Rob, who in turn handed it to Mike.

"Thanks for coming out, but I'll pay the interest on them for a bit longer. The cattle are worth far more than this. I'll auction them first," Mike said.

When the men were gone, Rob called Derek and told him what happened. Derek said, "Son, the jet is coming to bring supplies to the hospital. I'll ask Bob Sawyer to come up there and take a look himself. That way we'll have another opinion. Bob will contact you when and where to pick him up."

"I'll be waiting Dad, thanks."

"Our ranch manager is coming to take a look. The jet is coming this way, and he'll hop up here and take a look himself."

When Bob saw Rob he said, "Don't tell me anything about what has been offered. Just show me the cattle."

When he had thoroughly looked at them he wrote his figure, and it was almost twice the amount the other fellows had offered. "Mike was correct, Rob. She knows cattle and what she is talking about," Bob said.

Bob continued, "Oh, yes, you and Mike are to come with me back to our ranch. You have to go to Seattle with your dad. You fellows can drop Mike off in San Francisco on the way."

On the way into town to turn the truck in, Rob said, "What had you rather do, go to Florida with the jet or stay at our ranch until the jet brings Dad back?"

"What are you going to do?" Mike asked.

"It really doesn't matter to me. You will see the ranch when we let Bob off, and if we go to Florida with the plane you'll see our place there. That's called a two-fer in the South."

Mike said, "I want to do whatever you'd like me to."

"I really want you to meet my mom and see our Florida operation. Have you ever visited Florida?"

"No, just photos of all the tourist traps you have in the state," Mike answered. "We can go to Florida if you want to."

"Then that's settled," Rob answered.

Rob called Derek and made plans for a visit to Florida and dinner with Kit. Derek said, "We might as well invite Doc and the Bishop in, too, don't you think?"

"Sure, and while we are inviting, what about Mae for color?" Rob asked.

"I can handle that," Derek said. "Be safe, Son."

23

The plane arrived just at dusk. Derek, Kit, Doc, and the Bishop were waiting. Kit was all eyes as she disembarked.

When Mike stepped out of the plane, Derek took her hand and introduced her to Kit. After a few pleasantries Doc tried to take over with, "Now, Mike, the Bishop and I will take you over to where we live. There are some old fogies who want to become acquainted with you. You'll have fun!"

"You'll do nothing of the sort, Doc," Kit said. "Mike will go home with me where she belongs, and Rob will go to his place and take a bath. When have you had a bath, Son?"

"Oh, I think I just missed this morning," he said. "Maybe two days."

"Now, Rob, Mike will come home with me while we are getting dinner together. You bring Mae with you after you have thoroughly bathed," Kit said.

"Do I stink to you, Bishop?"

"Pretty rank. In fact, so rank I don't know how someone as lovely as Mike has stood it. The air conditioning in the plane must have blown it away from her."

Doc said, "I must ask Mrs. Davidson if this is a coat-and-tie dinner she has planned?"

Just as Derek was beginning to answer the question to the contrary, Kit said, "Yes, it will be, and Derek will have to change, too." Derek simply looked at Rob with a blank stare like a cornered animal about to be slaughtered, but was aware of and resigned to it.

When everyone arrived, Mae went immediately to the kitchen to supervise. Mike came out when she was dressed. She looked lovelier than ever in one of Kit's best dresses. They both wore exactly the same size clothing. In fact, both never looked better to Derek and Rob.

Seated around the dinner table, it was a contest from beginning to end between Mae, Doc, and the Bishop as to who could charm Mike the most. At times, it would almost result in a shouting match between the three. It was a good-time evening, and everyone enjoyed it.

Rob was planning to take Mae, Doc, and the Bishop home when the evening came to an end, but the Bishop remembered they had not sung "I'll Fly Away."

He said, "We can't leave without singing our theme song. Come on, Rob." And back to the piano they went. The group gathered around the piano, sang the song, and adjourned for the evening.

After the group had left, Kit went into the bedroom Mike was to occupy. "Everyone who has met you has had nothing but glowing remarks about their time with you. Ours is an unusual group and one that has known tough and easy times. Derek came in talking about how well you handled the function in San Francisco."

"I don't believe I've ever had a better time than with your group. Everyone was so nice and treated me with such kindness. Not the usual haughty behavior most entertainers exhibit," Mike said.

"Ours is a bit different, Mike. The group Derek and Rob visited was our associates. We do all sorts of things together for others less fortunate, and it is like old-home week when we are together. Even when I was Derek's personal assistant we were together with the group they visited in your hotel ballroom the other night."

"You worked with them?" Mike asked.

"Yes, that is how we met. We traveled constantly until we were married, and after the kids arrived I worked from here. Actually we lived at Bath Pond, where Rob now lives."

Kit was drawn into a deep conversation about the foundations and how Derek fit and some of the folks who had preceded them. Naturally, Mike wanted to know lots about Rob. Kit accommodated her and told her everything she wanted to know about his past. They talked until late into the night and even after Derek went to bed. It was close talk between a mother and a young woman about the mother's son.

When Kit went to bed she roused Derek and told him she had been talking to their probable future daughter-in-law. "Naw, it's not that serious, Kit. I've been with them, and I know," Derek replied.

"Mark my word, it's serious," Kit said. "It's called a woman's intuition."

24

Mae invited everyone to breakfast the next morning. She really put on a spread of everything imaginable, including a selection of fresh fruits since someone had mentioned Mike liked fruits of all kinds.

Doc and the Bishop were there prior to Rob getting dressed. They were sitting at the counter drinking coffee when Mike and Kit arrived. Derek had already been to the office and was coming out to Bath Pond for breakfast, too.

Mae had spiffed the place up, and Rob showed Mike his office and living quarters and the bedroom units for guests. She was impressed that Mae had a helper.

Mike was thoroughly taken with the living quarters, which anyone would enjoy. The structure was built around a beautiful small lake. Initially she thought it was a swimming pool until she studied it for a moment. The concrete embankment that held the house off the water was the key to its safety. When the sun hit the water or the underwater lighting was turned on, one could actually see the springs that fed the clear, clean water to the lake.

"Rob, if I lived here, my chair would be the one in the shade over there, and I'd look at this beautiful water all the time," Mike said. "Correction, until I got hungry enough to get something to eat."

"Well, that refrigerator is filled with snacks if Doc and the Bishop haven't emptied it," Rob replied. "We can take a dip when you are ready before we have to leave."

"I don't have a swimsuit," she replied.

"We don't use one here. You should see all these old men swimming," Rob replied.

"I really don't want to see that. Do you swim with them?"

"Sure, we all do, except when Mom's here and we have to wear trunks. But here is something you should know. Everyone who has had a part in the foundations, except the original Gregson couple, has a portion of their ashes in the water. The thought behind it is that this way, we will all be together for all time," Rob said.

Mike was about to reply when Derek drove up and said, "Good morning. Mae has already called me and told me to get my britches over here, so here I am." With this he kissed Mike, "Good morning, lady."

"Watch it," Rob said. "Mom's looking out the window, and you know she's jealous."

Mike had never experienced anything like the banter that went on around the table. It was a good time for over an hour that finally ended when Evelyn came into the kitchen. "I don't know what we've got all this expensive equipment for if you won't use it." Saying this, she walked into Rob's office, finding the door closed and knowing it was soundproof. "Who closed this door?" she yelled.

"I did," Kit said. "I'm sorry you had to make a trip over here. Why didn't you phone?"

"I knew Mae would have some leftover breakfast, and I needed to tell Derek that Bob Sawyer wants to talk to him."

Derek immediately went to the conferencing center in Rob's office. "Hi, Bob. What's up?"

"Derek, those cows at Mike's home place turned out to be fine animals, marked and branded with proper identifications. I think her dad must have spent a lifetime building this herd, and it would be a shame for them to disappear in a cattle auction. Plus, all of them will calve within two months. Why not bring two-thirds of them here and leave a third there if she doesn't want to sell them? Put a trailer on the place, and send one of our older families there to look after them. Leave the horses there. What do you think? If you agree it would be better to move them now than wait until the calves are born."

"Hold on, Bob, let me get Rob in here." Derek went to the door and called Rob, who promptly came. Derek asked Bob to repeat his statement, and Rob went blank. He didn't know what to say.

"Dad, she needs money for the bank. Where will it come from?" Rob asked.

Derek walked away from the screen and looked out the window toward the cattle grazing. Deep in thought, he turned and said, "Tell Bob we'll be back to him before the day is over." Rob relayed the message.

Rob turned to look at Derek, who motioned him to a chair. "Son, this conversation is between us, okay?"

"Okay," Rob replied.

"Do you have intentions for Mike? Have you made plans that you may or may not have discussed with her? You need to talk to me now, if you will, and I'm not trying to put words in your mouth. I just want to know your thoughts, whether you finalize them or not," Derek stated.

"Dad, I have thoughts of asking her to marry me, but then I have second thoughts since I've only known her for a few weeks, though I know in my heart that I love her," Rob replied.

"Whatever you decide between the two of you will be the answer. Your mom and I don't want to influence that decision. That one is yours. We need to decide about the cows in Wyoming. That is my purpose for asking."

"What do you have in mind?"

"You heard Bob. If you were to marry Mike, maybe you could buy some adjoining land and we could bring the cows to our place until then," Derek replied.

"Dad, she still doesn't have the money she needs," Rob said.

"Mom and I will advance whatever she needs to get the bank off her back and solve that problem, or you can go to the bank and borrow it. There are many, many ways to handle a problem that seems like a mountain to Mike, I'm sure. Certainly it is a burden for her, and she is concealing it well."

"When are we leaving for Seattle, Dad?"

"Tomorrow morning," Derek replied.

"I'll try to have an answer by then," Rob said.

Derek walked out of Rob's office, turned, and said, "Tell Bob we'll talk to him tomorrow about this."

Walking back into the breakfast room, Doc and the Bishop were leaving. Mae and her helper were cleaning up, and Derek said, "I have to go to the office since I see my boss has left. How long has she been gone?"

"About ten minutes," Kit said. "I'll talk to you later in the evening about tonight."

"What are your plans for the day, Mom?" Rob asked.

"I'm headed to the drapery people and try to finish that chore. What are you up to?"

"I thought maybe Mike and I would ride the horses for a bit and then decide what we'll do. Dad says we have to leave for Seattle in the morning." He then turned to Mike and asked her about riding the horses, to which she answered in the affirmative.

Before going to the barn, Rob took Mike into the office to meet those who worked there. Actually, he peeped into Derek's office, and Evelyn was there. He tapped on the door, and Derek motioned him in.

Evelyn said to Mike, "Rob has some duties with his dad. Come with me, and let me show you our offices." They promptly left the room.

"What was that all about?" Rob asked.

"When I got back to the office our banker was out soliciting business. I told him you might be looking for a loan, and we discussed the approximate amount. He said tell you to write the check and call him, and when you are in town after the transaction come in and sign the note."

"Tell me the truth, Dad. You didn't endorse the note, did you?"

"No, the cattle will be the chattel. This is your transaction."

An hour later Rob and Mike were approaching the Big Swamp and rode up to a very large oak tree and tied their horses.

Yearling bass were schooling just off the bank. Rob, who was walking in front, turned, and his eyes met Mike's. He kissed her long and passionately.

"Well, Buster, I didn't know you had that in you. Do it again!" He did.

They stood arm in arm for a short period and sat down on a log. Just as they did, a frog jumped out into the water and a bass snagged him in mid-air. They sat in the same spot saying nothing, yet both knew the other had something in mind to say.

Just as Rob was about to speak, a herd of wild hogs happened up behind them and a young boar grunted at them. The horses spooked, broke their reins, and ran toward the barn. Rob didn't know what to do, yet he wasn't about to let the hogs hurt Mike, so he moved her behind him.

When the boar stopped his forward movement and turned to face them, Rob and Mike backed into the edge of the water. The few hogs that were in the herd moved hastily toward the horses while the boar faced them. The piglets were squealing and making an awful racket. Quickly Rob thought he might scare the boar off. To do this he picked up a palmetto root and threw it at him. He missed, of course, and the boar didn't move. Then it started a slow forward movement toward Rob with his head lowered. Rob walked toward him, and the hog stood his ground. Rob kicked him in the nose, thinking he might be able to break one of the two-inch tusks off and the hog would leave them alone.

When Rob kicked him in the snout and the boar recovered from the unexpected lick, he charged them. Rob and Mike backed into the water about up to their waists. When the boar reached them, Rob grabbed one ear, pushing it away from him just far enough away to straddle it and grab the other ear. He then pushed it under water and held it there until it stopped bubbling. Rob's main concern has always been hurting a hand since the piano was what he did best.

When the bubbling stopped, Rob turned to Mike and said,

"Come around me and get out of the water." When the bubbling had completely stopped and the hog was no longer putting up any fight, Rob turned him loose and pushed him out into the lake and came ashore.

Just as he turned around to see where the hog went, a large gator grabbed the hog and took it down again and out to the middle of the lake. Several gators were in a frenzy fighting over a part of the hog to eat. They watched until the gator fight stopped.

Rob squatted down in the edge of the water and washed his hands and arms free of the mud. He stood, and Mike was in his arms. "Oh, Rob, that hog scared the daylights out of me!"

"I wasn't exactly at ease, but I did all I could figure to do," Rob said. "Mike, you've got mud all in your hair. Where did it come from?"

"Don't know, but let's get out of this swamp," Mike said.

The pair stopped at an artesian well with potable water and washed the remaining mud off themselves. Both waded into the reservoir and sat down and got rid of the mud from their clothing. The water was clear and of drinking quality. Rob then ducked his head under the water and shook it. When he came up, Mike was doing the same.

They sat for a long time in the reservoir and talked about the hog incident. All the while they were watching the hogs eat oranges that had fallen to the ground from the company grove about a half mile away.

Mike slid over to Rob and sat on his lap while getting the last of the mud off his forehead and his hair. While she was doing that, Rob asked, "What is the chance that you would marry me?" She immediately stopped washing his face, held his face in her hands, and said, "Yes." They were locked tight in an embrace when a herd of otters piled off the bank into the reservoir.

This was more than Mike could take. The otters ran around them and some across their laps. She had no idea what they were, and it scared her again almost as bad as when the boar attacked. "This is why we carry a Winchester with us in Wyoming. You've just about gotten me killed before I can taste a bit of your wedded bliss, my future hubby."

They got out of the water, and Rob picked her up and was carrying her when Derek came flying across the pasture in a pickup. "What happened, the horses throw you?"

"Dad, I proposed to her, and she almost drowned me in the Big Swamp Lake. This is a mean woman, and a tough one, too!"

"What did she say?" Derek asked.

"I said 'yes,' Dad," Mike said.

Derek stepped out of the truck and hugged both kids and kissed them, completely ruining a light tan Palm Beach suit he was wearing. They walked to the office and sent the paddock employee for the pickup. Rob told Derek about the hog and their morning.

When they walked in the office, Evelyn was over at Rob's office and was talking to someone in Derek's office. Derek turned his conferencing unit on and interrupted Evelyn. "Sorry to interrupt, but I have a bulletin for Kit. Is she still there?"

"Yes, sir," she said.

"Please get her and Mae and you to the unit," Derek said. Derek also turned the intercom on broadcast.

When everyone was situated, Derek said, "Ladies and gentlemen, may I present my son, who has an announcement."

Rob stepped in front of the unit and said, "I'd like each of you to know the newest member of the Davidson family, my spoke-for wife, Mike. You are all invited to the wedding." Mike stepped in front of the unit and kissed Rob, and the office went wild. Doc and the Bishop had come over for coffee and heard the announcement, They pulled the couple apart, and each kissed her as well. The Bishop asked, "Have you two been fighting already?"

Mike answered, "I almost had to drown him in the reservoir before he'd say yes!"

25

When Mae heard the news she said, "Oh my God, get Doc over here. I'm going to bed."

Within an hour everyone had gathered at Bath Pond. Doc had revived Mae, and she was all talk about how she was going to a wedding for once in her life when she had nothing to do. "Have you received an invitation yet? How do you know you're going?" the Bishop asked.

"Rob said everyone was invited," she said. "Didn't you pick that little tidbit up?"

Kit was in one of the guest rooms with Mike, helping her get cleaned up from the Big Swamp, and Derek was with Rob. Derek said, "Son, I checked your account this morning, and you've got more than sufficient funds to cover Mike's cattle loan. Why not talk to her about it, pay the loan off, move about two-thirds of the cattle prior to calving to our place, and leave the rest there? Bob suggested moving an older couple up to Mike's place in a trailer to look after the place. Why not talk this over with her?"

"I don't mind doing this, but why not just sell them?" Rob asked.

"Bob says, after close study, that Mike's father has been working on this herd for many years. It is a fine herd of cattle, and they are marked and branded. Got all of their shots, and none have any sort of sickness. We'll just keep them separated, and maybe you can pick up some land, buy or lease, joining what she already has, and we'll move them back when the time is right."

"We've got to leave early tomorrow for Seattle, right?" Rob asked.

"That's right, and I'll go commercial and take Evelyn with me. You take the jet and deliver Mike to wherever she needs to go and meet me there. Tonight, since we should celebrate, why not invite everyone in and have a party here at Bath Pond?" Derek suggested.

"Who's in charge?" Rob asked. "We've got so many bosses now, it's difficult to know if someone should be told or someone should be asked."

"Let's announce that we've made the decision. We'll order the trimmings, and the two of us will have a cookout on the dock. We'll pipe music out there and have a great time," Derek proclaimed.

"Okay, you do the telling," Rob said. "They won't listen to me."

After Derek's announcement Mae said, "Nothing doing. I don't mind a cookout, but we'll do the trimmings right here for the master of this house. The two of you can cook the burgers."

The place was filled with people from the office and friends, and dance they did. Mae kept Doc and the Bishop dancing constantly. She turned her spot in the kitchen over to Evelyn, who protested wildly. Kit was in a daze with the news that had hit her so suddenly, but as the evening wore on she livened up and had a good time with everyone else.

Ali got use of a conferencing center and called in and spoke to Rob, Mike, Derek, Kit, and almost everyone else. Some of the employees didn't know her.

As they were calling the evening to a close, Rob was thanking everyone for being so nice and coming over to celebrate their engagement. Just as he was concluding his remarks, Mae was standing behind Doc and the Bishop, and she pushed them into Bath Pond. "Yo' swimming naked days are over now. There is another woman in charge here now." They boiled up sputtering and couldn't get over the fact that they'd been pushed in. To be on the safe side, Mae went into the kitchen.

26

The next morning the pilots who'd brought their wives over for the party were worn out. Rob and Mike were tired, too. Because of this they were late getting off, and the pilots were doing their best to make up the time.

Rob and Mike were talking about the previous day and reliving some of the moments. Several times Rob thought about the nap he would have before the night's performance.

Rob talked over his paying the note off at the bank and moving a portion of the cattle down to their place, buying more land, and moving them back. Mike would have none of it until they were married. She was determined about it and felt she could keep the bank off her back until after their marriage.

Not wanting to upset her about it, Rob finally said, "It's up to you. They are your cows, and I would feel much better if you do what you had rather do. It is not worth getting upset over. At least you have the assurance the bank isn't going to get them." She agreed.

They landed in San Francisco an hour ahead of time and had more than made up the lost time. Mike thanked the pilots and got off with Rob, and both headed to the car rental counter. When she had safely secured a car, Rob kissed her and both were on their way.

Derek was waiting on Rob with a car in Seattle when he arrived. Derek said, "Not easy leaving Mike in San Francisco, was it, Son?"

"Sure wasn't, Dad. She's adamant about not taking any money from me until we are married. She thinks she can keep the bank off her until then. We'll be in a mess if those cows begin calving before we can get them moved."

Derek said, "You can cross that bridge if you need to. Right now we've got some business to tend to here."

The evening was a late one when the finish finally came. Derek and Rob left the band members to finish up. Rob boarded the red-eye to Washington, D.C., and Derek headed home. The pilots had turned in and slept most of the day so they were rested.

Rob landed about mid-morning and hailed a taxi to the Corrections Bureau. He had shaved on the plane and put on clean clothing prior to leaving Seattle. Even so, his clothing was wrinkled, and he looked as if his eyes were suffering some sort of terminal disease.

He was able to get into an assistant administrator's office. The person's name was Jonathan Cook. After a few preliminaries and Cook finding out Rob's occupation, Cook asked Rob what the meeting was about.

"Mr. Cook, our Foundation is fortunate in that we have aligned ourselves with all sorts of assisted-living facilities and other organizations of wealth that keep a steady supply of funds headed our way. These folks take care of those in hospitals and nursing homes who need someone to call them, or to write them a note or visit occasionally. The strange thing is that those volunteers doing the visiting are getting far more from this effort than the people receiving the visits, though the volunteers are indeed the source of lots of necessities for the bedridden. When we go by a nursing home that our folks are associated with, we always stop and entertain them if it is a decent hour.

"We help carpenters, plumbers, electricians, technologists of all kinds, nurses, nurse's assistants, and all sorts of secretarial prospects get their licenses through a seminar company we have hired in Chicago. This is nationwide, and we handle the graduations from Florida or with our traveling orchestra. We have several hospitals of our own, and we have several assisted-living facilities that we own and operate.

"I'm here today to ask a favor of you. We have been studying crime among young people, vandalism by high school students, and various other problems with kids today. We've found that single moms just can't cope, and even some couples can't cope with their kids.

"Here is what utopia would be for us. We have an increasing number of doctors on staff, registered nurses, and a bishop, as well as a nationally recognized internist.

"Since we are entertainers with a purpose, we'd like to videocast into selected prisons for a test run. We think we can talk even the most hardened criminal into writing a note to delinquents at our expense, encouraging a change in behavior. Our doctor will offer a medical moment, and the bishop will give a devotion. We will do this from our studio in Florida and videoconference to a screen that we will purchase and place in the prison facility. Our purpose is to encourage your prisoners to positively influence young folks, and the bottom line is to change them if possible. We think the prisoners will get as much from the effort as the young people will, if they will cooperate."

"Mr. Davidson, didn't your group entertain a few years back at a ballroom in one of the downtown hotels, and the president awarded some medals to your group? And didn't your dad entertain at the White House the next evening?"

"That's exactly right, and that crowd illustrates the type of audiences we entertain. For instance, we did one in Seattle last night. If you were to look at our schedule, it is doubtful you would believe we could fulfill it."

Rob continued, "Mr. Cook, if we had permission to come personally to one of your facilities and talk to those whom you would allow—and pardon my lack of knowledge, but I know nothing about what is expected of someone who enters a prison—and your administration officials could attend, perhaps we could work out a program?"

"Can we just be 'Jon and 'Rob'?" Jon asked.

"I'd like that," Rob answered.

"Rob, I know what you folks have done in the past. My parents were present at the Washington event we just talked about. I was their guest the evening your dad performed, and I must say he is a fabulous entertainer. I think I understand what you are asking. Would you go home and write me a proposal that I can present to higher officials, and let's see where we can take this? This type of program might accomplish a great deal for both of us."

Rob invited those in a decision-making capacity to Florida for further discussions if they were interested. Because of his preceding day and night, Rob got a cab to Dulles and a flight to Orlando.

When he was awaiting the flight, his cell phone rang. "Rob, it is unbearable without you. I just wish we had more time together."

"So do I, Mike. This past week is a blur in my mind, and I miss you more than you can imagine."

Mike continued, "I want you to know how much I appreciate your offering to help me out at the bank. Bob Sawyer is correct in that my dad worked a lifetime building up his herd. It is a herd he was proud of, and so am I."

"Listen, Mike, since there is considerable value at your home place and a herd of cattle just before calving, why not let me send an older couple there just to look after the place and take care of the cattle? We'll put them up in a house trailer on the property. When they are no longer needed, they can move back to our place."

"Truthfully, Rob, there should be someone there, and I can't take care of it. Could we do that and put it on my 'account'?"

"Money is not a problem. Bob says someone needs to be there who knows what needs to be done. Why not let Bob take care of this, and we'll worry about the money later?"

"Okay, let's do it that way, and whatever the costs are will go on my 'account.' Deal?"

"Deal," said Rob. "I'll call Bob when I get home."

"Where are you? In Seattle."

"No, Washington, D.C., at Dulles headed home."

"You rode the re-eye to Washington last night after we said good-bye?"

"I did, and just the sound of your voice has refreshed me immensely. Thank you for calling."

Arriving home Rob went directly to his videoconferencing machine and dialed up Bob. "Bob, I tried to buy Mike's cows to get her off the hook at the bank. She said no! She caught me in D.C. earlier today and took me up on letting someone move to the place, live in a trailer, and do whatever needs to be done to the place and for the cattle. Can you handle this?

"Sure. I've got an older couple who would love to do this. Consider it done," Bob said.

"Do me this one favor. For whatever the costs, don't charge her for the trailer, but rent it to her and rent her laborers. When you know the true costs, divide it by two and send her that bill 'on account.' If she sends you a check, hold it. I'll take care of the costs when that time comes," Rob said.

"You've got it," Bob replied, and hung up.

Derek came in just as Rob hung up. Rob filled him in on the conversation with Bob and the appointment with Jon Cook in Washington.

"Son, I've thought long and hard about this project. To keep you from being completely exhausted all the time let's convert this office into a studio. It is already soundproof. And if we follow through with the Bishop's wish to call it the Little River Mountain Cathedral, we'll get a photo, or an artist, to resurrect this studio to look just like the cabin and mountains out west. Doc can have a corner with medical equipment, and the Bishop can have a pulpit, and we can have a lectern and stage here as well. We'll record the program and videoconference it to each participant."

"Boy, you have been thinking, Dad," Rob said. "When we get the couples thing going, which the Bishop is bird-dogging, we can use the same concept maybe. I understand we can have a conversation with those on the other end if we secure sophisticated enough equipment?"

"Son, I'm worn completely out, and I know you are, too. Let's take a dip and go to bed before dinner," Derek suggested.

"Suits me," and both headed for Bath Pond. After the swim and drying off, they both went to Rob's bedroom and to bed.

Kit called Mae later in the afternoon. "Mae, where are Rob and Derek?"

"They talked for a while after Rob got here. The jet had just landed. Derek came over worn out, and they took a swim and went to bed in Rob's bedroom. They are sound asleep."

"Mae, they need rest more than dinner. Don't bother them, and let them sleep all night if they will. I'll be at home," Kit ended.

"Yes, ma'am," Mae replied.

27

The Bishop and Doc found out Derek and Rob were at Bath Pond spending the night. With this news they showed up at breakfast time the next morning.

"What is it you ol' birds want?" Mae asked.

"Since you already have house guests, we thought you might want to invite us to one of your lovely breakfast settings. And besides, you know the Bishop and I can keep a lively conversation going," Doc said.

"You thought wrong. My guests are not house guests, they are boss men," Mae said.

"Now when they come out—they are now in the shower—if they invite you old men, I'll feed you."

"Mae, don't be too tough on, did you say, your 'house guests'?" Derek asked.

"No, I said you were boss men, not house guests. Now, do you want me to use your groceries to feed these bums?"

"Once more, how about it?" Derek said.

"You're the big boss, and I can handle it," and with this said she turned from her counter seat and coffee and yelled into the kitchen, "Fix two more plates, we have guests." She then smiled at Doc and the Bishop.

The Bishop said, "Mae, you are getting too tough in your advanced age. You need to lighten up on Doc and me."

"Iffin I did, every time I look up you'll be sittin' here waitin' on breakfast."

Rob came out. "Why can't you folks be quieter in the early morning around here so a fellow can nap?"

"You've napped since five o'clock yesterday afternoon while I was on tiptoes all the time. You both missed dinner, and your daddy is in trouble at home, but I've rescued him already."

"Kit called, didn't she?" Derek said.

"She did, and here she comes," Mae said. "She doesn't look happy."

Kit brought Derek a change of clothing and said, "I thought you'd need these based on how I know you looked." With this she kissed him, and everyone in unison said, "Aaaaaah, she kissed him!"

After breakfast was over, Rob said, "Fellows, I visited the Bureau of Prisons or whatever it is called in D.C. yesterday."

"We thought you were in Seattle with your dad," the Bishop said.

"I was, but the red-eye brought me to D.C., and our red-eye brought Dad home. Now, as I was saying before you interrupted."

"Bishop, let the boy talk," Doc said.

"I just thought that since he left here with a woman he might be confused," the Bishop said.

"He was confused when he left," Mae said.

Rob tried again. "I was successful in talking to a junior administrator who thinks our chapel idea with prisoners might work. I explained the entire thing to him, and he wanted to run it past his people. Dad and I talked it over yesterday afternoon, and we think that since my office is soundproof we could do it all from here. We would do it by two-way videoconferencing. The object would be to encourage inmates like tax evaders to get involved with kids who are getting into trouble and maybe have an effect on their future behavior. The Bishop would have a devotional. Doc would have a medical moment. We might play and sing, and Dad might talk to them and encourage them as well as get them to writing."

"What'll I do?" Mae asked.

"You dress up in your finest and be the first member of our audience," the Bishop said. "Be sure to wear a hat. I like hats, don't you?"

Mae replied, "No. I always knew I was cut out! I feel like I've been double-crossed. I come up with all these ideas, and you have all the fun. And to think the president made so much fuss over me."

"Okay, Mae, next time we broadcast, you have a song rehearsed and you can sing it to the group. Rob and I will accompany you."

"I don't sing. I talk," Mae said.

Derek said, "We'll talk about it, okay?"

"Okay."

Evelyn walked in, and Mae said, "I hope you don't want breakfast, because if you do you'll be suckin' wind. These folks have eaten everything I have in the house."

"No, I've had breakfast. Coffee would be nice."

She handed a sheaf of papers over to Derek for his signature. He took time to read and execute them.

"Rob, we are overloaded at the office trying to keep up with your work. It's about time you had someone over here to take care of yours, and I've got just the person."

"Who is it?" Rob asked.

"What about Mae?"

"No," Mae yelled. "I'm insulted enough with Doc and the Bishop. I don't need more grief from someone who is gushy in love. My job is to run this house and feed everyone who comes along."

"Well, since Mae said no, I'll send someone over whom I've been working with and familiarizing her with what you do. Your mother has already approved her, and she has passed all her tests from me. Keep your eyes open for her."

"Who said I needed anyone?"

"I did," she replied.

"Yes, ma'am."

28

Rob called Lineer at Trident in New York. "Mr. Lineer, what's the possibility that since my office is soundproof, we could decorate it like the mountain woods in part of it, a church chancel in another, and a medical examination room in another, and broadcast from there?"

"It is totally possible, but expensive, since we'll have to have expensive equipment in every place you broadcast and terrifically expensive equipment in the office. My assumption is that you will want two-way receptivity?"

"Can you come up with a proposal we can read and understand, and give us a price for the system?"

"Sure, but we'll have to know how many outlets you'll need and whether you will want a portable system since you might have the opportunity to broadcast to a place where you won't have a regular broadcast," Lineer said.

"Let's figure on twenty-five outlets plus the studio. Can you do that?" Rob asked.

"Sure, give me a few days."

Rob worked feverishly for about a week on the proposal for the prison system. All the while he was working on it, another group was on his mind.

Rob went to Derek's office and closed the door. "Dad, I need to talk to you. You have a few minutes?"

"Sure. Let's walk out into the pasture. I need to exercise my legs a bit," Derek said.

They walked over to the flowing well and sat down. "Now what is it, Son?" Derek asked.

"You remember, I visited the Corrections Bureau a few days ago, and while I was there I passed a group of wounded war veterans in a park, each with an attendant. This group badly needs our help if we can figure a way to do it. Have you ever thought of that?"

Derek said, "Son, yes, I've thought of it, and I've also thought of the fact that we can't fulfill the needs of everyone with whom we come into contact."

"Maybe what we should do is prioritize the groups and work from there," Rob said. "Do what we can, and let the rest go for now. And before I forget it, could you get Mom to decorate the studio in my office?"

"I've already thought of that, and she's working on it. She wants us to go with her and get the layout."

"What about next week?" Derek asked.

"That's day after tomorrow, since today is Saturday," Rob answered. "I can make it."

There was a call from Bob Sawyer waiting for Rob when he returned to the office. "Hi, Bob," Rob said. "I hope nothing is wrong out your way?"

"No, just reporting that we have two-thirds of Mike's cattle here. They are fine, the trailer is in place, and our custodians are already there. For the time being we feel it best to keep her cattle separated from ours just in case either has a disease we know nothing about. Our vet is coming out tomorrow to have a look-see at both herds."

"Sounds as if you've been on the ball," Rob answered.

"We have, and I just wanted you to know the job went off smoothly. Mike's dad knew what he was doing with these cows, and you should remember to keep the proper bulls with them and keep a certain amount of the offspring for the future. You'll do yourself proud."

"Thanks, Bob. Dad and I were just talking, and we are planning on a trip out next week. Mom is coming to take a look at the cabin area. Let Azzi know, will you, please?"

"Sure," and they both hung up their phones.

Derek was sitting in front of his conferencing unit, and Rob told him of the conversation with Bob. "That's good he knows.

Now I won't call and alert him. Do you want to pick up Mike and bring her in?"

"I've thought of it, Dad, but haven't spoken to her. I'll give her a call, and maybe I can meet her someplace. You and Mom take the jet, and I'll go commercial."

"I'd planned to do that already. Evelyn is spoiled," Derek said with a chuckle.

Rob asked Mae to have a meal over the weekend for Doc and the Bishop at his office. She asked, "Is this a board meeting?"

"Yes, it is," he answered.

"I thought I was on that board?"

"You are. I failed to remember. Set a place for yourself."

Doc and the Bishop came over a bit earlier to enjoy a swim. They had a wonderful dinner, and Doc asked, "You know, I've never served on a board that had no fee for a director. Has any thought been given to whatever this fee might be?"

"You mean we get paid?" Mae asked.

"We'll have to take this question to the board that is just above us. We don't have the power to set fees," Rob said.

"That means no, Doc," Mae said as she shook her head from side to side.

When the meal was concluded and the table was cleared, they continued around the dining table. Rob said, "The purpose of this meeting is that we've gotten more planned than we can handle, I think. We've talked about a weekend each quarter to broadcast to couples having marital problems, and maybe once annually meeting them in four different quadrants as outlined presently with a night out. We've talked about an effort to softer inmates in prison writing notes monthly to juvenile delinquents. Maybe we can figure a way to get inside some of the prisons to entertain them a bit and to express our appreciation. We need to get a relationship developed between the inmate and the juvenile to turn the juvenile around. Now, while I was in D.C. recently talking to the prison officials, I found another group that is desperate: wounded military personnel and their families. They have more need than just about any group I've seen. The sad part is their recovery is going to be lengthy. The military has been lacking in all our efforts, except one time when the Bishop had me help him out.

"Now comes the question: How much is too much if we mostly utilize this studio that we will begin next week?"

"Rob," Doc said, "I've seen those boys in military hospitals who are wounded, and many of them have long periods of convalescence. Some will make it, and some won't. Some will make it and become something less than desirable citizens because of their wounds. They are a worthy group, and if we could assist them it would be wonderful."

"Doc, you and Rob both have to consider that at least three members of this board are elderly, and we can't hold out like Derek and Rob can. Maybe even Doc and I should just assist in getting it started and the two of us plus Mae become advisors to the board," the Bishop said.

"Does an advisor receive the fee like you said?" Mae asked.

"The money is exactly the same," Doc said. "Probably nothing!"

This statement caused Mae to throw her head back in disgust.

"Consider this," Rob said. "Suppose we hire a writer to write the scripts for the couples' retreats, the prison project, and the military effort—a really great writer who will take direction and the three of you offer all the assistance you possibly can until that person can handle it. Not having to write the script would lessen the load considerably."

"You are right about that, Rob," the Bishop said. "The only thing that would blow Derek's mind is to have to stick to a script, and I think it would yours as well. Scripts are not something you are used to. However, if the writer could come up with a general direction we could all, in the beginning, follow the theme whether we stuck to the script or not."

Derek walked in just as the Bishop said that he wouldn't stick to a script. "You are correct, Bishop. I have never yet had a script. I am a seat-of-the-pants type of performer. But you are correct, too, that a writer would at least aim the effort in the right direction."

Because time was limited, Rob flew into San Francisco. Mike met him at the airport, and Rob chartered a plane to take them to the ranch. They had time to catch up on conversation and to talk on the way to the ranch about their future. Wedding plans even entered the conversation.

Because it was mid-afternoon when everyone arrived, and because they needed to be at the cabin at just the right time, they drove to the site. Mike and Kit sat in the right place in front of the cabin. They took the four boys with them, who gave their rendition of "Memories" from the Broadway hit *Cats*. It was breathtaking, and both women sat mesmerized at the sounds they were hearing. Derek and Rob actually had not expected anything so beautiful.

Derek said, "Son, you sing something and allow the boys to back you up."

Rob discovered that the boys were facing a different direction between two mountains instead of bouncing the sound off one. When the group sang, the sounds were better than they had remembered hearing them before.

Derek said to Kit, "The purpose of this trip is not to sing but to allow you the opportunity to determine how the Florida studio should be developed. You look around and tell us what you think." She walked across the water and into the woods, being careful not to disturb any of the young trees and bushes growing there. After all, no one, at least up to this point, knew for a fact what was causing the beautiful sounds, so nothing was disturbed.

When she walked back to the cabin, she said, "We need the same photographer we had when we did the Carter project in Atlanta for the media. He can do a much better job than I, and we could build from there."

"Can you find him, Evelyn?"

"Sure. His brother was the financial man for the foundations at the time. He is living on the south ridge, and it won't be difficult."

In order to give Rob and Mike some time together, Derek asked Pepe to bring a couple of horses to the cabin and allow them to ride them back. Derek carried the rest back in the pickup.

Azzi fixed a wonderful meal, and afterward everyone gave Rob and Mike all the space they could. Rob and Mike chose to sit around the pool and talk until very late.

When the party started to break up the next morning, Rob said, "We have an announcement."

Of course, everyone in the party tried to appear surprised, yet their surprise came out fake. "What's the announcement?" Derek asked.

"Mike and I have decided we'd like to be married as soon as possible. Since Mike's degree is in public relations and not in doing what she does at the hotel, we think she should be given a shot at writing the script for everyone when we begin conferencing from Florida," Rob concluded.

Kit, of course, went to Rob and Mike and not only congratulated them verbally but offered more hugs than they had figured on. Derek and Evelyn were right behind them, and Azzi was also in line.

Pepe took Rob and Mike to a small airport, where a charter picked them up to transport Mike back to San Francisco. Rob was with her, and then he took a commercial flight home. Mike stayed with Rob as long as she could prior to his flight departure. The thought of marriage was so new that they had no idea of the plans they should be attempting to finalize.

29

Before arriving home, Derek decided the studio would be free-standing and away from the Bath Pond complex in which Rob lived. When the concept was laid out, Kit decided she would take over the construction and decoration.

More than one half of the studio would be the Little River Mountain Cathedral, with a photo of the area as wallpaper. There would be a hallway opening up into Doc's examining room for his medical moment, and also farther down the hall a door opened into a chancel area with a lectern for the Bishop's devotional. This area could quickly be transformed into a stage area from which various audiences could be addressed—with appropriate floral decorations, moveable bookcases, and chairs. The entire studio was soundproof and would have the same projection equipment as a first-rate movie house. The projection equipment was located in the appropriate places on tracks around the side of the walls and across the ceilings. To project the professional sound, they were expecting that all of the cameras would be mounted on tracks that an operator would move automatically from a control room. The sound would be digital.

When the jet landed at home, Evelyn received word for Rob to call Trident in New York. She immediately text messaged him to this effect. He was now on a commercial airliner headed home.

The messages was from Bob Lineer. Since the conversation could be lengthy and since there were two talkative and also somewhat nosey individuals sitting in the same area, Rob decided to wait.

Knowing that Lineer didn't bother with frivolous talk, Rob stopped in the airport and called from a private booth. "Rob," Lineer said, "Tapton has hit the mother lode maybe with his sound engineering, by figuring a way to distort the sound in a studio that duplicates the natural sounds at the cabin on the ranch. We'd like permission to come to your Florida operation and experiment a bit with you, if that's okay."

"Sure, when do you want to come?" Rob asked. "Today is Friday, and Dad and I both have to be on the road Monday. Can you make it tomorrow?"

"Let's say two in the afternoon, tentatively. I've got to run this past Tapton and be sure he can make it."

"I'll wait to hear your final word," Rob said as he hung up the phone.

Rob went straight to Derek's office. "Dad, I've just spoken to Bob Lineer from Trident, and he says Tapton has engineered a method by which he can reproduce studio sound to come out just like out by the cabin. They want to come tomorrow afternoon and show us. I'm waiting for confirmation now. Can you make it?"

"Sure," Derek said.

Doc, the Bishop, Kit, and Mae were sitting in Rob's office to hear the sound. It was determined that Rob would sing and Derek would accompany him. Rob sang a hymn, and Tapton recorded it normally. Rob then sang it again as Tapton adjusted the sound.

The second time Rob sang the hymn, it sounded to them just like music at the cabin. It was a magnificent sound. When the song was finished, everyone listening was completely dumbfounded as to how it could be done. The engineering put a rich quality in Rob's voice that was unbelievable and duplicated exactly, as best they could tell, the sound by the river at the cabin in the West.

Derek told Lineer and Tapton about their plans for a freestanding sound studio. They both approved and asked for permission to engineer the studio to their standards, to which they received an affirmative reply.

When Lineer and Tapton left, Derek said, "Kit, I'm exhausted from the week. Let's call it a week and go home." She agreed, and they promptly left. Before they did, Derek said to Rob, "Son, we do have one problem: when we are on the road we don't sound like this studio sound. Therefore, we will always have to record with the sound in the studio if we are here. On a stage someplace we'll do the best we can on our own."

Rob replied, "Well, Dad, it has worked so far. You've been mighty successful with just a naked voice with no enhancement."

Doc and the Bishop were soon out the door, and Mae asked, "Well, it's just the two of us now. What do you want to eat?"

Rob called Mike and told her all about what had happened and what their plans were for the new studio. "The great thing about it all is that we can do most of the work from here and not have to travel."

"What about me? When will I see you?"

"Won't you be my wife and won't you live with me here, and won't you be writing the scripts for everyone?" Rob asked.

"You're right. I keep forgetting that our home will be there."

When the conversation was over, Rob announced to Mae that he was whipped and was headed to bed. "So am I. These executive decisions I've been required to make are killing me!" she said. Both had the lights out shortly after dark.

PART THREE

Ecstasy

30

All Rob had thought about in terms of marriage was Mike. None of the planning had entered his mind. All he knew was he wanted Derek to be his best man. Also, he and Mike had previously had a short conversation about where they were going to live and how the Wyoming property would be handled.

Because of the economic situation in the United States and the world, the hotel Mike worked for in San Francisco laid off everyone in the catering department but Mike. She had absolutely no help, and the grind was exhausting. The work was sixteen- to twenty-hour days every day. The hotel wasn't doing all that much business, but with no assistance it was more than she could handle.

When Derek found out about it, he said to Rob, "Son, I don't believe I'd let them take advantage of Mike like they are doing. If you are going to be married, why not tell her to quit and come here? She can live with us until the wedding."

"Truthfully, Dad, the schedule is about to get her down."

Derek and Rob were in his office, and he asked Evelyn to come in. When she did, Derek asked, "Evelyn, take a look at our schedule and determine when from our viewpoint it would be best for Rob to have a month off. Coordinate that with Ali's studies, and get back to us as soon as you can."

When she was gone, Derek turned to Rob and said, "We won't have to stick to Evelyn's schedule, but we've got to begin someplace."

"Thanks, Dad. I wondered the same thing, but didn't know how to begin," Rob said.

Later in the afternoon, Evelyn came into Derek's office and said, "It looks to me like since Easter is just around the corner and since Ali will have that time off anyway, she wouldn't have to miss any of her medical obligations. Wendy also takes Easter every year, too. There is one thing."

"What's that?"

"If this occurs it will put a load on you. What a strain you'll have," Evelyn said.

"It appears that is the way of life around here. The good thing is the studio will be complete when Rob returns. If they will accept Easter, the travel will slow for me."

Rob wasn't able to get Mike until around midnight. "What's the possibility that you could turn in your resignation now, come here and live with Mom and Dad for the few weeks, plan the wedding for around Easter, and then we'll be off someplace for a month?"

"Can we afford a month honeymoon?" Mike asked.

"We'll mortgage something," Rob said. "Really it is a break in our schedule. Ali can come home at Easter, and Wendy can be here. How does that sound to you?"

"Sounds great to me, but how will I get to Florida and move those things I have here there?"

"That's what Evelyn is for. She will take care of that," Rob said. "Do you think two weeks is sufficient for notice to the hotel?"

"Sure I do," Mike said.

"Let's shoot for two weeks. My schedule can change a number of times before then, but that can be the constant you work from. How's that?" Rob asked.

"Perfect. Let's do it," Mike agreed.

Since Mike lived in the hotel, all she had was clothing and a few other personal items there. Her keepsakes were in Wyoming, and there wasn't time for her to get them prior to going to Florida.

Evelyn had trunks sufficient to hold her clothes sent to the hotel, and a moving company picked them up as she left. Her commercial airline ticket had already been delivered by a travel agent.

When she walked out of the hotel, a car was waiting that took her directly to the airport. She boarded an Orlando flight, and Rob was standing at the gate awaiting her arrival. It was a happy homecoming as she arrived at her new home.

Rob delivered her to Kit and Derek and had a meal planned for that night. The entire evening was spent discussing the upcoming plans for their wedding.

31

Kit and Mike landed in Worland just after noon. The pilots unloaded their belongings and had the plane pulled into a locked hangar since it was loaded with their particular travel gear. Derek said most of his and Rob's clothing was kept in the plane.

The pilots loaded their suitcases into the back of an SUV and drove them to the Saunders Ranch. Derek would have none of Kit and Mike going alone to an isolated ranch. Plus, some items would require some heavy lifting.

When they arrived in the long valley looking toward the ranch house, Mike noticed the house had been painted and the bunkhouse had a fresh coat of stain. The barn was painted, and all the equipment had been locked inside. The house had new doors and locks. There were flowers growing in all Mike's mother's beds. It was a storybook setting. For the first time, Mike saw the new house trailer a respectable distance back from the mailbox at the entrance to the driveway.

"Who did all this?" Mike asked.

"I think Rob might have had something to do with it," Kit said. "Do you like it?"

"Oh, yes. My mother and dad would be so very proud of the place they slaved to build."

Pepe's parents were the caretakers. Their names were Juan and Nita. They were nice and polite, and very proud of the way the place looked.

Entering the house, Kit said, "Oh, Mike, this looks so much like the house in North Carolina I was reared in. It reminds me so much of it, and it looks like a very livable home."

"I always enjoyed it, and my parents were very proud of it. Their ancestors lived in sod houses out on the prairie. It must have been a horrible existence."

The pilots took some things out to the barn and were back

talking to Mike about the woodworking equipment there. They asked all sorts of questions about it.

"My dad made most of the furniture you see here. He was a master craftsman to the point that others hired him to make furniture for them. My mother made our clothing and all the other cloth items you see here. She even sat at night and crocheted the table coverings and the bed coverings. Look in the guest room here at the bedspread she made. To me, it is a prize."

Kit looked at the spread and said, "This is one of the prettiest spreads I've ever seen anywhere. She must have been a real talent."

"She was," Mike answered. She turned to the pilots and said, "You must remember that in winter Dad had to work in the barn a great deal because of the weather. It gave him the perfect opportunity to do what he enjoyed doing with his woodworking hobby."

The pilots asked Juan where the cattle were. He said, "Mr. Sawyer came and carefully selected the cattle he wanted to take to Poppy's Ranch and left about seventy-five here for me to look after."

The pilots also wanted to know how far down the valley Mike's property went. "We own over the mountain behind us and only down about five hundred feet beyond the mailbox."

"If you owned the entire valley, we could put an airstrip here without a great effort," one pilot said. Nothing more was said about the airstrip.

The pilots went into Greybull to eat and spend the night. Kit and Mike were up most of the night looking at various items Mike's mother had made. By the time the pilots arrived the next morning, everything was packed and ready to be loaded into the SUV.

After good-byes to Juan and Nita, they were off for the airport in Worland and home.

32

Rob arrived home very late that night and went straight to bed, realizing that Mike was with his parents and probably asleep. He was asleep in a matter of seconds when he finally got to bed.

The next morning, after he showered and dressed, Rob came to the kitchen where Mae, Doc, and the Bishop were in a scrappy argument.

"Now, you old men have got to understand I've got this wedding to run, and you are not going to show up around here every time you think Mike might be around and particularly when you want to take a dip. I don't want her having to dodge your rusty butts in the water. It just ain't right for her to have to see such a thing. Therefore, until she is married to Rob, I have decreed that she will not stay here. When it becomes her home, I will advise her to keep you two run completely off."

"Now, Mae, you don't mean that," Doc said. "She'll like for us to come over and have breakfast with her occasionally."

"That's right, Mae," the Bishop said.

"Yeah, I know you. If she gives in once, like I have done, you'll be here every time she looks up," Mae concluded. "Won't she, Rob?"

Rob said, "That will have to be up to her. If she is going to run you a close second for your boyfriends, that'll just have to be her business. It could turn into a first-class catfight."

"Boyfriends? These birds?"

Derek walked in about the time Mae said this and asked, "What's all the ruckus here, and where is breakfast?"

"Better watch it, Dad. Doc and the Bishop have Mae's hot buttons, all of them, stuck in meltdown mode," Rob said.

"All I want is breakfast, not an argument," Derek said. Mae turned and huffed off into the kitchen where the cook was.

It was a good-time session with everyone gathered around the table and Mae sitting at the counter. When the group was finished with Mae, they started in on Rob with all sorts of questions. It was an unbearable tirade that Rob was hard-pressed to keep up with. Not one of the questions they asked would he have ever answered in his wildest imagination.

After breakfast Evelyn called and asked both Rob and Derek to go to the conferencing unit. It was a never-ending list of problems. They were in the middle of this when Kit and Mike walked in. They had news that Ali would be with them for a week over Easter.

The Easter season was filled with happy days. Not too much traveling, but more problems than could be solved. Actually Rob was looking forward to leaving his dad with them when he was away for the honeymoon. While he was grown, a vacation was never in his plans or had he ever been away for just a good time, a restful time. When he traveled, he worked. That's what travel meant to him.

Rob and Mike had decided they just wanted family attending their wedding, but that was not to be. Everyone at the ranch would want to come. Both Rob and Mike had friends all over the country, and there was the problem of seeing to their accommodations, though they had plenty. The Carter folks would all want to come since they worked so closely with the Davidsons. So, for these reasons and the fact that Mike had no family, they decided to hold the ceremony in Sammy's Sanctuary, the chapel dedicated to the memory of Dr. Sammy Squires, in the hospital. Derek got Tevo Taylor to come and sing. But more, Gus and Anne Squires had put a white concert grand Steinway in the chapel, and occasionally someone in the group dropped by to play it. To play on this wedding day, Rob wanted Ali to handle all the wedding music. She did a magnificent job and, of course, acted also as maid of honor.

Since it was Easter, Mike and Kit decided on Easter and calla lilies with lots of greenery. The Bishop ushered in Kit, and when he went to the chancel area, Doc gave Mike away. Derek served as best man. Ali was maid of honor. Just those associated at work and involved in the foundation's work locally—plus the Davidsons' closest friends—were invited. These folks filled the small chapel.

Everyone but Mae thought it was a happy occasion. She blubbered and snorted her nose the entire ceremony. In fact, it got so bad that the Bishop had to stop one time and look at her. After that embarrassment, she got it under control. She was the only lady with a hat. It was a flowered arrangement of a pillbox nature.

When the ceremony was concluded, the couple only wanted the same group to gather at Derek and Kit's home and have a catered affair. It was a very plain wedding with lots of flowers that were distributed to those in the hospital having no flowers.

So, as Rob and Mike requested, there was nothing to prepare and nothing to clean up. The honeymoon began as soon as they arrived at the airstrip at Bath Pond and headed toward Poppy's Ranch. The pilots even closed the door to the cockpit and promised not to open it.

What Rob and Mike didn't know was that Derek had chartered two other jets and took Ali, Wendy, Doc, Mae, Evelyn, and the Bishop with them to the ranch also. The employees there were planning a gigantic western celebration, which included a barbeque and a mariachi band, and everyone who worked there was included. The four boys who were close to Rob had planned the musical celebration, which included lots of singing and dancing.

The dancing went on until the wee hours, and everyone was so exhausted they had to quit. All the females had to dance with Rob, and the males with Mike. Doc, Mae, and the Bishop thought they ought to dance with everyone, too. Evelyn also had a blast. The pilots were as close as family and were always included in every kind of celebration the Davidsons had.

The phone was ringing for Evelyn at daylight the next

morning. The problems at home necessitated everyone going home as soon as they could assemble for breakfast and make their way to the planes. The planes had to stand by for a long time, because everyone was ribbing the newlyweds unmercifully. Mae, Doc, and the Bishop were full of it, and everyone enjoyed the good banter together. It was truly a happy time, without any soreheads, resulting in a memorable occasion.

Once everyone who was leaving was in the air, Rosita said to Rob, "I have the cabin clean with provisions, if you wish to visit there." Rob looked at Mike, and they decided to drive over and decide what they wanted to do for the balance of their honeymoon.

Opening the door to the cabin, Rob was astounded that Rosita had removed the twin beds and put a king-sized bed there. "Rosita doesn't miss a trick. Look at this, Mike," Rob said.

"You are right. Rosita never misses a trick."

Both were tired and decided to take a nap and then decide what to do. Actually they slept all afternoon. When they were awakened by some animals outside, Rob thought the thing to do would be to introduce Mike to the pool under the waterfall even though it was quite cool outside. She was a good sport about it and tolerated it better than Rob.

When they returned to the cabin, they saw Pepe leaving. He brought a scrumptious dinner for them that Rosita had prepared, with all the trimmings. Another meal fit for a king.

The next day they rode around among the cattle until they located some of Mike's cows. The cows seemed to recognize her, but then they couldn't be certain. They were fat, and some had calves with them.

They decided at that moment that they should drive to Mike's home place. Pepe took them to a rental car outlet, and off they drove. It was actually only about a four-hour drive, but they took a couple of days getting there.

Rob told Mike of the conversation the pilots had with him about buying the rest of the valley and putting a landing strip there. Rob and Mike discussed this at some length, yet reached no decision as to what they wanted to do.

When they finally arrived, Rob was astounded at how well the place looked with the new paint job. Juan had made lots of repairs that were needed, and all the flower beds were in first-class condition. Juan was very proud of his work, and the more the young couple bragged on his work, the more he showed them.

Much to Rob's surprise, Juan had totally repaired all the fences on the ranch, which had been in horrible disrepair. He'd repaired the roof of the barn and the house also.

Mid-afternoon Rob and Mike walked up to the top of the mountain behind the house. The cows gathered around them, since Juan had encouraged them to gather around him. They were beautiful cows, some with calves. Rob looked down the mountain on both sides, but mostly on the side containing the home and the long valley. "How many acres are in that long valley in front of your house?" he asked.

"I think somewhere around five thousand," she replied.

"Wouldn't you really rather keep this place than sell it, since it is your home?"

"No question about that. But you must remember that taking care of my parents and buying enough feed to get the cattle through the winter a couple of years wiped us out. I was barely making it on my own, and there was no way I could keep it—hence, the decision to sell," she said.

"Do you know if their estate is settled?"

"Not totally. The attorney had some deed easements and restrictions that were standing in the way. Plus, there was the money thing again. The only way I can close it is to sell it," Mike said. "You married a woman in debt. Now, since we are talking debt, how much do you owe?"

"I don't owe a dime. I don't own anything, and I don't know what I make. I usually don't have any cash on me, only a credit card. How's that for starters?"

"If you don't owe any money, you don't know how it feels to be up all night wondering how you'll ever pay the land taxes and all the other expenses that a place like this requires," Mike said.

"No, and I'm sorry you have had the experience. We'll take measures to fix this." After saying this, they walked farther and then turned around and headed to the house.

When they were in smelling distance, Rob said, "I don't know what it is, but something is beginning to smell very good."

"Nita cooked your mother and me a few meals while we were here, and she is as good as Azzi," Mike said.

Walking in the front door, Nita told them dinner would be served in about thirty minutes. If they wanted to get cleaned up, there was plenty of time. With this, both bathed and changed clothing.

When the semi-banquet was concluded, they sat on the porch for a while and then decided to walk down the road in the valley. No one else lived in the valley, and it was the perfect wintering pasture for cattle. The property included the mountains on either side of the road, and their place was located at the end of the road up on the side of the mountain. *A perfect place to hide*, Rob thought.

Rob and Mike didn't leave the place for a week. Actually it took them that long to get rested to want to do anything. Rob traveled so much that moving about wasn't of interest. Mike just wanted to do what he wanted, and she felt like home wasn't calling him. Both were very satisfied to remain there.

Once they were headed back to Florida, Rob said, "What would you say to having your home in the mountains renovated and put in modern appliances—and a shower—and think about buying the additional land and keeping it?"

"I'd like that if we can afford it. My family worked awfully hard to get it where it is today, and though it isn't much by comparison to what you've been used to, it was their dream home and my home."

"When we get home, locate an architect in Worland. Get the architect to go out and draw a floor plan of the home, and then a plan of a proposed renovation. Be sure it has a shower, preferably two, and more than one bathroom. We'll keep those things that are important to you, and we'll buy the rest of what we need to make it into a first-class ranch house," Rob said.

The newlyweds landed in Orlando, rented a car, and drove down to Marco. He did call Evelyn as he left town and asked her to alert the caretaker at Marco that he was headed to the fish camp. He wanted privacy, the place spotless, and a cook.

They lay in the sun and ate. They looked at the Gulf, but didn't take the boat out of the boathouse, nor did they fish. They simply enjoyed each other.

33

The newlyweds pulled in late in the afternoon, sunburned from head to toe and a few pounds heavier and very much in love. The trunks Mike had shipped from San Francisco and Wyoming were still unpacked and had been moved to the living room.

Mae walked into their bedroom and said, "Well, now, I guess you plan on coming in here unannounced and expect a banquet waiting for dinner?"

"Quite frankly, no. We plan on taking you to the Club for dinner if you will get yourself straight," Rob said.

"I don't want to go to the Club. I can fix a whole lot better food than they serve," she replied.

Rob turned to Mike and said, "You see anything wrong with Mae fixing dinner?"

"No, that would suit me just fine. I'm almost too sunburned to be up and about," she said.

"Let's take a dip, and at least that will make you feel better." Both started to undress and look for their swimsuits.

When they started out the door, Mae said, "Watch for them two grumpy old men. I don't want my darlin' Mike exposed to them right off."

Rob asked, "Are you going to invite them over for dinner tonight?"

"No," came the firm reply, and Rob said no more since they had already talked to Kit, and she knew they were home and had an idea she alerted Doc and the Bishop.

The swim made them feel much better, and they were sitting on the dock in the shade drinking a soft drink when Derek came over. It was like old-home week even before they were finished hugging and laughing and the kidding was finished. Mae came out and said, "I guess you plan to stay for dinner?"

"Didn't you invite everyone?" Derek answered.

"No, I didn't invite anyone. This pair just comes driving up without any warning and expects supper."

At just this time Doc and the Bishop drove up.

"Oh no, here are the grumps," Mae said.

"Why didn't you tell us they were coming home, Mae?" the Bishop said.

"Who knew?" she replied.

"Well, I'm glad I checked with Evelyn then," Doc replied. "You wouldn't have invited us to dinner if we didn't have friends in high places over in the big office."

"You still haven't been invited. It might be the big office, but the talent and most of the power is housed in this office, and I guess all the food is here. You're all invited. Call yo' mother, Rob."

"Here she comes with Evelyn," Mike said.

"Well, I'll swear. Here it is, an old woman like me run over by everyone on the place and some imported from the old folks' home. You'd think this was the Club," Mae said.

"Mae, this food has the Club beat," Doc and the Bishop agreed.

Derek said, "Mae, don't let them rile you. We'll all help, and we'll do the cleaning up. We want to hear about all the juicy parts of the honeymoon." Everyone agreed.

"I don't need no help. I was expectin' you folks, and we'll serve at the usual time." Mae turned to walk in the kitchen when Doc and the Bishop ran over and tried to hug her. She wiggled around, got the advantage of them, and pushed both in Bath Pond and kept walking. Everyone fell out laughing at them.

When the kidding ended, Rob went to his closet and got both a pair of his shorts, a T-shirt, and flip-flops, and when they had changed they sat on the dock and laughed and talked until dinner was served.

When everyone had left but Derek and Kit, they went into the living room and sat for a short while.

"What are your plans for tomorrow?" Derek asked Rob.

"I need to show Mike around the settlement and where the bank is and a few things like that. We also probably ought to buy her a car since she is on foot. I plan to be back in the saddle day after tomorrow. Is that okay?" he asked.

"Sure it is. Your schedule looks terrible for the next few weeks. Also, we have concluded all your instructions regarding Wyoming, except you and Mike will have to decide on the reconstruction of the home there. Evelyn has all the plans in the office. We are looking for a company to put the landing strip in, and then it will be time to bring some cows back from Poppy's Ranch."

"Gee, Dad, you've been busy while we were away," Rob said. "Thanks."

Mike said, "I only wish my parents could see the place now. It looks so lovely, and I'm sure they would be very proud of it. You have concluded the purchase of the valley?"

"Yes, and you folks have a few pennies left in the bank, but when Kit finishes decorating, you will certainly be in the hole. That's her long suit," Derek concluded.

"Well, I want to express my appreciation to whomever did what. I know it is lovely, and the additional land will not only accommodate the plane but will allow us to put more cattle there," Mike said.

"You're more than welcome. We enjoyed doing this, mostly through Bob Sawyer. He is a whiz at doing things like this, and he says you have almost a full calf crop. He's wondering now if he should feed out the calves and put them on the market along with the older cows. I told him that decision would come from you folks when you arrived home. Be sure to touch base with him soon. That would really be the source of some operating funds for that ranch."

34

Since Mike was now the scriptwriter for everyone who spoke for the foundations' public relations activities as well as the writer of the advertising, Rob decided to take her to Boston on his annual visit to one of their assisted-living facilities. Evelyn took her to the tailor and had her outfitted in several appropriate dresses and gowns. Kit would have taken care of this little duty, but she was completely wrapped up in a long-distance renovation of Rob and Mike's western home. Rob worried that his mom was getting carried away with the renovation.

Rob and Derek's usual planning left an extra day in Boston to visit with Ali. This trip was no different. Their visit to the group was similar to most other occasions as well. The older residents they started with were gradually dying, and new ones were coming on the scene. The foundations' field men were constantly schooling the newer residents about what the foundations were all about and helping the residents get started with the foundations' programs.

Ali and Mike spent most of the day together. They actually had lots in common and enjoyed the day just talking, with a bit of shopping thrown in.

That night during dinner, Ali said, "Dad and Rob, I have an announcement."

"She's in love, Dad," Rob said.

"No, nothing that alarming, I can assure you. You both know I graduate the latter part of the month. Wendy and I have been talking when we get a chance. Both of us want to come home. Of course, Wendy has retirement in mind and moving into her folks' residence at the assisted-living facility. My thought is a bit different. I want to begin a pediatric surgery center with Casey first, and then gradually move around to each of our hospitals with the same plan. No plans at this time for any physical structures, but just use what we have. What do you think, Dad?"

Derek and Kit had spoken of this day often since they missed Ali every day. Derek stood and walked around to Ali on the other side of the table. She stood, they embraced, and both shed a few tears.

When he was composed, Derek said, "Nothing would suit us more than to have you home and working with the foundations. Your mother and I talk about this all the time, wondering which way you'll jump when you finish all your specialties."

Rob was in line for his hug, and he said, "It will be great to have you home, and we'll look forward to having you on the road sometime with us."

Mike already knew about the announcement and said, "Ali and I have been talking today and believe Doc and the Bishop wouldn't mind bunking together in the Gregson unit. If not, we'll have Mae to convince them." This brought a laugh and lightened the moment for everyone.

When the evening was finished, Derek said to Rob, "Son, you are visiting the federal prison tomorrow that Mr. Cook arranged in Washington. Will you be home tomorrow night?"

"Yes, if they don't lock me up," Rob replied. "It will be the first time to have the opportunity just to talk to prisoners, and I plan on being home tomorrow night. I'll have to let you know when I'll arrive."

Derek, Mike, and Evelyn left early, headed back to Florida. Rob flew down to Washington and took a car to the prison. The prison was expecting him and didn't offer any resistance. The fellow who met Rob told him the prisoners would be waiting for him in the dining room since it was the one place large enough to hold all the prisoners.

First Rob had to pass through security. He was led into a room with a couple of guards waiting. One said, "I'm very sorry, Mr. Davidson, but I must ask you to remove all your clothing."

Rob hadn't even thought such a thing might occur, but since this visit was something he wanted to go well, he began to undress. When he was completely naked, socks and all, he was asked to bend over. When the search was over, trying to lighten the moment he turned to the two guards and said, "I'm sure glad I don't have you fellows' jobs!" The two guards looked stoically at him, not cracking a smile. "I was just trying to have a little laugh with you," Rob said. Not one smile came to their faces. Rob walked out not knowing whether to be embarrassed or mad.

One guard said, "Please leave everything in your pockets but a handkerchief here, including your tie and coat. You can come back here and redress prior to leaving."

When Rob was introduced, his acceptance was on the mild side of blah. He told the prisoners about how older folks in assisted-living facilities had a passion for writing to those in hospitals and homes who were depressed and what just writing a note did for them. Rob's request was that each of those in the audience would write a kid in a juvenile detention center to encourage them and to outline what prison was actually like.

His response was fairly close to nothing. When he had said about all he could, he spotted out of the corner of his eye an older upright piano. He walked over to it and discovered it was in fairly good tune. Sitting down, he played "Rocky Top." The response to this was better than it had been with his speech. He thought privately that maybe he could reach them through this old piano. He still had twenty minutes left.

"Anyone have a request?"

"Can you play 'Rhapsody in Blue'?" one prisoner asked. He asked in such a manner that Rob had the thought that he was just playing with him sarcastically.

"I'll try," he said.

He began with all sorts of kids' songs and would catch himself and then start another kids' song, making all sorts of mistakes. He caught himself again until he finally got to the request about five songs later. The result was that he had loosened up the group, and they were laughing a bit and booing his mistakes. He then played the request, and some stood and cheered.

Ironically, they wanted to sing. They sang all sorts of songs and enjoyed doing it. They were warming up to him, and finally, when his twenty minutes were coming to a close, he said, "We have a closing song that we always use wherever we happen to be. I'll sing the verses since we have no songbooks, and you sing the chorus." They agreed, and he broke out with "I'll Fly Away."

They sang it with gusto, and the experience was very enjoyable. When he told them he would have to leave, Rob asked the prisoners if they would think about what he had asked, and maybe the officials would let him come back again for a songfest.

The guard in charge dismissed the prisoners and allowed them—at least those who wanted to—to come by and shake hands with Rob. Almost all of them did.

When Rob was redressing, the guard said, "I've never seen that group open up to a person like they did you. Why don't you send the writing paper, stamps, and kids' names and addresses, and I'll pass them out. Maybe a few will begin. Then when you can make it back, call and we'll allow you back in. You might have hit upon a therapy for the hardened criminals. You should know that none of the ones you were with will ever be free again."

"Wow," Rob said. "I wonder if we should pitch the program differently—maybe following the age-old adage, 'It is in giving that we receive our greatest gift'?"

"I'll have to leave that up to you," the guard said as he opened the door, letting Rob out.

Mike was waiting on Rob in Orlando. They had dinner and went back to Bath Pond. He was anxious to tell her about his day, and she was anxious to discuss it. She agreed to put the prison program in its proper context and offer some angles for him to follow.

A variety of angles were required since they had determined with the assisted-living facilities that different areas of the country responded in various ways to their acceptance. Prisoners would be no different.

The next day, Rob was telling Derek about his day at the prison, and both had a real conversation going. They talked more than an hour about it—about how very many were incarcerated in prisons, and that the number of teenagers incarcerated in juvenile delinquency centers was astounding.

Derek said, "You know, Son, both of us could go when time permits and maybe take Doc and the Bishop, only to the tougher prisons, and maybe we could do both a service. In fact, why not get the four boys at the ranch to go visit with the juveniles and begin using them this way and let it take them where it will?"

"That's good, Dad. I'll get my chief scriptwriter right on this project." When Rob said this, Mae walked in and said, "Ask the ol' man if he is coming over for lunch."

"Mae wants to know if the ol' man is coming over for lunch."

"Get her over to the unit." She ambled over and looked at him. "Mae, you know your youngest son is older than I am. Why did you call me 'the ol' man'?"

"Because you are the one who pays me all this money, and that makes you eligible for this title."

"I'm very sorry, but I can't join you today. Thanks." Hearing this, Mae walked out.

35

Rob visited Derek the next day and asked if they planned anything special for Ali's graduation.

"I don't know, Son. Have you talked to Mom about this?"

"No, sir, but I figured you had. We are all going, aren't we?"

"I've asked Evelyn to mark it off everyone's calendar. We need to have some sort of celebration, and perhaps even enjoy some of Ali's friends at school. Maybe Mike and Mom could handle this?" Derek said.

"You are serious about sending out the boys at the ranch to juvenile facilities?"

"Yes, but you'll have to go with them the first time. Can they get by just on what they have?" Derek asked.

"I think so. The real problem is developing a spokesperson who will follow roughly our script and find a way to encourage them to respond to the prisoners. If they will, it might do them some good."

Derek asked, "Have you spoken to any of the administrators of the juvenile facilities and determined their willingness to allow their kids to participate?"

"Only a short period by phone, but the acceptance was favorable," Rob said.

"Tell you what: You get the four boys on the conferencing unit and describe the program and get a feel if they want to tackle it with your help initially. If they do and Mike can get it on paper for them to prepare from, you can go out there and work with the kids a day or two. And maybe you can also go to your place and see if that airstrip is finalized and what it's like. By that time the sound studio will be finished at Bath Pond, and we'll begin there. We've got a ton of money invested in that studio and will have another ton in screens in various meeting places unless we can determine a way to use just a few screens and have our quadrant managers move them from place to place," Derek said. He continued, "But there is this to be said about the entire concept. Our comptroller says we can cover more ground with the studio, and the expense of operating will be drastically cut. So this may be a great move economically."

"Mike has the script almost finished for the juveniles and the convicted felons. I'll talk to the boys this afternoon, and the rest of this week isn't bad for me," Rob replied.

"Okay, Son, have at it," Derek said.

When Rob arrived home, he announced to Mike, "We have to go west to both places, come home and prepare for Ali's graduation, and then come back home and begin broadcasting in the new studio. Broadcasting doesn't have a live crowd, and this is the big problem."

Mike said, "Sit Mae over there when you are broadcasting, and at least someone will be there to gripe and kibitz about what's happening."

36

Rob and Mike left on Sunday afternoon via commercial airliner. They switched in Dallas to regional and flew into Worland. From there they rented a car and drove to Greybull.

The airstrip was complete, and it was a masterpiece. It ran north and south and was perfect for the jet. In fact, it had plenty of room left. There was a hangar there, but nothing but a small amount of jet fuel. Derek preferred that the jet be thoroughly serviced when it was refueled, and they had all of that worked out at Poppy's Ranch.

Nita had dinner almost finished when they arrived. When Mike and Rob had unloaded, both sat on the front porch and looked at the countryside and the new airstrip.

"Do you know what is on either side of the mountains that ring the valley with the strip?" Rob asked.

"Not really. I'd been over there with my parents when I was little, but because of the animals I was never allowed to play there alone," she said.

"What kind of animals?" Rob asked.

"We've seen wolves, coyotes, and a few times bear, and on one occasion a cougar. The same animals inhabit this area as at Poppy's Ranch, so you'd better take a firearm everywhere you walk around here, particularly early and late," Mike said.

After dinner they walked up the mountain behind the house and then around the top of the mountain on the east side of the strip. The view was magnificent, and no animals were present.

The renovations to the house were almost finished, and Kit and Mike had accomplished a great deal. A few pieces of furniture needed purchasing, and Kit thought she and Mike could get them while Derek and Rob were at Poppy's.

Around noon the next day the jet landed for the first time, and it was a perfect landing. Kit was alone since she'd dropped Derek off at Poppy's.

"Where is your dad?" Mike asked.

"I've got to get back to Poppy's since the two of us don't ride together. Company rule."

The pilots were complimentary of the new strip. According to them it was situated perfectly in the valley.

They ate lunch with Nita and left Kit and Mike to buy furniture and recommend some alterations to the contractor. The jet took off and transported Rob to Poppy's for a meeting there.

Evelyn and Derek were in the office working when Rob arrived. The boys were in the large room by the bunkhouse rehearsing.

Rob went into the room, and it was like old-home week. They sat down, and Rob explained the entire prisoner/juvenile delinquent program to them and what their job would be. He carefully compared it to what was done with the assisted-living facilities and every other program the foundations had going. Rob carefully explained to them the program and the method he might use to get the message across to juveniles—namely that some adult prisoners would write them a letter describing their lives in prison and the juveniles were to discuss their situation with the prisoners and begin a conversation of sorts by mail. This would be one method to help juveniles.

After the explanation Rob said, "Okay, fellows, let's practice what should be said in the stand-up presentation. The musical part I'll leave up to you, and you find the key that will unlock their voices to sing with you. If you keep probing long enough, you can find their hot button to join in."

There was really only one choice, and each agreed that the bass in the group, George, would be the spokesman. George would travel with Rob for a few days and observe him and the method by which he related to various audiences.

After this discussion, they adjourned to the living room where the piano was located. Rob had the boys singing with him, switching from one genre to another. Once the country music was winding down, he switched to pop, jazz, gospel—both contemporary and traditional—and anything else he could think of.

When they were beginning to get tired, Rob said, "Now you've traveled all day, or maybe done a show in the morning, you have a radio show at noon and another major performance that night. A nap is a must in the afternoon, and a fresh set of clothing. The tailor will work out clothing that is as wrinkle resistant as possible, but the rule is that for major performances we do not sit down after dressing. The crease in your trousers should show. We have worked now about four and one-half hours. Are you a bit tired? With your agreement to build stamina for performing, let's begin at the beginning of a Broadway show and sing it to the end."

The boys groused a bit, but fell right into the show songs they picked and did a rousing performance for Rob. He commented, "You've done a great job by having to sing too much this afternoon, but envision now having to fly most of the night to do a morning show halfway across the United States. You've got to be up for the show without drugs and alcohol, which we never use under any circumstances. How do you do it?"

Bob said, "By working out and a cold shower." The other boys agreed.

Derek walked in and said, "You boys have been wailing all afternoon. I've got a song for you to sing for me. Sing 'God Bless America' in half-notes."

Derek stopped them in mid-song. "One of the voices I'm hearing is sticking out. Each of you should not hear your own voice but the voice of person next to you. Sing the song as you normally would, except in a much, much slower tempo."

This time they got it right, and Derek let them go for the

day after profuse bragging on them and congratulating them on the fact that they would be representing the foundations.

Rob said, "Dad, I think we've got a fairly good quartet for its purpose. It'll take lots of monitoring."

"I sure hope it isn't more monitoring than we can handle," Derek replied.

Before leaving the next morning, Rob and Derek gathered the boys. Derek told them, "You keep practicing your singing, and George, you keep practicing your lines. Always remember, we use no notes. Most important, remember you are only booked by our booking office, no one else. You will not hire yourselves out for an evening to make some extra money. You work for the foundations, and I think I can guarantee you won't want any additional work. And you all already know: no drugs or alcohol. There won't even be a question if you are caught using them; you are out. Understood? And one last thing. You are decent-looking young men. In fact, when we finish dressing you, the girls will be after you when you perform away from delinquency centers. If either of us ever hears of you responding to their requests on company time, you will be fired on the spot. What you do with the ladies on your time is your business. You are thinking that I'm hard. I'm not hard at all. You will never know who is watching who will cut you out of an opportunity too valuable to miss. Are we clear as to what will be acceptable?"

All the boys were in total agreement. "Yes, sir, we understand," George said.

37

Derek, Kit, Rob, and Mike all went to Ali's graduation ceremony. It was a memorable occasion since she had worked twelve years on her schooling. Ali was very happy to be coming home.

Wendy was also retiring after the ceremony. Age was creeping up on her, and she was ready to slow her pace. She was still planning on moving into the quarters her parents had in the company's assisted-living facility.

When all the festivities were concluded and everyone was at home again, the Bishop called Rob and said, "Rob, our board needs to meet and include your dad. Doc and I have some words to share. You set it up, since we are available at any time. We think the social chairman should not be a part of this meeting."

"Is that Mae?" Rob asked, and received an affirmative answer.

After talking to Derek, the meeting was scheduled later in the afternoon in his office. Rob picked up Doc and the Bishop and delivered them to his dad's office. Derek closed all the doors to his office and asked Evelyn for privacy.

The Bishop said, "Okay, Doc, you start."

Doc began. "Fellows, you've had all sorts of work plans since I've known you. On several occasions I've cautioned you from a medical standpoint and encouraged you to slow down. You listen for a few weeks, and then it's gangbusters again. A lesson doesn't stick until you become flat and unable to continue. The point is that one of these days you'll each be flat, and no one can help you. Now you are going into becoming involved with couples who are having problems. You are trying to become involved in a prison ministry with felons and kids. You are already involved with more assisted-living facilities than I knew existed. You are assisting carpenters, plumbers, electricians, nurses, and single moms and dads schooled in all sorts of professional activities. And now you're creating a broadcast studio that will reach everywhere called the Little River Mountain Cathedral. The programs from this studio will have a medical moment and a short devotional. The latest is the four boys out west. When is it all going to stop? You and Rob can't handle all of this. I know you have quadrant managers, and I know you have the electronics company in New York and the Carter folks in Chicago. But the way you two operate it is 24/7, and you never stop, always on call."

Doc just stopped and looked at them all. Derek, Rob, and the Bishop looked at each other.

Derek said, "You make a splendid case for my retirement, Doc."

"I'm not talking about retirement. I'm talking about a plan of action to be able to handle it all."

The Bishop spoke up, "Doc, you've made a wonderful beginning for our case. You see, fellows, we are on the outside looking in, and you're looking at it oppositely from our point of view. We have a suggestion for you to consider."

"Our ears are open," Derek said, "and you know we value your opinion."

The Bishop continued, "Bring the four boys here, and get them the best voice and elocution coach you can find to work with them. Both of you could do this, but you don't have time. Let them work out of this location. Then, go the last mile with the broadcast, and do as much as is absolutely possible from here. Set up a schedule where you are working only about twenty hours a day instead of twenty-four, and try to take it easier. It might surprise you how modern technology could be helpful. This might be crazy, but Rob could probably be a part of the boys' work in detention centers. He could work from here, and they could travel."

"Now you are talking, Bishop," Rob added. "Dad won't ever become a granddad if I can't stay home more."

Derek said, "You fellows have always been there for us.

You are always thinking in our best interest, and we do appreciate it. Rob and I have a conference call coming in right now. Why don't you just sit where you are, and we'll continue in a few minutes?"

Derek's conferencing unit beeped and came on, and Trident engineers in New York were beginning to discuss the new broadcast center. Sanjay Tapton was also brought in from Los Angeles. The bottom line according to Tapton was, "The way you've constructed the building, we think your cameras can run around the room on tracks on the walls and from the ceilings. You will also have a teleprompter with every camera. We can put in a control room that handles the sound and the cameras. This would require one professional and one helper. The only problem is that unless you have a mobile camera or two, you won't be able to broadcast from other locations. You would need at least two cameras and the two men you already have to broadcast from other locations and feed it back to your studio. We think this would be considerably less expensive and do you a more professional job now that we have the sound thing whipped."

Derek looked at Rob, who was nodding his head in agreement.

"Sanjay," Derek said, "you know we've already talked about exactly the same form of operation. If you can make the studio work as you say you can, go for it. At the same time, it is up to you to hire the men we need and tell them they might be all over the U.S. and at any given time without notice. And you'll need to train them so that they can train us. And for a while, at least, you'll need to be here with us until we get our feet on the ground."

"I can handle this. We've got some folks here who want to move their families to Florida."

"If that is it, proceed," Derek said.

Derek turned to Doc and the Bishop. "There, we've already followed your instructions, and we do appreciate your kindness by sharing your thoughts. The only thing left to do is to put up a wall around the dock at Bath Pond. Otherwise we'll have everyone who comes out wanting to take a swim. We'll leave the east side completely open and fence out the rest on the west side."

"Dad, let's landscape the part between the studio and my living room and maybe put a fountain there, and a decorative masonry fence between the buildings," Rob said.

"Sounds good to me," Derek replied. "Now, I'm going for a dip." And everyone followed.

Later that evening, Kit invited Rob and Mike to have dinner with them since Ali was home. They just relaxed and had a good time together.

"Well, what's next?" Rob asked Ali.

She said, "I've already talked to Casey, and he is arranging a pediatric surgery department within each of our facilities, and I will be one of the surgeons. One day I'll be your boss!"

"Where will you live? Here with Mom and Dad, if Casey allows you to stay permanently?"

"I haven't figured that out yet, but I can't live with others with my schedule like it will be. I might even have to roll you for the jet occasionally, Rob, and travel to the other facilities," she said. "How would that suit you?"

"Well, you just gotta do what you gotta do. If it isn't available, the airport hasn't moved," Rob answered.

38

Derek met Rob at Poppy's Ranch. The purpose of the trip was to discuss with the parents of the four boys taking them to Florida for their home base, training them extensively, and allowing them to be an integral part of their troupe. They would be monitored; provided housing, meals, and show clothing; and allowed to conduct themselves as adults. If they couldn't act as adults, they would promptly be sent home.

Derek made it very clear to the parents that no alcohol or drugs would be allowed. If caught with either, that particular young man's relationship with the foundations would end, and he would be sent home.

The parents asked all sorts of questions, and the group thoroughly talked about every conceivable aspect of their program. Of course, all the parents seemed appreciative of the chance their sons were receiving and wished for success.

When the meeting was concluded, and the parents and the boys had asked all the questions they thought necessary, Rob and Mike went by car to their place in Wyoming to check on the renovations. Derek and the four boys returned to Florida. Each boy had very few belongings. Derek and Evelyn conducted business as usual all the way home, and the boys laughed and talked about fishing and hunting in Florida. Most of all, they were excited about the opportunity, and Derek was happy to have the chance to offer it to them, especially given that each had only a high school education.

Mae was required to hire an additional assistant in the kitchen to help feed the boys. She was well aware that her energy was not sufficient for anything other than talking to Doc and the Bishop from time to time. She was worn out, and she knew it. Mae remained with the Davidsons because she didn't have any place else to go. Her next move would be to the assisted-living facility with Doc and the Bishop. In fact, she should already have been there, but felt she was doing a service where she was. Truthfully, she was a pleasure to be around, and the chance to provide a useful service was her greatest joy.

Derek brought the boys over to visit with Mae, even though they had already met her, and outlined what they would be doing and where. They were to live in the visitors' quarters at Bath Pond; rooms had been constructed for three more people.

Derek then took the boys to their rooms and told them to come over to his office when they were unpacked. Unpacking didn't take long, and they were off to the main Foundation office.

Evelyn brought in a fresh pot of coffee. The youngsters, coming from where they did, drank nothing but coffee. That was their drink of choice, even instead of soft drinks.

When Derek entered the room, Evelyn had already poured him a cup and one for herself. She was sitting at the table talking to the boys and answering their excited questions. Gently she changed the subject and gracefully turned the spotlight on Derek, who explained the following to the new troupe:

"Boys, listen closely. You work for Rob, not me, although Rob also works for me. However, I'm always willing and interested in talking to you about whatever you wish. He is going to get a tailor here to measure each of you for the clothing we will require you wear. Each of you has a room that has been assigned to you, and we expect you to take care of it. Additional employees have been added to that complex to take care of you in terms of food. You will be asked to keep your room clean and always tidy. Rob will hire a voice coach for you—not to teach you how to sing but just some of the finer points that you are not yet aware of. I expect a minimum of two hours practice each day you are at home, Sundays excluded. We have a workout room, and each of you will be required to use it under the direction of a person from the YMCA, who will come out and show you what you are to do and how much you are to do. You will be expected to run every day. We are hiring you to be the same size you are now, not to blimp out on us. If you blimp out, your clothing won't fit."

After they'd talked for more than an hour, Derek heard the jet land. He was aware it was bringing Rob and Mike home.

Before the conversation was over, Kit, Doc, and the Bishop along with Rob came in the back door. Kit said, "I'm glad you folks could assemble here today because I have an ultimatum to deliver. It will be carried out to the letter." When she said this, Derek, Evelyn, Rob, Doc, and the Bishop all were surprised by her candor. Continuing, Kit said, "Now that we have four additional males on the premises and since the work will be heavy there are two additional announcements. Number one is no one will be allowed to skinny-dip in Bath Pond any longer. It is just too public a place, and the ladies who now work there shouldn't have to endure that. And number two is that the boys will have an etiquette expert work with them, and I might include some of the rest of the members of the crew in that class. More on this later. Are there any questions?"

Everyone in the room but Evelyn and the boys really gave Kit a hard time about using suits to swim. It was a tradition and all sorts of other reasons surfaced, but she held firm and won out. They all agreed in the end that she was right, and they would follow her instructions.

When Kit was finished, Derek said, "Boys, stay with me just a minute along with Rob when the madam here is finished with her ultimatums."

When everyone was finished and gone, Derek said to them, "Boys, we will not put any personal restrictions on you. If you can conduct yourselves appropriately, there will be none. If we have to watch you, the next step is to catch the jet back home. I will not tolerate behavior unbecoming a member of our out-front team, and you already know what these restrictions are. When you are in public, you are representing this Foundation and each of us, and it must be impeccable behavior. Does each of you thoroughly understand that?" The agreement was unanimous.

"While we are talking, I personally want you in as good a physical shape as is humanly possible given the schedule that you will probably have to maintain. From being on the ranch where each of you grew up, I know the fad there is gold teeth. I can see a few here. Believe me, I am not in any sense making fun of your gold teeth, but here is what I want you to do. I want each of you to visit our dentist, who will cap each of your teeth with white porcelain. Your teeth will look just like mine." Derek then showed them his teeth, which were perfect. "Your teeth will also look just like Rob's. Show them your teeth, Rob."

Derek actually thought he would embarrass the boys, but they felt sufficiently fulfilled by their association with the Foundation that they didn't feel that way. "Dental hygiene is something we must maintain," he continued. "In fact, you will need mints with you at all times. Here's the reason. We sometimes are caught thinking we'll do just an hour show and wind up with two. If you sing and sweat for two hours, your breath, through no fault of your own—it might be something you ate—could become a bit rank, and when a nice-looking woman wants to hug you or dance, a lingering odor is not something you want her to remember you by."

"Now," Derek continued, "other than the dentist, how many of you have ever had a complete physical examination?" Not one had.

"Okay, Rob will set that up with Dr. Cagle, our head physician. We don't think anything is wrong with you, but we want to make sure.

"The last thing is that we want you to eat properly. There will be absolutely no binge eating when you are on the road performing. It is better to be a bit empty than not be able to get your breath." The boys got a laugh from this. "Additionally, after your tailor-made clothing is completed, that is the size you will remain. If you become larger, your clothing will not. So watch your weight."

Evelyn took the boys to the accounting department to officially work them into the Foundation as employees. They were then told to wait in the lobby, and Rob would take them back with him, or they could walk. They left walking and were joyously happy as they went back because of their good fortune to have found a way to utilize their talents and not be forking a horse running cattle at the ranch. Three generations of each boy's family were ranch hands before them on the same ranch. The boys were determined to succeed with the break they had been offered.

39

Everyone thought the studio was much larger than they would ever need. The walls were on rollers and could be changed with little effort to enlarge or diminish a studio. The cameras ran on tracks around the edge of each room and the ceilings. All the cameras were controlled from a console in a control room by a trained technician. The volume and mix of the sound were controlled from there as well. Each camera had a teleprompter to be sure each participant knew what was coming next. Only in unusual circumstances were words ever placed on the prompters, since Derek did not want the singers to rely on them. The words should be memorized, he felt, and sung from the heart. The reason? Most people can't read in such a way that the words become free-flowing. Plus, no one would have teleprompters on the road.

There was also a soundproof practice room with no chairs. The room had its own piano and keyboard.

Before Rob left the office, Derek called him back behind closed doors. "Son, just because the boys live in the same complex as you doesn't mean you have to watch them. If they can't behave as they should and approach their duties in a professional manner, they might get to catch the plane home."

"I was going to talk to you about that since Mike and I live there. We plan to eat in our apartment and have some sort of life to ourselves when possible. Since the boys are only twenty years old, I know they will want to get out occasionally if we are not on the road."

"Wait now. This new studio is supposed to keep us from working on the road as much as possible," Derek said. "I think you should ask Mike if she will have installed a bulletin board in a central location that has everyone's schedule on it as far in advance as possible. Do you think she can handle this for us?"

"Sure, I think so. I'll talk to her about it and get her to work it out, and we'll come up with a design everyone can understand."

Derek continued, "Son, we are setting out on something that really could be a bear. Not any more so than the jet is, but we are continually adding more. To start with, for the next few days I think you should find out which of the boys can really nail a note, loud, clear, and right on the button. The next note should be one-half step up or down, the third one-half step up or down, and the fourth likewise. Teach them to harmonize better, and slide up and down the scale, never moving until the harmony is perfectly correct. When they have conquered this, I want to hear it. Also, talk to them about not being nervous around either of us."

"Yes, sir, I can handle this. They already know most of this, but in places they're a bit rusty."

PART FOUR

A New Adventure

40

The first day using the studio, all sorts of strange people were there to ensure success. The boys had practiced almost nonstop for a month. They were ready for assisted-living-facility functions and graduation ceremonies for all sorts of schools that the foundations sponsored and in every location. A special program was developed for prisons and schools for youngsters in trouble. Each of these required a different approach.

Extraordinary attention was used in preparing for single moms and couples having marital trouble. In fact, this aspect of the work was so difficult, Derek was already preparing for live conferences to be able to better assist these groups with their problems. Via teleconferencing, they were guessing at the probable problems unless they could determine the best manner for feedback. The idea was bounced around that Derek and Rob would have a teleconversation with these folks, and through this talkback idea develop a useful approach for back-and-forth discussion.

Mike moved into Rob's office to work. When he needed to practice, she moved to the kitchen counter.

When the preliminary sketch of the program was being honed into the finished product, Mike called Derek and Rob over to discuss what they were setting up. "If you will come with me to the scheduling board, I'd like to show you what we have planned," and everyone followed her.

"Stop here and study the board," she said. The longer they studied the board, the more both could see that they were terrifically overloaded. "We don't have a minute to spare from the studio, and still we have those programs we've promised to do in person. You tell me when and where we should put them in. The way it is set up now, no one will have time to go to the bathroom!"

"Son, she's right," Derek said. "Everyone is overloaded. If someone is sick, what are we going to do?"

"Well, Dad, we'll do just as we always have. We can do it ourselves," Rob replied. "We don't have any alternative until we are free of this logjam."

"You're right, we could do that. I thought that the purpose of the studio was to cut the work so that we could have more time for ourselves. Now we are scheduled to begin in two weeks, and we're grossly overloaded."

Rob said, "Dad, let's give it a try now that the Carter folks have agreed to assist with the screens on location and see how it goes. If we have to make adjustments, we'll just do it. We can't let it whip us now."

"You are correct. I think we are ready to begin. Take Mike, and let her see the finished product of your home in the West, and drop the boys off at Rosita's to visit their parents. I'll talk to Doc and the Bishop about their roles. Truthfully, their roles can't be too extensive due to their ages. I've got Doc talking to Wendy, and we can always fall back on Ali and Casey to see if they will assist when needed," Derek concluded.

"That's a good lick, Dad. You are right not to forget Ali, though with her just beginning it might be more difficult for her than Wendy."

41

The boys were excited about going home for a short visit. They had practiced hard and long and fulfilled all the requirements Derek had laid down. All had a burning desire to be sure they did all that was asked of them. Their voice, diction, and etiquette lessons had paid off. They were different young men. They had new clothing, new teeth, and new haircuts that were alike. It was very evident they all had new bodies from the trainers they had. Astonishingly, they were each the exact same size. They were clean and wholesome-appearing, and ready to give it their all. Most of all they were grateful to Derek and Rob for the chance to work with them, and someday to become as professional as they. Just before the boys stepped out of the plane, Rob said, "Boys, remember what you were taught in diction, etiquette, personal hygiene, and all of that. Use it here since you don't want to allow yourself to slide backward from what you've been taught."

Rob and Mike dropped them off at the ranch to the happy arms of their families. Everyone had lunch with Rosita, except the boys, who were anxious to get home. Rob had promised the boys that when they were picked up, they would spend the night and the boys could sing for their parents and everyone on the ranch who wanted to attend.

The runway at the renovated home was perfect. The pilots were to be back in six days for them.

This was the first time Mike had seen their home since the decorators were finished. Both Mike and Rob thought they did an excellent job under Kit's supervision via telephone. She had a modern kitchen installed; the master bedroom was spiffed up a bit, even with a bathroom that looked sinful; and an extra bathroom was added to the other bedroom. It was just the perfect place to relax for a few days.

Almost at once Rob felt lost. The reason why wouldn't come to him immediately, but it dawned on him in the middle of the first night. There was no piano there. Using all the restraint possible, he didn't mention it to Mike since she was so carried away with being at home, for her, as a change.

Arriving back at Rosita's, Rob took a nap and was ready for their concert prior to dinner being served. He had secretly made provisions for them to have a poolside party after the boys sang for their families.

When the boys came to the main house, Rob told them, "Boys, you each have a tux in the closet of the plane. Bring them to my bedroom, and you can change." They were elated to be able to show off their clothes and newfound talent.

Rosita had all the families seated in the living room, and everyone else from the ranch was sitting on the floor without shoes. At precisely 7 p.m., the boys and Rob walked in dressed as if they were on stage. He could see the parents, who were elated because their sons were given such an opportunity and had gotten this far with it already. The boys walked through the living room to their area in front of the piano.

Rob played an introduction that no one knew; actually he made it up as he played. The purpose of the introduction was to give the boys their pitch with the last note. With the pitch, Bill solidly nailed the first note with the word "There's"; then Bob a quarter note later sang "There's" solidly one-half step lower; then Butch and then Bang both one-half step down and one-quarter note later. They held that harmony until Rob was satisfied with it and the volume was where he wanted it. Two beats later they sang "There's a Place for Us," to everyone's great applause. The ranch people had never heard that kind of talent and didn't expect it from their boys. They were elated beyond description. Before the crowd was able to get over their thrill, Rob broke into "Bridge over Troubled Water" and then "I Need You Now."

When they finished the third selection, Rob stood and

said, "We are very, very proud of the boys' progress since their move to Florida. We hope you are, too, of the manner in which they sang tonight." Of course, the applause wouldn't end until Rob stopped it, but he couldn't stop the tears of some of the boys' closer relatives. They were proud beyond description of something they never expected to hear. They were convinced that Rob was the one who had recognized their talent and polished it.

"Because of the schedule ahead of us, we have a closing number and then we'll all have dinner together," Rob said. The first word, "Some," was held just like the beginning note for their first selection, except this was for "I'll Fly Away." The boys' harmony was perfect on their first night out, which thrilled Rob to no end.

When Rob got the crowd quieted down and ready for dinner, Derek walked out of the hallway from the bedroom, entering the living room to loud applause. "Thank you, folks. We wanted you to hear the progress your boys have made. I especially wanted to hear them myself tonight, but not with their knowledge that I was here. Boys, you were perfect in your presentation, and I know your parents and friends are very proud of you, as I am." When he said this, he hugged each of the boys and Rob.

Around the pool a bit later, Kit asked what Rob thought of the house in Wyoming. "It is great, Mom. Mike fell in love with it immediately and is thrilled with it. In fact, she hated to leave."

"What did you think?" she asked.

"While I like where I live, I liked it as well. I would have enjoyed the stay more if there was a piano there." Neither Kit nor Rob said any more about the house.

42

Everyone was on hand at the studio Monday morning at 10 a.m. It was the only dress rehearsal they would have unless they were really in need of more, but this was the only planned full dress rehearsal.

Mae, Kit, Evelyn, Mike, Wendy, Casey, and the cooks from the kitchen were their audience. Doc and the Bishop were dressed in full regalia for their stage debut. Sanjay Tapton and Bob Lineer were very much on hand. Tapton was riding herd over the technician whom they had hired to run the control room. Lineer was directing the entire production. Lineer was sitting in a soundproof booth with the ability to speak through an earpiece to each person involved in the production.

Because it was their first practice run, it was being sent live to Chicago to the Carter Communications Center, and about two hundred of their employees had gathered to offer their opinion. It was a tense moment for everyone but Derek and Rob. Rob had total confidence that, based on their past performances, he and his dad could handle most any failure. Derek was in apparently good shape, too.

The lights were blinding and hot. Lineer wanted all the performers to stand on stage to allow their eyes to become accustomed to them. He did not want them squinting. In fact, the backstage area was just as bright to allow their eyes to get used to the glare.

Because it was hot, Derek and Rob started to perspire the minute the lights came on. It was miserable until they had grown reasonably accustomed to the uncomfortable nature of the entire setup. The dressing rooms were directly behind the stage, and a tunnel was placed down both sides of each wall for everyone to enter unless they were going directly on stage.

They were using the set of the Little River Mountain Cathedral. Kit had selected blooming plants in such a manner in front of the curtain that they looked natural and as if the entire wooded scene was natural and blooming. The scene appeared to be a rustic chapel back in the woods. The setting was very real, and without the knowledge that it was a stage prop there was no way to tell.

The red lights located strategically around the studio came on as the signal for Rob to begin the piano and everyone else to silence themselves. Rob took parts of several beautiful pieces and put them together as the door to the chapel slowly opened. He was sitting there with the four boys standing in front of the piano. Rob's music was a cross between classical, contemporary, and spiritual. His last note was the boys' pitch, and they did the same program they presented at the ranch. The only change was that Derek was announcing, and when they finished the first song the camera panned to the window and one could see wind blowing through the trees outside, which stunned everyone. Derek came on camera first and outlined to the Carter folks in Chicago the intent of the program—a dry run so to speak. This was Derek's place to speak, and he lavished accolades on the boys, who were dressed in white tuxes with a red cummerbund. Derek was dressed the same, except his cummerbund was black.

Derek then introduced Doc, and the camera made its way down the hallway of a clinic setting and into a doctor's examining room. Doc was sitting on the examining table. "Good morning," Doc began. He then delivered about a ten-minute presentation on handling stress in the workplace. What no one knew but Derek, Rob, and Mike was that Doc's script was on a teleprompter. The Bishop had a teleprompter as well.

The camera panned back inside to the boys. Rob played an introduction, and they began to sing "Bridge over Troubled Water."

Derek simply said, "Ladies and gentlemen, it is my pleasure to present the Reverend Doctor Roger Hornsby, Retired Bishop." The applause was real in Carter's auditorium and canned inside the Foundation studio. The Bishop stepped up on his platform and moved behind the pulpit. He then delivered a ten-minute devotional developed for business people, which was well received.

The camera panned back to Derek, who stated that one of their most requested songs was "I Need You Now," and the boys sang a terrific rendition.

Derek took the opportunity to praise the boys and the musical talents and promised they would continue to be closely associated with entertaining the Carter Communications Group. He gave Rob the signal to close with their usual number, "I'll Fly Away," except Rob sang the verses and all six, including Derek, sang the chorus in very tight harmony.

Lipton faded out the Mountain Cathedral. The credits rolled, and the program signed off.

The performance was taped in regular sound and the sound of the wilderness from the cabin out west. They all sat down, viewing and listening very carefully. They felt one sound was just as good as the other, and the total production performance was just what they were looking for. Lipton felt they could do much more to spiff it up a bit, including the sounds of the wind and animals.

When the official postmortem concluded, everyone went into the dining room for a catered lunch.

Later that afternoon, Derek decided to go back to Bath Pond and take a look at Rob's schedule of performances, both live and studio. The truth was that the live performances were really going to overload the group, given all the studio sessions that were already scheduled.

Derek said, "Son, I can still do some of this from time to time—either in the studio or live. Don't overload yourself and the boys."

"I expect to call on you, and it could be at the last minute,"

Rob said. "You know, Dad, I am normally not uptight about a performance, but this morning whipped me for some reason. I'm hoping it was because it was just something new and different and worried about the boys. They did well, I think."

"They did. I was surprised at the magnitude of their improvement. Their ranges are different, their sounds are coming from their toenails—nothing nasal—and the body trainer has gotten results. Kit shouldn't see them in the pool; they are total muscle. I'd probably be with them with the trainer."

Rob said, "If Mom saw them in the pool, you would be signed up again with the trainer like I had to do. I was hoping to be through with him until Doc caught me one day at Bath Pond. Let's take a dip?"

On the way to the pool, Derek said, "Why not send one of the boys to get Doc and the Bishop? They'd like to be with the boys and enjoy them, plus a dip."

"Butch, how about going over and asking Doc and the Bishop if they'd like to come over for a dip?" With this, Butch was off in Rob's car.

As soon as they arrived, Mae was on them. "Don't think you ol' birds will weasel in on the training table. They feed you softer food where you live now. It is much better for ol' men."

"Mae, please don't be so hard on us. It is difficult enough getting old, but a good meal once in a while is necessary to keep hanging around and doing for nothing the job we are charged with doing," the Bishop said. "Couldn't you possibly squeeze us in? Can't you do that? We'd sleep better tonight."

"It would be a big help, Mae," Doc begged.

Mae had known that Kit was looking at catalogs with Mike, and Mae asked that she and Derek stay and have a little celebration for the boys. Of course, no one was hard to talk into staying. So they ate, talked, bragged on themselves, and sang.

Doc said, "Boys, we are having an in-house good time tonight. Bragging on ourselves really has no place for professionals of any kind. This word is as a favor to you. If you develop this habit, the first thing you know you will begin to believe the rubbish and your performance will slip. Dwell on the mistakes and other ways you can improve, and your performance will continue on the upswing."

Derek piped up. "Doc is entirely right, boys. This job was thrust upon me, and all the mistakes I made in the early years I had to live with them. However, for every mistake I made, I tried to work on it until the correction was second nature. Doc is telling you right."

The Bishop said, "I've never made a mistake!"

Mae screamed out, "Whoever is responsible for this ol' bird who's never made a mistake being over here, take him home now. Why, even I can think of one mistake I've made."

43

Just as Derek sat down at his desk the next morning, Rob came on the conferencing unit. "Dad, what's the possibility you can drop by sometime this morning?"

"Do we have problems?"

"Some slight problems, but nothing we can't correct," Rob replied.

Mid-morning Derek walked over for a bit of exercise. "Morning all," he said, pouring himself a cup of coffee. He sat down by Mae at the counter. "How are you today, Mae?"

"Not good. I had a terrible night. Didn't sleep good. It must have been something I ate."

"You are the boss over here. How could that be?"

"I don't rightly know. It must have been something those old men did to me. I could be poisoned."

Rob walked in, "What's her trouble?"

"She says Doc or the Bishop poisoned her. She's made bad enemies when a minister of the gospel would poison her, and a man who had taken an oath to save lives then poisons her."

"She's finished," Rob piped up. "Can you come into the office?"

"Sure," and Derek said to Mae, "I'll check on you on the way out."

"Are you going to leave me here to die alone?" He kept walking, and Mae mumbled, "I guess so. It's a bad thing when an old lady has to die by herself." After saying this, she turned and walked into the kitchen.

Mike was standing in front of the scheduling board that covered almost one wall of the office. She said, "It appears that we've gotten too many performances lined up for our available time."

"What do you plan to do about it?"

"That's why we called you," Rob answered.

Derek asked, "Do you have any suggestions?"

"I've got a question," Mike stated.

"What's that?" Derek said.

Mike asked, "Is there a possibility that all these broadcast programs be simultaneous? Could all the prison programs be simultaneous? If the possibility arose whereby one of the heavy contributors might be having a special night, then you could either broadcast separately or do it live as in the past," she offered.

"Do you have any better suggestion, Dad?" Rob asked.

"Not at the moment—remembering, of course, that the one constant we have is last-minute changes. My off-the-cuff remark would be to try to get everyone we are trying to improve our outreach with on the board, and to take a copy of the board to the downtown office of the schedulers. Allow them to set up the performances, schedule them, get the screens up, keep everyone on their toes here, and expect many, many changes. Their job is to coordinate our performances with the ultimate locations. They are to talk to each transmittal receiver and provide us with feedback as to acceptance, quality, and any suggestions for the future. You are not to try to do this from this office. Rob, you concentrate on quality of performance and stay ahead of the chart. Also, find a fill-in for Doc and the Bishop. Neither can hold up to this schedule. Casey can find someone who can fill Doc's place, and maybe the Bishop can suggest someone to replace him. Now, see how easy that was?" Derek asked.

"What if a prison, for example, has a conflict on the night it has scheduled? Can we simply take the recording of that night and play it when they can take advantage of it?" Rob asked.

"Sure, that's an idea for all performances. Record them and play them at their appropriate time," Derek countered. "This way you might not be fighting a schedule all the time."

Later in the afternoon, Rob dropped in on the Bishop and

Doc. Both had been dozing and were now in a heated argument over a World Series game that was broadcast sometime in the 1930s.

Both welcomed Rob and asked him to be seated and have some refreshments of his choice. "No, thanks. I really don't have that much time to visit. There is some business we need to discuss. We've got some scheduling problems that haven't been resolved as yet, but we almost have them."

"Tell us about them," the Bishop said.

"The truth is, we've got more performances than we can schedule for the next year, and we are taking steps to combine most of them. For instance, all the prisons will be recorded at one time. If they don't go out live at the time, we'll play the recording when they can allow them. Then when we do live presentations we can cut out the time, just record a number of performances," Rob explained.

"That sounds reasonable to me," Doc said.

"Here is the thing. If we do everything we've planned for the coming year, you two will be way overloaded. Dad and I think the two of you need stand-ins for those times you don't want to, or maybe don't feel up to, completing a performance," Rob said.

The Bishop turned to Doc and said, "They are afraid we are going to die!"

Rob turned red. "Dying has never entered our mind. We all get tired, but you fellows are older and we certainly don't want to have any part in allowing you to overload yourselves."

Doc said, "Rob, the Bishop is kidding you. We all know we don't have many performances left in us, and you are right. We should find substitutes and be sure they are trained in what we've set out to do. Do you agree, Bishop?"

"Sure, you're right. No sense even discussing that. We should find the right people—people who can even do a better job. But Rob, I want you to know I've had fun and continue to have fun with you fellows who are much younger. I feel invigorated around you, and I, for one, am thankful for the opportunity," the Bishop concluded.

"I feel the same, Rob," Doc said. "You are right on target, Son, and there is no animosity here with your thinking."

"The last thing we would want to do would be to hurt either of you. This is just something we have to face, but we want you two around for a long time yet."

When Rob started to leave, both the men hugged him and reassured him of their love for everyone and the opportunities they'd been given.

Thirty minutes later Derek called and thanked them for being so nice to Rob. He also reassured them they could remain as long as they were able and wanted to. They also had a private agreement that Doc and Casey would begin looking for a replacement. The Bishop had some connections to help him locate someone who would agree to fill in for him when the time came.

44

Rob called a meeting for the boys, their sound man, and camera and light technician. Rob was uncertain as to what the outcome would be, but he knew it had to happen.

Seated in the studio, Rob said, "Fellows, we are fixing to have to go to work. When we crank up there is no stopping unless an emergency arises, and then we'll have to work through it. So listen carefully." For this he asked Derek to sit in.

"First, we're overscheduled. To compensate we'll do all the recording for Carter's graduations for the year. Dad will want to say a word here probably to each one of them.

"Second, we'll do the prisons and the reform schools. From time to time we might mix them up a bit.

"Third, we'll do the nurses' graduations. In all these recorded sessions, they might be different than when we do live presentations. We will go to some of them. If you are hankering to travel, hang on, you'll get enough.

"Most of the traveling will be done on the weekend, and special events during the week to upscale assisted-living facilities. And from time to time there will be all sorts of performances which will surface that we will be compelled to comply with for many reasons. You will go to places you've never heard of, and some you will not want to hear of again.

"Here is the point. You fellows must broaden the scope of selections that you can recall and sing perfectly at a moment's notice. We will do all the practicing possible. If Dad goes with you, it will be when he mounts the stage when you know what you will do. This can be an unnerving experience, believe me. However, he will never do anything to embarrass you in public. He might embarrass me, but never you: count on it.

"So, we are about to set up a schedule that we will attempt not to break from—five days each week. If we don't go out on the weekend, we will work in the morning on Saturday, until we are broad enough to do the job. Of course, we want the lights and sound to work by. This way we can become accustomed to working with lighting and sound men. We will do all our recording in the morning if possible, to look fresher."

Derek said, "We've got stacks and stacks of music that must be gone through. You need several favorites to fall back on, and you need some that no one else can do better. I know you can't read music like we can, so you get to make some selections you like and can do well, and we can get you the music and then memorize the words. The point is these words won't stay with you from now on. One must go over and over them often. When we are in public or recording in places other than our studio, and the studio is where you will record most, you will always be in the appropriate dress. For practice, you work it out with Rob. Whatever suits him will suit me."

Rob asked, "Any questions?" Those questions they asked led to others, and they had quite a question-and-answer period.

45

After a few weeks the schedule leveled out. It was determined they could, in fact, record better in the morning, since that is when they had the most energy. Rehearsals were always in the afternoon. If they traveled for a Saturday performance in another city, they traveled late Friday and into Friday night. Since recordings were in full dress, they had to know in advance who they were recording for. For example, for the boys' reformatories they recorded in sport coats and ties—and not all the same. But all the coats were the same distance from the floor, always. They simply dressed for the occasion. With the lights as hot as they were, the dry cleaners had a steady delivery since everyone was constantly changing clothing. Sometimes recording required those involved to change to two different styles of clothing.

Clothing became such a problem that a wardrobe person had to be hired. The wardrobe supervisor made a few changes and began to switch the clothing about, dressing the boys in suits of various colors, various sport coats and pants, and occasionally if a situation presented itself whereby an open-neck large collar was the answer, that's what they used.

Kit always handled Derek's clothing, except that he did have some clothing in the boys' dressing room. They kept recording clothing in a large dressing room that all of them used. Derek and Rob kept their clothing there as well, and the supervisor took care of theirs also, including Doc's and the Bishop's. Everyone presented in the same clothing they recorded in.

The clothing was worked out, and the rehearsal schedule was refined to the point that they were in the studio a full day every day but Wednesday. Wednesday afternoon was off, and the boys could do anything they wanted to. If the boys traveled, they were usually out over the weekend. If not, they worked Saturday morning and had the afternoon to do whatever they wanted. Strangely, they tended to hang around close to the compound. After they became known, they didn't enjoy the notoriety that it brought. They were pretty much loners.

If the boys were home over the weekend, they were always in church in the settlement. They didn't perform in church to give themselves some relief, since they were more religious than anyone had thought. They did like to bring their friends from church out to Bath Pond and swim or dance to CDs. There was never a discipline problem, and the boys worked very hard attempting to polish their talents.

When they performed and Rob or Derek was playing solo, they enjoyed dancing with those in the audience and never hesitated. They were wonderful dancers after Kit made them take lessons, and those in the audiences looked forward to their coming.

In the studio a closely held secret was that Mae could play a juice harp, Doc could play a mouth organ, and the Bishop thought he could play a bass fiddle. They developed little antics that included them occasionally. However, they usually adhered to the script.

The boys took one week off per quarter and one month off each year. Their destination was home to the ranch. Derek and Rob worked every week and tried to be at home as much as possible at night. If Rob was out of town during the week, Derek practiced with the boys and did the shows with them. It was a wonderful arrangement. Rob also filled in for Derek on the road when necessary.

Occasionally Rob and Mike were able to slip off to Wyoming and to visit and eat with Rosita at the ranch. Mike was busy keeping everyone on schedule at Bath Pond. She did none of the scheduling with clients, but made sure the boys were up and ready and on time.

The only surprises were between Derek and Rob on the road. Their ability always added to a performance, and everyone enjoyed them tremendously.

Their schedule was usually at home for the week and the weekend. If they traveled, it was not as often as formerly, though still fairly regular.

PART FIVE

The Big Time

46

One late afternoon, Rob was diligently going through old music for the sole purpose of keeping their presentations fresh. They were now where they could remain home most of the time and travel was at a minimum, which was a great relief. Attending to important matters was very difficult while away from the office.

Derek walked in and said, "Son, put all that away and let's talk a little."

"Sure, Dad, what do you want to talk about?"

"We are missing a big bet, I think."

"What is it?" Rob asked.

"With you doing most of the performing with the boys and the old men, I have been given the chance to sit back and observe. The bet we are missing is that the boys have so much more to give than we are asking."

"How so, Dad?"

"I believe with the proper training, we can take them to a much higher level. I know that with our elaborate sound system, we can do a great deal just by jiggling the sound, but those boys have talent we haven't scratched that needs developing naturally. They need to stand on their own. They stand out on songs like 'A Place for Me' and 'Impossible Dream,' 'The Prayer,' and all the really classic songs of our day. Each has a magnificent solo voice, and their harmony is wonderful."

"Well, if they are that good, what's the problem?" Rob asked.

"I think we need to hire a high-powered voice and performance coach. I've taught them all I can, plus not having the time to devote to it, there isn't much more I can do. I want to bring someone in to observe and not mention to the boys why he or she is here. After a few weeks we'll have a private conference and discuss the possibilities for the future and how we can develop them further. What do you think?"

"Don't forget, Dad, we have so many programs going now that we are getting to the limit of what we can invest without going over our limits with cash. Every area is growing and we are stretched thin, yet I know we have those standing in line needing us and we are virtually helpless because of lack of time," Rob declared.

Derek walked into the Robert P. Wagner Music Building at his alma mater and asked the receptionist if his old voice coach Vincent Bender was still actively working.

"No, sir," the receptionist replied. "Dr. Bender lost his wife, traveled for a short while, and now lives quietly in his little bungalow. Would you like his address?"

"Yes, please," Derek replied.

When Derek knocked on his front door, Dr. Bender immediately recognized him. "Derek Davidson, what a pleasant surprise. Won't you come in, please?"

After an hour of exchanging pleasantries inside the disheveled little home, Derek asked, "What are you doing for fun, Dr. Bender?"

"Just sitting here waiting on tomorrow. That's about it," he said.

"Would you be interested in doing something constructive for me?" Derek asked.

"What did you have in mind?"

"Let's go some place for a bite to eat, and we'll discuss it."

They went to the college cafeteria, sat in the corner, and talked until well into late afternoon about all the things Derek had going and what he wanted to do. Dr. Bender was interested and decided the effort would at least give him something useful to do. They agreed that Derek would send a driver for his automobile and bring it to Bath Pond.

47

The first night, Rob got Dr. Bender moved into the assisted-living center with Doc and the Bishop. When he was almost settled, Rob took him to the airstrip to meet Derek's arrival. The jet was overwhelming to Dr. Bender. He was unable to quit talking about it.

That night, Kit fixed dinner for Rob, Mike, Derek, and Dr. Bender. They had a good time just talking about Derek's school days.

"Rob, I'd like to hear you play and sing," Dr. Bender requested. After his performance, Dr. Bender said, "Derek, your son is much, much better than you ever will be. He can play better, too!"

This statement sent Rob and Kit to the ceiling with laughter after observing Derek's doleful face. "Dad, I still like your singing," Mike said.

"Thanks, darlin', it's nice to know I still have one friend. I'll get even with Mr. Rob on payday."

Derek took Dr. Bender back to his quarters and introduced him to Doc and the Bishop. "What's he going to do?" Doc asked.

"One thing is he'll teach you how to play a harmonica and the Bishop to play his bull fiddle," Derek answered. "Since he answers to me, if he says let you go that's it."

"You can't do that to a man of the cloth who is already a master," the Bishop said. "Anyway, we now have two docs and a bishop. That's fairly close to the Three Stooges."

"You are right. Dr. Bender's presence and reason for being here are not known to the boys from the ranch. You fellows have a good time with him, but keep him away from the boys. His seat is in the sound booth, and Rob will have an earpiece for listening to him."

"Does Mae know about Dr. Bender?" Doc asked.

"Not yet. I was afraid he'd leave if exposed to her too early. Dr. Bender is on a special mission known only to me, sort of as an undercover agent," Derek said. "We will introduce Mae to him later in the week."

"Look, fellows, please call me Vince," Dr. Bender said.

The next morning Rob and the boys were to record a commencement exercise for electricians and carpenters, plus a dance. The Bishop and Doc didn't have to be in the studio until very much later in the morning. The commencement was to be for 10 a.m. When Derek slipped Vince into the sound booth, they both sat down and listened as the boys warmed up prior to their performance.

"Derek, does one of the boys, or more than one, have a cold?"

"Not to my knowledge," Derek replied.

"You go down there and tell them 'good morning,' and see if one does. Ask if necessary."

Derek came into the studio whistling and carrying on with his usual banter. "Hi, boys. Everyone feeling good this morning?"

"Yes, sir," they responded almost in unison.

In first-grade conversation, he nosed around among the boys and tried to read them for cold symptoms. He sat down on the bench and talked to Rob for a minute. When he got up to leave he said softly to Rob, "Dr. Bender is in the studio. Keep your earpiece in."

When Derek was back in the booth, Rob had the boys singing scales and camp songs. They appeared as if they felt good, and they were happy and enjoying each other.

Derek said, "They appear in good shape to me. Rob hasn't detected anything."

When the practice was over, the boys, Rob, and Derek went to the dressing room to change for their performance. They all wore black tuxes with red cummerbunds.

The Bishop and Doc came in with a cup of coffee for Vince.

"We didn't know how you liked your coffee, so we just brought the fixings."

"Thanks, fellows. Boy, this is a state-of-the art facility, isn't it?"

"Wait until the exercises begin, you'll see a show," Doc said.

When the moment was precisely right, the automatic door locks did their duty, and the studio announcer turned on the appropriate lights and said, "We are now ten, nine, eight, etc. seconds away," and continued the countdown.

At the exact necessary moment, both Rob and Derek began "Pomp and Circumstance." When they arrived at its familiar melody, the graduates started processing to the front of the auditorium in Kansas City. They could see this on a massive screen down front of the studio and the musicians could see one located at the back of the studio. The way the screens were aligned in Kansas City, it appeared in the studio that the musicians were inside the hall with the graduates. Actually, to Vince it felt like he was sitting with the graduates' family members. It was simply unbelievable what they were doing with electronics.

When they got to the melody that most people know, Derek switched to the keyboard and played it as an organ with Rob continuing on the piano.

The boys only sang "The Lord's Prayer" at the end of the ceremony. When the ceremony was over, a camera followed the crowd outside into the hallway, and the doors opened to a large room with a buffet lunch ready to be served. There on the stage was Rob dressed in a white coat and a black cummerbund, as were the boys. The boys were performing "Somewhere over the Rainbow" when the crowd walked in. The younger folks in the crowd immediately began dancing after Rob moved center stage and congratulated the graduates on behalf of the foundations and invited them to dance.

Rob also told the group they would remain on stage until mid-afternoon, when they would have to leave for another engagement.

When Derek and Vince were alone, Vince asked, "Derek, do you know if one or more of the boys has a hearing problem?"

"No, I don't," he replied.

Vince asked, "Does the hospital close by that your Foundations own have an audiologist?"

"Sure," Derek replied.

"Take the boys and Rob, and each of you have your hearing checked as soon as possible. I think someone singing during the commencement exercises has a hearing problem."

"How do you know that?" Derek asked.

On the third day of Vince's visit, they introduced him to the boys and Mae. His first question to the boys was, "How much formal musical training have you fellows had?"

The answer, of course, was "None, except Rob and Derek."

Derek piped up, "They're correct, Vince. Rob brought them from a ranch we have in the West. They are actually cowboys, singing cowboys."

Mae interrupted. "No one has told me yet what this old man is doing here. Now, every time I turn my head are his drawers going to hit the ground before he goes into Bath Pond? I've got enough of old men around here who want to be looked after."

While Vince was embarrassed beyond words, the Bishop said, "Now, Mae, you really hurt Doc, and we thought you sort of felt like we were supposed to come over for lunch a few days a week, or breakfast and sometimes even dinner. You let us go swimming, too, didn't you?"

"Yes, but Kit stopped that naked-butt swimming when the boys came. The sight was just overwhelming," Mae said. "Who is this bird?"

"This is my college professor who is visiting," Derek said.

"How long does he plan to stay?" Mae asked.

"That's up to him. We've got him watching Doc and the Bishop over at the assisted-living facility," Derek said.

"That does it, he ain't going nowhere," Mae said, as she walked into the kitchen.

48

It was into the next week before Casey could get the audiologist around to the four boys, Rob, and Derek. When the results were in, they were given to Vince.

Vince asked Rob, "Is there a soundproof room with a piano in it except the studio?"

"Yes, sir. My office is soundproof, and it has a piano that has just been tuned," Rob said.

"Can you get your dad to join us?"

Rob picked up the phone and called Evelyn. "Evelyn, can you tell Dad the 'big boss' wants him in my office pronto?"

"Is your mama over there?"

"No, Dr. Bender wants to see him."

"You might just relax. He has an office filled with bankers right now, and it will be at least an hour."

"Dr. Bender," Rob said, "Dad has an office filled with bankers. It might be an hour before he gets here."

"Okay, get the boys, and let's go to your office," Dr. Bender said.

When the boys arrived, Dr. Bender said, "My presence here has been largely kept undercover. Knowing that you boys possess immense talent, we want to give you every opportunity for each of you to develop yours to the utmost. It took me most of the first day to determine just from listening that someone in this group has a hearing problem. I should say a very slight hearing problem. I could tell when you were harmonizing. Therefore, I asked that everyone's hearing be checked. What we've got is nothing to be frightened of. The problem is something that affects singing, not everyday living. It is nothing to be frightened of, but if it gets worse we'll know where to look and who to look to, and we'll fix it."

Continuing, "I will play four notes that should harmonize. Listen to them on the piano." He played them slowly through two times.

"Now, tenor, you hold this note.

"Now, lead, this one.

"Now, bass, this one.

"Now, baritone, this one."

Everyone knew at that moment it was the baritone who wasn't hearing appropriately. "This is nothing to be upset about. Most singers have just a bit of impairment. Rob, you sing the baritone, and we can demonstrate just how little the impairment is."

Rob sang the note with the rest, except the baritone. It was noticeable.

"This is noticeable to us, but people in the audience can't pick it up unless they have a trained ear," Dr. Bender said.

Derek came in as Vince was saying this. "Glad you're here, Derek. We've determined the baritone has just a bit of impairment noticeable only to an old bird like me." He then demonstrated to Derek the regular baritone singing and then Rob taking his place.

Derek said, "No one will ever notice that, as Dr. Bender says, unless it is someone with a trained ear. I've known it, but didn't know who it was and didn't mention it because I was afraid it was me." The boys laughed, and Derek did want to lighten the moment since they thought someone was out.

"What's the solution, Doc?" Derek asked.

"A suitable aid while he is singing. Very simple, and it will make all the difference in the world after I give them a few lessons not associated with the hearing. This is step one, and an easy one to get past."

When the session concluded, Butch, the baritone, went into Rob's office while Derek was still there, "Can I speak to you, Mr. Davidson?"

"Sure, Butch." From observing him, Derek knew he thought he was out of the group.

"Does this mean I'll have to go home?" he said as a tear rolled down his cheek.

"Not at all. You are in and will be as long as we exist. Keep working, and everything will be okay. Do you believe me?"

"Yes, sir. Thank you, sir," and Derek put a bear hug on him as he started to leave the room.

Rob's private line rang, and it was Casey. "Rob, what is this about some singer who works for you needing a hearing aid? What I'm looking at we would normally overlook."

"Case, his slight impairment is interfering with his harmonizing with the group he sings with. He is a real professional, not an alley-cat wailer like you used to be," Rob concluded.

"Thanks, I'll get even with you on your next physical. It'll be time for every medical test I can think of that is unpleasant," Case concluded and hung up.

49

The recording sessions went on continuously for almost a month. It was an unusually busy time.

Dr. Bender went with Rob and the boys to the Atlanta assisted-living facility that was a foremost supporter. Everyone was dressed, at curtain, in a tux on stage and within the dining room, including Dr. Bender.

Derek came on a commercial airliner with Doc and the Bishop. It was actually a good-time affair since Dr. Bender was starved for companionship since the death of his wife.

Dr. Bender didn't sit while they ran over a few numbers in advance of the evening. He continually walked and listened without saying a word.

Derek took the Bishop and Doc over to a nursing home to entertain them. Dr. Bender came over later.

When the patients saw Derek coming in mid-afternoon they begin clapping. Since he had been there many times, he could recognize also the loss of some of his greatest admirers and was taught the hard way never to ask by name where someone was. If they weren't there, it was a good possibility the person was deceased.

He sat down at the piano and started to play the "William Tell Overture." When he finished, he went into "She'll Be Coming 'Round the Mountain," and everyone who could get into the room began singing. Doc had been with him, and he started with his harmonica as well.

Dr. Bender was amazed that patients on stretchers, in wheelchairs, and in beds were rolled in. He couldn't imagine someone doing something like this.

Derek played until dinner was announced, and then those who wanted to hug him were accommodated. Doc and the Bishop did the same and waded out into the crowd. Some came over to become acquainted with Dr. Bender, who didn't quite understand what was happening or how to handle the situation.

Outside, Dr. Bender asked, "What was all that about, Derek?"

"The group we'll entertain tonight are well-heeled, up-scale folks who live in a facility you won't believe. We've talked them into writing notes on a regular basis to these people we've just performed for and calling them to determine their needs. They bring over presents on their birthdays and holidays, and this is the basis on which our entire outreach had its beginnings all over the United States. Sadly, some of these folks won't last out the day." Vince noticed Derek's eyes cloud up.

Doc and the Bishop took Vince with them to their table. Vince had never seen another place like it. He estimated that three hundred to five hundred older patrons were having the times of their lives. There was a small orchestra playing for the group to dance.

A deep voice interrupted the group, "Ladies and gentlemen, Derek Davidson." Thunderous applause followed. Derek stepped through the center curtain, dressed in his tux.

"Ladies and gentlemen, we have a wonderful night planned that I know you will enjoy. Before we begin serving dinner, I've asked Bishop Hornsby to offer the invocation. Bishop, if you will stand you will see a microphone coming down from the ceiling." Sure enough a wire was coming down.

The Bishop delivered an eloquent invocation and sat down grumbling about why Derek never tipped him off that this would be his duty. He liked to plan his remarks.

The orchestra began with a slow dance tune. An elegantly dressed senior citizen grabbed Derek, and off to the dance floor they went. Before the evening was finished, all the old men were dancing and having a wonderful time, including Vince.

When the dishes were cleared away, Derek again addressed the group. "Ladies and gentlemen, it is always so nice to visit with you since you are so gracious with your southern hospitality. We have a little surprise for you this evening. A group of youngsters will perform, and then we will dance a bit more if you wish. My son, Rob, found this group in the West, and we think you will be pleased with these young men."

With the curtains opening, Rob began playing the introduction to "There's a Place for Us." It ended to a standing ovation. This young group with little experience received the shakes almost from the applause. They were going to perform for an hour and end with "The Impossible Dream." The crowd would have none of their conclusion until they sang "I'll Fly Away."

Rob approached center stage after the last song. "Thank you, ladies and gentlemen. I must confess that this is the first time out for these young men, and we are very, very proud of them. What did you think?"

There was another standing ovation that wouldn't stop for the boys.

Derek took his place at his piano, and Rob sat down at another. They both began playing a song that was suitable for a western line dance. The boys knew it was going to happen, and it was their note to load up on breath mints and wade out into the guests and make themselves available to dance. These kids were in their early twenties, and ladies ninety years old were trying to dance with them. It was a riot until the evening ended.

Derek and Vince took the jet home. Doc, the Bishop, and the boys spent the night until the jet arrived the next morning.

On the way home that night, Vince said, "Derek, we have no way of knowing what is going on in those boys' minds tonight. Can you imagine where they came from and compare that to where they've arrived tonight?"

"They began singing backup standing hidden behind the piano for Rob at the ranch one night at a managers' meeting. Rob and I—at that moment—thought if we could ever develop their talent, we would have struck gold, and I still think we will."

"They've got the raw material. Now the problem is getting it out of them in presentable fashion and keeping them humble," Vince concluded. "Yet, Derek, there is another thing about which I'd like to comment."

"What's that?"

"Now that I've been here only a few weeks with you and witnessed the outreach of what your foundations actually do, it is like something that couldn't be written as truth. There is not a mind in existence that could conjure up what you are doing."

"There was," Derek continued, "a country farmer boy from Mississippi, now deceased, who started it as a personal mission while he worked for Jay Gregson. His motto was 'Keep it simple.' We did, and now you see what we've got. While he claimed to be just a country boy, he was anything but that, yet he was the gardener and proud of it. Jay Gregson picked him up at one of our hospitals after being injured. He was from Mississippi, an honest man, and he had an education. If you could have known Gregg Gregson and his wife and Gus Squires and his wife, you would have been amazed at what they could do. They did it all for nothing, would not accept pay for a show of the nature we do, and yet we couldn't spend the money that came in. For example, as a favor to one of our donors living in a Birmingham assisted-living facility, I played for her birthday party on the way home from the Northwest. She sent me ten thousand dollars as a gift. I gave it to Kit to turn in, and Greg put it in my bank account. It bought my parents a tombstone and a piano for my mother's church in Georgia. Later the same woman from Birmingham sent the foundation $25 million at her death. We've gone from one place to the other and became friends with folks just like this. People who were fabulously rich, and I hadn't the faintest idea what my salary was—truthfully! The Foundation provided me with credit cards, and Kit took care of everything else since she was my assistant."

"I like what has happened and only wish I could have played a part in the development."

"You can get everything the boys have to give, and you will see great results."

"I can't believe when I met you in college that one day you and I would be a part of such a fantastic organization, and I know it took hard work to get it here," Vince concluded as the jet rolled slowly to a stop at the home strip.

50

Vince suggested installing screens and automatic cameras in all the primary broadcast facilities. The idea was to broadcast with sight and song feeding both ways. This allowed performers in the studio the opportunity to speak to those attending via state-of-the-art sound systems. On very special occasions, performers traveled in person as in the past. This cuts down on travel time and fatigue.

While at first glance this seemed like a mountain of money would be needed to set it up, actually it boiled down to less since they were not spending large sums running the jets all over the country. Plus, this type of performance wouldn't be as tiring as travel every day.

Performing from the studio and limiting travel also provided time for practice and planning instead of yelling inside a moving plane. All the programming seemed fresher. Everyone looked energetic. Everyone had more time and more free time to rest and some different activities. Most of all, they wanted to become involved in community activities. Up to this point they knew only few of the locals and were involved in nothing but traveling and singing away from home, or in the studio when they were home.

The greatest disadvantage to traveling less was that the performers, all of them, seemed to be gaining weight. Doc became more involved with the performers in this regard, and the kitchen employees began to have to pay attention to him. The meals became more nutritious, and less was served. Additional exercise was prescribed, and at first everyone was just a bit irritated by it all and managed to sneak extra food. After Doc caught this happening a few times, he became more stringent. Everyone eventually came upon a workable agreement, including Derek and Rob.

Before Doc imposed the diet, everyone ate all they wanted, including Doc. Now they were all hungry all the time. One of Doc's greatest problems was from Mae. She was opposed to broiling anything. Her vegetables had to have fatback in them. The meat had to be fried. Desserts had been served with every meal. Now everything was wrong. Her entire cooking regimen was nothing like she knew how to do in a kitchen.

"How do you know these boys wouldn't sound better if they had a little meat on their bones?" she asked Doc.

His reply, "They might! The problem is they wouldn't live as long. You were never anything but skin and bones. You probably had stomach worms and maybe still do. I think we should run a test for worms on you." In very short order, Mae had disappeared and was scarce around Doc for a few days.

Derek called Doc and asked, "Doc, how long do you feel it will take to begin to get everyone into some plan for weight reduction?"

"Well, Derek, if they won't slip around and eat, maybe a few weeks to begin to recognize visually their weight loss. You can disguise the weight as long as you restrict them to the camera. But a public appearance will require new clothing."

Rob was sitting in front of the conferencing unit when Derek came on. "You busy, son?" he asked.

"No, sir. What can I do for you?"

"Can you bring the boys over to my office, along with Doc and the Bishop, in about ten minutes?"

"Yes, sir. We'll be there."

When everyone was sitting around Derek's conference table, he remained at his desk. He shuffled through the papers on his desk and came out with a blank sheet of paper that everyone else couldn't see. He studied it for a few minutes and said, "Fellows, according to our calculations we have almost forty thousand dollars in clothing for you. The truth is, you've about eaten your way out of the best clothing money can buy, and if you don't lose weight we will have to buy more to fulfill our obligations. I don't want to buy more clothing. I know if you continue to gain weight, Doc tells me it will affect your health—maybe not in the immediate future but in the years to come. How many of you want that?"

No one answered.

"Then it's settled," Derek said. "How many of you will not stick to the diet and lose these extra pounds? let me see your hands." Not a one went up. "Now, Doc, will you report to me regularly—collectively and individually—the weight loss?"

A hand went up.

Butch asked, "Tell us what 'collectively and individually' means, please."

Doc piped up. "It means your fat rear end and Bob's fat butt individually and then everyone together."

Butch asked, "How are you going to weigh my belly and his butt?" Evelyn was sitting in her usual place with a smirk on her face when Derek realized the situation and motioned her outside. When this happened, the boys got serious looks on their faces. Weighing a belly must be quite an undertaking, they thought.

"I will discuss this privately to keep from wasting Derek's time this morning. Is that satisfactory?" Doc asked.

Rob almost exploded trying not to laugh and embarrass the boys over such a trivial thing, but seeing the seriousness of this he was well aware he had to hold it. He did manage to, until the boys left and everyone who remained laughed out loud.

When no one was left but Rob and Derek, Evelyn came back in and asked, "Where did you get your cost figures for the clothing?"

"I just pulled it off a blank page. It's probably a bit high, but I was trying to impress the boys," Derek answered.

"For your information, it was low. I don't think you need to know how much the clothing really cost." After this remark, she turned and walked out, leaving a blank face on Derek and Rob.

PART SIX

Mission Accomplished

51

Ten full years had passed since the boys from the ranch joined the musical group. Over that time they developed into top-flight singers. Of course, Derek and Rob remained out front with their ability and did all the program execution. They were subjected to every kind of venue possible and excelled in them all. Not a single audience had been disappointed in their stage presentations. Their audiences grew with every return visit. The boys had grown into men; all were married with families, but to the foundations' people, they were still "the boys."

The best thing the boys had going for them is they realized the break they had been given through hard work in sometimes difficult circumstances. Because they did, they were never quarrelsome about the work. They never tired of the work and always appeared to an audience that this was the place they wanted to be. They played to the audience as if they were the only group they wanted to entertain and were always very well received.

Derek had figured out the best approach to the schedule. During the winter, late fall, and early spring he worked the South and Southwest when at all possible. This way the weather seldom kept any of their prospective attendees at home because of snow and weather.

When the social season in the East and Northeast arrived in mid-spring through summer and early fall, everyone came home from the South or wherever they wintered and were ready for a night out.

It was the week before Thanksgiving, and the entire troupe of entertainers was scheduled before their very best assisted-living facility in Boston. Everyone there was ready for a night with the foundations that meant so much to them. This gathering was always held in the very best ballroom in the city.

During an intermission, a very nice-looking, well-dressed

young man took the liberty of stepping onto the stage in front of a stand-up microphone. Both Rob and Derek saw what was happening, yet from their position they were defenseless against stopping him.

The very large crowd immediately recognized he wanted to say something. Being well groomed in expensive clothing, the room became noiseless.

"Ladies and gentlemen, there is a good possibility I might get locked up for taking this personal privilege. I hope not, because my purpose is to tell you something you really have no way of knowing that affects you personally and benefited me immensely."

Hearing this, Rob and Derek relaxed a bit, and the boys sat down since they were motioned to. Yet the young man was a total surprise to everyone.

"About ten years ago, I was locked up in a house of correction because of theft of electronic gadgets from other people's automobiles and selling them for cash to buy all sorts of things I didn't need. The only reason I'm standing here tonight is because of you folks. It's true that I didn't use guns or knives, so hard time was not an issue, and my age also played a part. You wonder how you helped me? It's simple. I got a letter from a hardened criminal in a full-fledged prison outlining what his life was like, what his days were like there. There was paper and an addressed, stamped envelope within his letter with the request that I respond to his letter. When I received his letter I was in lockup. That is, I had misbehaved in prison, and they took exception to it and removed my privileges." While he was pausing after saying this, the crowd chuckled.

"Because of my circumstances, four more years of what I was going through, I read, reread, and studied his letter. I gave it considerable thought. Looking at his message from every angle, I responded. I awaited his response about a month, and finally one day another letter arrived with paper, stamp, and an envelope addressed to him."

"One year later, as a result of his encouragement, I was released with my promise to go to college. I worked my way through college and became a licensed certified youth counselor. This opportunity came to me because of your generosity. My purpose this evening, as a party crasher, is to let you know how deeply appreciative I am to you for your thoughtful kindness."

While he was trying to replace the microphone, Derek and Rob walked up on either side of him and turned him toward the audience. Derek asked, "Young man, would you tell us your name?"

"Yes, sir. My name is Chad Mizner, and I live in Dedham. I've been working for the state now almost a year and feel I can tell I'm making progress with those I am trying to help."

Rob said, "Chad, I am Rob Davidson, and this is my dad, Derek Davidson. Let me tell you, if God himself had asked me what I wanted to happen tonight here with this group, your appearance here would have been it." The crowd exploded with applause.

"Are you married, Chad?" Derek asked.

"No, sir, but I do have a serious girlfriend here with me," he said.

"Bring her out, and let us meet her," Rob said.

Very timidly the young lady came from the opposite side of the orchestra. She was also well dressed, and very shy. "This is Sherry McDonald." The crowd applauded again.

Derek said to Chad and Sherry, "You two stand here with Rob and me while I do some explaining to the group." Turning to the group, Derek said, "Some years ago, Rob came up with the idea that in the same way you folks began helping those in nursing homes who were abandoned, in like manner hardened criminals could become useful to those younger people in correction facilities. Rob went to Washington and received permission for us to entertain and talk to the prisoners. This was done to encourage hardened criminals to do something for their fellow man since they would never see a free day again. They could give a bit of time to a young person who had a chance to make something of himself. And now you see proof positive that the program, though long-term, must be working." More applause followed.

"We broadcast monthly to each of the prisons and make a personal appearance once annually. I must apologize that we did not make a big issue of it to you folks, even though a lot of your money is going nationwide in this program. We needed some proof. With this, and with your permission, I am going to ask Chad and Sherry to stay for the remainder of the night and join in the fun."

When Derek said this, Rob begin again with a rock-and-roll number, and the quartet encouraged Chad and Sherry to dance with them, plus the floor filled immediately. They were sucked into the spirit of the evening.

Derek allowed the program to come to its natural conclusion, yet before the closing song, Derek said, "Ladies and gentlemen, we will fully explain what has happened here tonight in the form of a newsletter. Be serious now: let me hear applause if you agree that working with inmates in correctional facilities is within the boundaries of what you would like to do—the same way you assist by drilling wells for those who need water, teach gardening to those needing food, help all sorts of people become certified in occupations if they will attend our schools and every other venture we are in, and you are aware of most of them. Give me some indication of your permission, please."

The crowd not only stood in deafening applause but then came down on the dance floor and continued without stop until Rob and Derek began the introduction to "I'll Fly Away." Everyone sang it with gusto to the complete amazement of Chad and Sherry.

When Robert Turnbull could speak to Derek, he took him aside and said, "Derek, you know I own a nationally distributed magazine. One of my reporters was asked to be here by the young man whom you assisted . He called me, and every photographer and reporter on duty tonight was here. We didn't want to make a big deal out of it until the young man made his move. I want your permission to tastefully tell the story again of the foundations' work and use this young man as an example if he will agree to the publicity. I want to do your activities proud and help the young man if possible. What do you say?"

"Mr. Turnbull," Derek began, "you've done us many, many favors. I personally have no problem with your proposal. However, Rob is coming of age to take on much more responsibility. He had the idea to do this with the prisoners, and it has proven a helpful thing for young folks who have a chance at the real world. Please ask him the same question for my sake. I have no problem with it since you've always been straight up with us."

Sherry McDonald came up to Derek and said, "Mr. Davidson, may I speak to you?"

"Sure," Derek replied.

"You can never know how much your Foundation's assistance has helped Chad. He had lost faith in the human race. He was mistreated by some of the other inmates, and his family had almost disowned him. Then this killer who will never see the light of day again pulled him into an interaction with him. You saw the results here this evening. We plan to be married when the money is sufficient. I teach, and Chad is trying to find something in his profession that will sustain us, and when he finds that job we plan to get married."

"Sherry, you need to mention this to my son, Rob. This was all his idea, and he has accomplished this almost by himself. Plus, for your private information, Mr. Robert Turnbull, who owns a nationally distributed magazine, is seeking permission as we speak from Chad to tell his story. Additionally, when the day of your marriage comes I'll commit to provide the music for it free of charge," Derek concluded.

Rob walked over to Derek wiping sweat. He was soaking

wet from the performance and now Turnbull's surprise. "Dad, guess what?"

Derek said, "I know what Mr. Turnbull said. What was your response?"

"I told him I'd have to discuss it with you first. What do you think?"

"I said I thought he should talk to you since this was your program. What do you think?"

"Well, Dad, Mr. Turnbull has always been in our corner, hasn't he?" Rob asked.

"He's all wool and a yard wide," Derek said. "I think you should turn him loose. And, by the way, I told Sherry that when they were married you would furnish all the music for their wedding free of charge."

Rob replied, "I want you there, too, and it will be very soon because a little publicity for Chad will get him the job he needs."

"Okay, son, you tell Mr. Turnbull to have at it, remembering Mike is with you tonight and you go on vacation tomorrow, remember?"

"Can you handle Turnbull alone?"

"I think so, except you might have to stay here an extra day so the plane can get us home," Derek replied.

"We can't fly commercial since I'll have our plane loaded with items for our home in Greybull. Take your time, and I'll bask in all this glory," Rob boasted.

Later, Chad and Sherry couldn't thank everyone enough, but finally left for their homes. It was a good feeling for the group to have such an unexpected surprise and then the expected publicity from Mr. Turnbull.

Evelyn caught up with Derek and Rob at the same time and said, "You two owe me, and you owe me big."

"To my knowledge, your check has never bounced, has it?" Derek asked.

"No, but I'll have two to four reporters and photographers

at the office at noon tomorrow. I've got to go home tonight," she said. "You might as well come with me, Derek, and let's talk about how far into our operation we want them since Buster here is going on another honeymoon."

"Okay, I can do that. The plane can get you before lunch tomorrow, Rob, and you two can report to Greybull in time for dinner," Derek replied.

52

Nita and Juan were standing about midway of the runway when Mike and Rob landed in Greybull. They slowly moved aside, much to the amazement and disgruntlement of the pilots.

The plane barely missed them, then taxied up to the end next to the house and turned around before cutting the engines. The pilot left the cockpit first, asking the copilot to "please run through the final procedures."

The pilot took Juan and Nita away from the plane and said, "What you two just did was very, very dangerous. I know you were anxious to see Rob and Mike, but as fast as we were traveling we could have been bottoms up in the driveway in order to miss hitting you two. While we are talking about this, never walk up to one of these engines until they have stopped rotating." By this time Nita was crying.

The pilot continued, "Nita, stop it! I know you were anxious to see Rob and Mike and here to help unload the plane, and everyone appreciates this. What you did was something you didn't know not to do. No harm done, I just didn't want you hurt unless Juan had to spank you for something you did." She smiled.

It was a happy homecoming that night. Nita had a sumptuous dinner prepared and insisted the pilots stay and eat, which they did. The pilots belonged to everyone and took advantage of all the home-cooked meals possible. They were part of the musical company and everyone's home.

After dinner, Rob said, "Nita, I'm going to bed, and I don't want to be disturbed until next week."

"Are you sick?" she asked.

"No, tired. I have to work while these pilots eat at all the fancy balls and stay in the very best hotels, living the life of Riley."

The chief pilot spoke up. "Who was it that snored from Boston to this strip? Aren't you glad you even knew someone who could find this little strip, from all the way across the northern tier of the United States?"

"Yeah, yeah, rub it in. Leave quietly while I'm in the shower. I need a bath," Rob said.

"You do, you smell like a boar hog," Mike piped up.

The next day Rob saddled a horse and rode up to the top of the mountain behind the house. Mike still couldn't get over the manner in which Kit had overhauled their home in the West. Nita was just as thrilled, and couldn't keep from talking about little things she thought Mike ought to see that really were of little value that Kit had done.

Rob thought the cows looked wonderful. The calf crop was growing out in fine shape as always. Juan was doing a great job here.

When Mike began to locate Rob for lunch, she found him on the front porch asleep. She didn't bother him, and he finally began to stir at about three in the afternoon. He skipped lunch, and after an early dinner he was back in bed.

A week later the jet buzzed the house. He opened his eyes and peeped up from the chaise lounge and saw it making a long circle and coming back to land. Rob lay back down.

The pilots were on the porch shortly with an armload of magazines. The front cover pictured Rob in a white tux with tails at a white grand piano and it appeared, at first glance, that he took up the entire cover. Opening the cover, they saw it was a double page, and Derek was dressed the same. Down on the dance floor were Chad and Sherry and the folks in Boston singing the closing song. The four boys were standing behind the piano, singing.

The article was most complimentary of the foundations. Mike, being the foundations' public relations person, wrote the article while they were flying to their ranch after the Boston performance and emailed it to Evelyn. Of course, it favored everything the foundations did and told the whole story. At the end of the story, there was penciled-in note from Derek: "Call me."

"Son, your mom and I left home and bunked up with Rosita in order to hide. The switchboard looks like a Christmas tree in the office. The Boston thing has good and bad connected to it. There are more requests for performances than we could get around to in a few years, and money is rolling in to keep up the good work from those we've never heard of. Son, there are lots of good people in this world."

"Dad, the money is good, but we just can't book any more performances, can we?"

"No, don't worry about it. We've hit a good lick in Boston with Chad and Sherry, and we'll talk when we are both home and had some thinking time. Will another week get you back on your feet?"

"Yes, sir," Rob said. "Ask Evelyn to have the plane pick us up a week from today."

"I can handle that. Rosita wants you to stop by for a day or two. She misses her baby."

"On the way home maybe," Rob said and hung up.

53

Chad and Sherry's wedding was in Dedham, Massachusetts. Rob, Derek, the boys, two keyboards, a harp, and several other instruments provided the music. The church had a magnificent pipe organ, and the organist was just a bit put out she wasn't playing as much, by request of the bride and groom.

Because of the recognition the foundations had received a few months prior, the church was packed with people the newlyweds didn't know who came just to hear the music.

By prior agreement the musical group was not mentioned to get the spotlight off them and put it on Chad and Sherry. The boys, Rob, and Derek did all the playing and singing. With two top-of-the-line keyboards along with their sound system, they put the church organ to shame.

The reception was in the church Fellowship Hall, and Rob provided soft piano music until the couple was out and gone. Derek had the church and Fellowship Hall decorated with flowers for the couple. It was breathtaking.

Two weeks later Derek received a five-page letter from the newlyweds in appreciation for what the foundations had done for them and their wedding. Showing it to Rob, Derek said, "All of this is nice and we certainly appreciate being recognized for our contribution, but look at the money they raised for our foundations and didn't realize it. In fact, if others stepped up and spoke out, we wouldn't have to scuffle for money."

54

Rob peeped in Derek's office and walked in. Derek was talking on the telephone and motioned Rob to pour him a cup of coffee. Rob responded and poured himself a cup also.

Hanging up the phone Derek said, "Hi, Son. What brings you over now after not having seen you in so long?"

"I'm afraid you are looking at an embalmed son, the way I feel."

"You need another rest?"

"Dad, we've got so much going, if we stop we'll get overrun. We are piled up with work. We were in fairly good shape until Chad and Sherry came along. Now folks want information about the foundations, and Mike is trying to get some together in print form that just explains what we've always wanted folks to know and not the inner workings of what we really do. Others want to hire us for their functions. Other types of facilities with all types of different faces want us to work with them. And now, of all things, the federal government would like us to entertain troops in hospitals in Europe from the war. How do you say no to the government?"

"When and how much does the government want?" Derek asked.

"I don't know. That's the reason I'm here. What do I tell them?"

"What do you think, son?"

"Initially, I don't know how we would squeeze them in. Second, our jet won't go that far," Rob said. "Yet I would like to find a way to give those wounded folks a little of our time, if at all possible. They've paid a terrible price."

"That would be nice. Let's think on that until lunch tomorrow. Ask Mike to join us and discuss the possibilities," Derek concluded.

"I can do that."

Rob explained to Mike over dinner the conversation he had with his dad. She agreed to the invitation. Then she said, "I've got another problem to consider on the back burner. Anna Gregson came over today after calling to be sure I was at home. Her kids are away in college, and she has a new interest in a man. When they are married she wants us to move into her home. It belongs to the foundations like ours does, and she wants us there. Plus, it has just been redecorated and is gorgeous."

"What if the marriage doesn't work out?" Derek asked.

"She won't be back. Too many bad memories from losing Bart in that house," she said.

"What do you think, Mike?"

"It sounds interesting in that we'd have a home instead of an apartment, and we'd need more employees to run it."

Rob replied, "There is always a catch. Have you thought about furniture for that big ol' house?"

"No, I haven't. We have no kids, so the furniture we have would almost do it," Mike replied.

The next day Evelyn was there, and lunch was brought in. After sitting and having fun while they ate, Rob asked Derek, "Dad, what do you think all the folks who have gone before us would think of what we've done with the foundations since their deaths?"

"Well, Son, generally I don't see how they could have too many gripes. It has doubled and is on the way to tripling in size and financial security since your arrival even. We are covering ground we never thought was possible in the early days. My great regret is that all those who went on before us never knew people like Mae, the Bishop, Doc, and particularly the boys who are with you. I think they would approve how you handle the road and the outreach through Mike. They would be proud of you. Particularly so would be Gus and Anne Squires, who were so talented. Greg would be happy with our financial status since that was his constant wrestle. I think we rate an A+. We've made progress by always moving forward. Don't you think we've done well since we've begun just a bit of a bragging session?"

Rob answered, "Yes, Dad, I do. I know we've traveled a lot of miles, and we've made inroads that I personally thought might be impossible. I'm happy if you are."

"I am. Now to the discussion of the hospitalized servicemen and women overseas. First, we've never done anything for those here, except minimally. We'll have to throw them into the equation somewhere. Why not do this: ask each of our quadrant managers to discuss the proposition with our contacts at each assisted-living facility nationwide, telling them what has been requested of us. You talk to the Carter folks. The idea is to have them give up some of our time in order for us to assist those hospitalized away from home. I also think that if one of our facilities gives up their night for a group overseas, the patients in the foreign country should write them a thank-you note. In order to facilitate the government's request, we will have to park the jet we now have and buy a larger one. We can do that if necessary. The one we now use is about worn out anyway. This way we'll have a spare. If we do get one to go overseas with, you'll need to check with the pilots to determine if they need any additional documents other than to update everyone's passport. The boys will need passports, I'm sure. How does that sound to you?"

"Sounds like you've thought it through. Before we commit, I think we need to get someone from the government in a decision-making capacity here and thoroughly discuss the entire operation so that we understand each other," Rob said.

"You are correct. Get the managers going, and you talk to Carter. You get a military official here, and we'll talk," concluded Derek.

Rob said, "One other thing is necessary to discuss. Anna is

planning on being married and moving. Her children are in college, and she has too many memories here. She wants us to move into the Gregson house. What do you think?"

"Mike, what do you think about it?" Derek asked.

"Even though we don't have enough furniture to furnish the house, I do like the idea since it has just been redecorated," Mike said.

"Suits me if you want to do it. Would you leave your office where it is?" Derek asked Rob.

"We would almost have to. I think we need to think and look some more at the idea of moving. However, I have no particular objection," Rob answered.

Mike said, "While we are here, I want to ask a question. Since I've been with the foundations, I can find no one with a historical record. Therefore, I assumed there wasn't one. I began to write one, and up to now I have almost a book. It will be a decorative coffee-table book. I already know what I want on the cover, but not a title for the book. I want the photo of the two of you in Boston that was on the magazine cover. Do either of you have any problem with that?"

Derek said, after Rob looked over at him, "I don't have any immediate objection to it, and I would advise you to keep writing, but at the moment because of our taxing peculiarities and nonprofit status, I need to talk to others who know about such things. I believe it would be okay but need a few days. Is that alright with you?"

Mike said, "Sure."

55

During the next month, every moment Rob and Mike had was spent with a few little renovations to the Gregson home. Both wondered how they would rattle around in this large home when they had been used to a small apartment. It would be a bit inconvenient, yet Kit and Mike had a great time out buying furniture. Kit was having nothing but the best, and the decoration had to be perfect.

While they were getting settled in the Gregson home, Ali was also moving up. She preferred to live in the private side of the assisted-living facility but had been elevated to CEO of all the foundations' hospitals. The good thing was that Casey was well enough to travel, and occasionally he either ran errands for Ali or went with her to settle whatever the problem was. While she enjoyed being the chief executive, the elimination of pediatric surgery from her life left a hole. After discussing it with Derek, he told her they needed her in surgery but had a far greater need for her in management. He put her there because he figured at sixty-six years old, he had a few more years to help her get her feet on the ground. She had to agree with his long-term planning.

Derek satisfied himself that they could visit overseas military hospitals. They decided on one trip each month, during which they would do two concerts.

With the overseas journeys came a new jet. With the new jets came two problems. Neither of their three runways were long enough. They began work quickly on the primary runway at home and finished it in short order.

The new jet had custom seats in it so those who were inside could lay back and take a nap if need be. Rob's seat had a fold-down desk, and he used it regularly.

The pilots had to be checked out in the larger jet, and they passed with flying colors. Since the chief pilot had flown much larger military planes, it was nothing new for him.

The first trip took them to England to a rehabilitation hospital. It was decided that all those servicemen and women living in the area could attend also, and the crowd began to multiply. Derek took the jet on the first trip, and Rob flew commercial. They could not carry their sound system and the pianos there would have to be sufficient, though they had asked that they be tuned prior to their arrival. Evelyn flew with Derek and operated the communications with the home office. Mike flew with Rob. Since she had gotten permission to finish the historical account of the foundations, her laptop was grinding the whole trip.

They arrived to a drizzling rain at daylight. The rain lasted all day and began to dissipate at about sundown. The boys slept just about all day, and Rob and Derek took a long nap that afternoon.

Walking out on stage that night, each of the performers was taken aback. Most of the men and women were sitting. A good 30 percent were wheelchair-bound and bedridden. Some didn't appear as if they were cognizant of what was going on. Their reception, however, was a rousing one, and those who could stand did so.

General Mike Mahoney came on stage and introduced everyone. The boys had on sport coats with large collared shirts, Levi's, and western-cut boots. Derek and Rob wore the same.

Derek took over as master of ceremonies. "Good evening, ladies and gentlemen. I can't tell you how honored we are to come here this evening and provide you with a bit of entertainment. You've got to know that the four boys standing here with me are Gringos from out west in the U.S. We found them cleaning the stables. They were singing out of tune, as they will tonight, and we brought them." This brought a laugh, and the boys acted embarrassed. The boys were the butt of every joke.

"My son plays at the piano. If he could learn how to play the piano, the Gringos might learn how to stay tuned and on pitch." It was one slam after the other, all to the guffaws of the service personnel.

When he introduced Rob, Rob stood and said, "The ol' man is never going to quiet down. I think we'll have some fun." He sat down, and the boys, Derek, and Rob sang all of the military songs as one. It went over big. They sang lots of their usual numbers and a few new ones. The general had asked that since the patients were mending, to hold the program to ninety minutes, which they did. Some patients tried to dance, but most did not.

After the program, all the performers moved out into the group of servicemen and women and wished them well. Some were horribly mangled and trying to get well enough to get home.

Arriving home, everyone was exhausted. Rob tried to schedule their upcoming appearances to allow ample rest time for the jet lag. They ran into a storm coming home and had to take evasive action in order to get around it. The boys were not thrilled with the magnitude of the storm over the ocean.

Keeping their regular schedules up and adding the overseas trip once monthly was taxing even on the younger men. Very soon, Rob encouraged Derek not to make the trip, and to keep Evelyn and Mike at home as well.

The overseas trips, while tiring, generated publicity everywhere. Mike was in charge of this, and she was doing a great job. Every news release she sent out had a photo of the boys and the audience. All the media resources used the materials. From this attention, money began to show up designated for trips overseas. Very soon the program was standing on its own feet.

Rob moved his office over to the study in the Gregson home, except when he was practicing with the boys. Instead of using old pickup trucks to get around the place, Derek bought a number of golf carts, which were perfect for transportation around the farm.

The Carter Group had a publisher for Mike very shortly. The editor assigned to her visited often with suggestions and changes that should be made. Some very prestigious people scattered across the United States jumped at the chance to endorse the work.

When the book was finished, no author was listed except "The Personnel from The Gregson Family Foundation and The Productive Life Foundation." There were one hundred thousand books printed, selling for one hundred dollars each. Every talk show in the United States was in play for someone from the Foundation to come and visit. This job fell mostly to Mike, and she did a great job since this was her field. The small jet became hers. It took her a little over a year to be halfway through her second printing.

56

Just as it had always happened, the Foundation boys got bogged down in their work and were going day and night. This time was no different. The new jet was nice and all of that, but it was a long haul to Europe—and then Asia—and locking it into a schedule was quite a drag on a person's energy.

Because the boys had not missed a performance, their resistance was low. When one was sick with a cold or some other minor illness, all got it. They were dragging. Rob was also sick.

Derek took charge and grounded the boys. He took one performance alone just to fulfill an obligation and give them some rest. He took Kit, and they had a little vacation.

When he had arrived home, Ali had taken charge of Rob and put him to bed with pneumonia. She visited twice a day and was a stern clinician.

Just when everyone was at their lowest, the switchboard buzzed Evelyn and said, "The night owl is on line five for Rob!" She went pale.

57

"Ali, I need to visit Rob. Is it okay?" Evelyn asked. The "night owl" call was Evelyn's signal to quickly locate Rob and report it.

"Sure, it's okay. He was much better last night. I'm just driving through the gate now to check on him. I'll pick you up," Ali said.

Both entered the house and caught him headed from his closet back to the bed. "A fellow can have no privacy. I'm going to Greybull to hide," Rob said.

Forcefully, Evelyn said, "You think so, but I've got news for you since the night-owl call just came in. I told them you're sick and would get back to them as quickly as possible."

Ali said, "You, my brother, are not going anywhere until your temperature has subsided."

"When, Sis?"

"Two days, maybe, if things go well."

Rob turned to Evelyn, "Evelyn, Ali doesn't know what's in Dad's future. Will you please fill her in while I call the general?"

No sooner than Rob was finished finding his socks, a shriek and a yell that would put a big-league cheerleading squad to shame came from the living room. Ali and Evelyn were ecstatic. They were laughing and skipping around the room when Mike came in from the study. Mike and Evelyn continued outlining the unbelievable story of the honors about to befall Derek. Mike was in the process of helping put it all together.

Rob spoke to the general for about thirty minutes and determined that in order to keep their secret, all the plans for the event would have to be by phone and personal email. No planning trips to confer since Derek would catch on to something out of the ordinary.

58

Inside the auditorium of the Langford Academy, not a seat was available. The dance floor was filled with patients in wheelchairs, and some even on beds with nurses by their sides. Few had ever seen the Grand Auditorium filled to capacity, certainly not those attending this day.

Derek and Kit walked in thinking he was going to play for the senior high chorus, as was the custom when they were in concert. There were a few people milling around in the hall, and the auditorium was abuzz with conversation as was always normal prior to a program.

When they approached the seats that had been left for them, Derek knew the program had switched on him when a piano behind the stage curtain hit four notes and four voices burst forth with "God Bless America." The curtain gradually opened, and the four fellows from the West were singing with Rob at the piano. On the riser behind the group were members of the various branches of the military, making up a stage filled with singers. To his amazement, a military color guard accompanied an army general down the aisle. Derek was so dumbfounded up to this point, he recognized no one.

The color guards set the flags during the third verse, and when the fourth verse began a director moved center stage. All the singers performed the fourth, including Derek's full orchestra that was positioned in the upper balcony. Immediately upon concluding, the director motioned the audience to stand, and the long military trumpets opened "The Star Spangled Banner." Everyone was asked to sing.

Upon the national anthem's conclusion, a small platform had been positioned next to the stage holding the singers. Rob introduced the chairman of the Joint Chiefs of Staff, General

John L. Kendrick. General Kendrick moved behind a small lectern that had been placed on the platform with his notes.

"This is an afternoon about which it can safely be said that another has never been held quite like it. The purpose is to honor a couple whose giving spirit has seldom been matched. We honor Derek and Kit Davidson. This is a complete and total surprise to the couple. For many months, only their son Rob had any knowledge of honoring his parents. The military demanded that since Mr. Davidson would not allow any payment for the frequent trips when his entertainers visited military personnel overseas, including flying his own plane, we should do something for him that would honor his good work. To this end, the United States government has done its best with profound appreciation."

While the general was presenting his opening remarks, two easy chairs were placed on the platform. Derek and Kit were escorted on stage by the military honor guard.

The general continued, "Derek was hired by Greg Gregson under circumstances we won't elaborate upon. One of their first duties was to figure out how to get water to Indians out west and others who were in desperate need of growing food for the table. They did it without any government intervention or interference. Their foundation furnished the money and know-how, helping those who wanted to help themselves dig wells. Those in the audience who were the recipients of such a gift please rise."

Scattered across the auditorium about forty Native Americans stood. The crowd went wild with applause. Both Derek and Kit shed a few tears as they stood to acknowledge their attendance.

The general said, "After water, know-how was needed to grow food for the table. A hotel was purchased here to train Master Gardeners. We've now gotten so many Master Gardeners that the United States has been divided into four quadrants teaching others who want to teach others how to garden.

Would those of you who can claim the rank of Master Gardener please rise?" Somewhere in the neighborhood of two hundred people stood. Derek and Kit stood again and recognized their attendance.

"One of the employees in the foundation who visited a small hospital here several times a week noticed the elderly were all alone, looking at the ceiling at night. He visited them for the purpose of giving them hope and someone to talk to. Derek went to a nursing home in Atlanta and simply walked in, asking the then-manager if he could play the piano for the patients in the solarium. He was privately looking for an ongoing program for elderly patients. Allowed to do so, patients from the entire nursing home congregated and sang with Derek without coaxing. One patient knew the entire *Sound of Music* score and was a professional singer. Derek encouraged her to sit with him at the piano, and it was a howling success. Ladies and gentlemen, the manager of that first nursing home, now retired, Sherman Smith."

Mr. Smith said, "My remarks will be very brief. No one person, including medical doctors, did our patients more good than Derek. He was in Atlanta often and never failed to stop by. He also never left with dry eyes. The patients not only looked forward to this but worshiped him." Smith turned and hugged Derek.

General Kendrick continued, "Someone hit upon a golden nugget when they discovered upscale assisted-living facilities and came up with the idea of the residents using their resources to help others. This group liked to party, and Derek was their man. He pulled all sorts of antics in only the finest ballrooms America has to offer, in all the states; even the president of the United States showed up at one of them. Theirs were high-class parties, and Derek was high-class entertainment. Those who know tell me this is when the big money started rolling into the Foundation to finance lots of other projects for the future. I'd like all those from such assisted-living institutions to stand."

The majority of the group stood and gave Derek a standing ovation that the general had to stop.

"These efforts also had to be divided into quadrants of the United States. Each quadrant has a manager to handle the Foundation's effort. Would you managers stand, please?" The four men stood and were thoroughly recognized.

"To make an evening that could go on well into the night a bit shorter, let me simply introduce the members of the Carter Corporation of Chicago and ask them to be recognized." They were seated together and had come in from across the United States. "These folks are the seminar leaders for the various classes offered to those who will take advantage of their expertise, including child care and other amenities.

"The Carter group is a seminar company that teaches—for the Gregson Foundation and the Productive Life Foundation—various classes on the steps to becoming recognized carpenters, electricians, nurses, and nurse's assistants, and helping students get their GED to gain admittance into college and to earn legitimate licenses to operate. So many became students at the Gregsons' expense. Graduation ceremonies are held quarterly by satellite, always hosted by the Gregson Foundation itself.

"They also assist hardened criminals in writing letters to younger folks locked in lesser penal institutions as a means of encouraging them take advantage of educational assistance, and when their incarcerated time is up, to become useful citizens. This program is showing remarkable success. To close my remarks, while in no way totally including all the good deeds Derek has accomplished—and I'm not trying to embarrass anyone—would all the folks who served their penal time, successfully concluded it and then worked themselves into some sort of effort to take care of their families, please rise?" About one hundred younger people stood.

"We also have a number of wounded servicemen who are coming home for further treatment in the audience, and all these up front in wheelchairs and beds. They wanted to come, and we diverted their planes to accommodate them," the general said.

When the applause ended and everyone was seated, the general said, "We are here today because the military would like to honor Derek for his role in giving a bit of home to those overseas fighting and to those in hospitals there as well. His work has been tireless, as has that of all of his group. This is our way to say, in a small way, thanks for all you've done for everyone." The audience stood with roaring applause as the general said, "Ladies and gentlemen, it is my pleasure to introduce to you Derek and Kit Davidson."

The crowd would not quit applauding and be seated. Derek turned to Rob and motioned in an entertainer's sign language all their own for the boys to sing "The Impossible Dream." When they concluded the crowd was seated.

As Derek approached the microphone, the crowd began applauding again. After a few minutes Derek quieted them and said, "You folks are a tough bunch." Then he noticed his employees from the West from the Barton Ranch as well as Greybull. "Would all you folks who work for the Foundation at Barton and Greybull please stand?" About seventy-five people stood.

Derek said again, "How did you get here? Answer that, Bob Sawyer."

Bob said, "We came commercial on your dime. We plan on eating on you tonight."

The crowd roared. "That's what I thought. I hope someone closed the gate so the cows won't get out." Another laugh erupted.

Rob butted in from the piano, "Dad, these folks in the audience have come from every state we work in. We've put them up in hotels and motels, and some even are staying with Mike and me, all on you. Isn't that nice?"

"Isn't it?"

Rob continued, "We've brought our A-number-one barbecue team from Barton, and we are going to feed everyone out back, including the wounded military, on the football field after this is over. It will be a grand time."

"I've heard many, many speakers in my lifetime who say, 'There really aren't words to express my feelings.' I've also thought *Yes, there are*, so many times. The truth is, tonight I don't have the words to say what needs to be said to you folks. It's true we provided the energy and maybe some of the talent accomplishing what we been about. Yet, truthfully, we've had fun every step of the way with some of the greatest people in the world, and you are those folks. Even though sometimes we couldn't put one foot in front of the other because we were so tired, our former bosses who were responsible for the program deserve the credit.

"The truth is, you are the people who allowed us to do what we've been allowed to do. If we've entertained anyone, for this we are grateful. If we've provided a bright and happy spot in your life, that's really what we've wanted to do. If we've provided you with anything you needed, we wanted to do this.

"I'll look forward to visiting with as many as possible at the barbecue on the football field. I'm grateful for the honor you have paid Kit and me this afternoon.

"Our benefactor, John Langford, told Greg Gregson's father, when he left his property to him, to 'do as much for as many as is humanly possible.' I've always had the feeling that God himself was working in me and through me to do as much for as many as is humanly possible, knowing that it is in giving that we receive our greatest gift."

"When tomorrow morning's work time comes, Kit and I will be retired. Sitting in my chair will be my son, Rob. Kit and I will visit our Little River Mountain Cathedral in the West and live off of the fat of the land until we are no more.

"Thank you for sharing our lives and being the friends you've chosen to be. Know that we offer sincere thanks to each of you and an invitation to visit at any time. We'll just be sitting on the front porch rocking and talking about all the good times we've had together." Derek offered his arm to Kit, who took it, and they exited the platform.

Rob was supposed to begin "I'll Fly Away," but was just sitting there dumbfounded when he heard what his dad had just said and saw tears streaming down his face. The military conductor tapped his baton on the piano to get his attention. Rob couldn't remember the introduction, and when the boys recognized his problem they sang the first verse without accompaniment. The military group joined in, as did the entire group. Rob came back to himself on the second verse.

Derek and Kit walked out to the football field and began picking at the barbecue and talking to those who came to visit. A wonderful way to end a celebration, visit with old friends, and make new ones.

It was also a great way to end a life of work and toil. Yet he knew that, as an entertainer, he would always have a spot since Rob would need him. The truth is that Derek knew he needed to perform since that was his life. Even more, though, he needed Rob, Mike, and Ali, and mostly he needed Kit.

About the Author

A native Floridian, Lowell Teal was born into a citrus and cattle family. After graduation from the University of Florida, his executive career began with an international agricultural marketing organization representing citrus growers and other producers nationwide. Fifteen years later he established a management/marketing/public relations consulting firm. Today the company is known as Austin Teal Corporation. He is the author of several books, including the four prequels in The BATH POND Series, *Bath Pond, Fortunes Crossing, Inherited Journey, Promise to Poppy,* as well as *A Happy Heart Is a Good Medicine* and *Company Stewardship.*

Lowell is married, father of two, and grandfather of two.

Other Books Written by Lowell Teal

A Happy Heart Is a Good Medicine

Bath Pond

Fortunes Crossing

Inherited Journey

Promise to Poppy

For more information please visit Lowell Teal's Web site:

www.LowellTeal.com